The Child Finder™ Trilogy Series
by Mike Angley

Child Finder™

Child Finder™ Resurrection

Coming Fall 2010!
Child Finder™ Revelation

Child Finder Resurrection

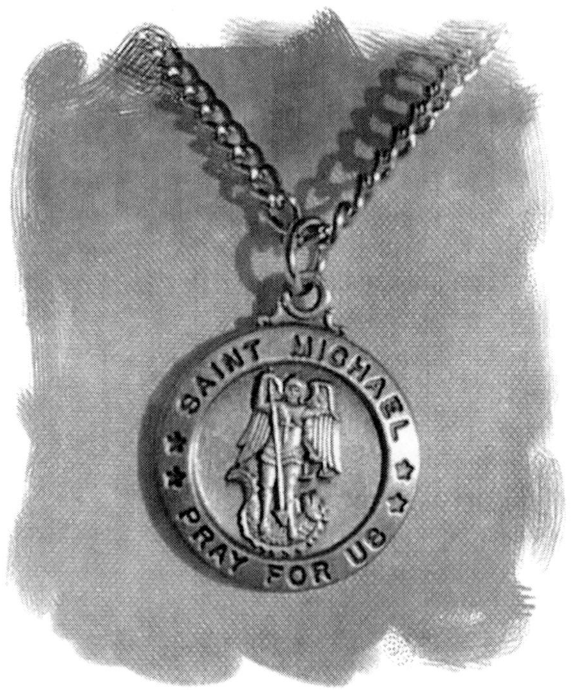

Mike Angley

TotalRecall Publication, Inc.
United States Canada United Kingdom

This is a work of fiction. The characters, events, views, and subject matter of this book are either the author's imagination or are used fictitiously. Any similarity or resemblance to any real people, real situations or actual events is purely coincidental and not intended to portray any person, place, or event in a false, disparaging or negative light.

ISBN: 978-1-59095-829-2

TotalRecallPress.com
1103 Middlecreek Friendswood, Texas 77546 281-992-3131 281-482-5390 Fax
6 Precedent Drive Rooksley, Milton Keynes MK13 8PR, UK
1385 Woodroffe Av Ottawa, ON K2G 1V8

Printed in the United States of America with
simultaneously printings in Canada, and
United Kingdom.

1 2 3 4 5 6 7 8 9 10

First Edition

This book is dedicated to my family…
to Evelyn, my wife of 24 years and our children: Kiernan Matthew, Kyle Patrick, and Meghan Nichole Marguerite. Thank you for your love and support, and may God always bless you and keep you well.

"Sweetest Lord, make me appreciative of the dignity of my high vocation, and its many responsibilities. Never permit me to disgrace it by giving way to coldness, unkindness, or impatience."

Mother Teresa

FOREWORD

Mike Angley knows his way around investigations. His background as a former Special Agent in the Air Force Office of Special Investigations enhances his ability to spin an exciting tale of intrigue. As a retired FBI Agent, I appreciate his attention to detail as he takes us through each drama-filled aspect of a case that carries life or death consequences. His "Child Finder Trilogy" mystery series first caught my attention when I read his debut novel, *Child Finder*™. He writes about a disturbing phenomenon in our society—child abduction—and enlightens the reader by describing how authorities solve this complex and dangerous crime using an investigative technique that will keep you riveted to the story.

As an author, I appreciate a well-written mystery and I knew after finishing his first book that I needed to read more about Mike's protagonist, Special Agent Patrick O'Donnell, and his unique investigative escapades. What also attracted me to Mike's distinct brand of writing was his ability to weave his strong spiritual foundation and love of family throughout his stories.

In *Child Finder*™ *Resurrection,* Mike does not disappoint! He introduces a killer so evil, you will want to jump into the story and fight the villain alongside Agent O'Donnell. The cat-and-mouse game between protagonist and nemesis will keep you on the edge of your seat.

Mike's insider knowledge about the government and its classified labyrinth of investigative techniques is both fascinating and entertaining. I enjoy his straightforward style of writing; it allows the story to move quickly; I had difficulty putting it down. If you hunger for a good mystery as much as I do, Mike Angley's trilogy will satisfy that urge. However, be forewarned…once you begin reading you may suffer from sleep deprivation. Enjoy.

John M. Wills

Author of the Chicago Warrior™ Thriller Series

Chicago Warrior™ *Midnight Battles in the Windy City*

Chicago Warrior™ *Gripped by Fear*

~ 1 ~

The dark alley was cool and seemingly empty. His footsteps made small tapping sounds on the dry concrete as he slinked along, countering his best efforts to stealthily and quietly clear the narrow passageway. With his back pressed tightly against a rough brick wall for cover, he held his cold, black steel 9 mm Beretta semi-automatic handgun at the ready. His mission was clear: capture or kill all three suspects...old Cold War-era former Soviet agents…armed, desperate, and deadly. They had just broken into a clandestine Air Force research laboratory in the heart of downtown Washington, DC and made off with critical satellite microprocessor technology. On the open black-market alone, the tiny devices would fetch a hefty profit, but in the hands of the Chinese government on whose behalf the men had stolen them, they were guaranteed to rake in an unfathomable sum. If they made it to China, they could cripple America's information superiority, giving the Chinese the ability to take down not just the nation's spy satellites, but the entire infrastructure of the United States. Banking, commerce, transportation, communication... everything was at risk of devastating damage.

Special Agent Patrick O'Donnell's hands trembled slightly as he crept along, anticipating an ambush, with his heart pounding so loudly he was certain the suspects could hear it thumping.

He approached a doorway, the dank and dirty back of a Chinese restaurant, the irony of the situation not lost on him. Remnants of rotten vegetables and the pungent shards of wilted cabbage draped over wooden crates stacked haphazardly near the doorway posed a small obstacle to his careful footing. The heavy garlic and ginger odors from the kitchen were not at all contained by the closed door. He cleared the doorway, and was just about to move beyond it when his right foot landed on a crumpled piece of paper. Its crackling sound shot down the otherwise silent alley and echoed loudly off the buildings in the narrow spaces. Startled, he looked down, a fatal mistake one of the suspects spied. Seeing that Pat was distracted, the man jumped from behind a large, green metal dumpster just fifteen yards ahead and aimed his revolver at him. Pat didn't have much time at all to react. No time to try to aim expertly. He quickly pointed his Beretta at the man and fired two rounds in rapid succession sending booming explosions ripping through the alley. It was a Hail Mary of an attempt at best, but it worked. The first bullet struck the suspect in the left shoulder, followed quickly by a second round to his abdomen. Two spent shells ejected from Pat's gun and made a sharp metal tinkling sound as they bounced along the solid pavement below. The man fell down and out of the way, his gun and his head simultaneously striking the ground hard.

Pat's pulse raced, certain now the remaining two men were nearby and getting more desperate as he inched toward them. They had the advantage, and he knew it…not just in terms of number, but because all they had to do was lie in wait. Pat was the one exposed…the one taking all the risk by moving forward and hunting for them.

He approached another doorway, close to a corner inside the alleyway, a T-shaped intersection among the mass of old, tall brick and glass buildings that made him feel small despite his six-foot-one-inch frame. He aimed his gun into the doorway, found it empty, and was about to press forward toward the intersection when he saw a figure pop out from around the corner to his left. He took but a half-second to assess things in the dim, flickering light from a neon sign near street side. It was another stocky, white male in his late fifties, aiming a semi-automatic pistol at him, barely five yards away.

The sudden muzzle flash was like a camera going off right in his face. The bright orange and white light reached his brain a split second before he heard the deafening volley of the hollow point round that ripped out of the suspect's barrel toward him. Just as the heat and pressure from the gunshot hit his face, Pat heard the bullet whiz past his left ear, nearly grazing his temple. Like before, he had little time to react. He pointed his gun and quickly fired two rounds. One struck the man in his chest killing him instantly, but the second one missed and glanced off a wall, ricocheting two or three times before stopping.

At the moment the ricocheting stopped, Pat heard a rustling sound behind him. By now his adrenaline was rushing like a flood. He turned quickly and aimed at the figure emerging from the first doorway he had cleared, the back of the Szechwan eatery with the wafting stir fry scent. But he was unprepared for the hideous sight before him. A demonic-looking man with a dark red face, piercing green eyes, and malevolent sneer, stood with his arms crossed, bright chrome Desert Eagle gun in his left hand. *This guy put on a disguise?* he thought, confused.

Pat's heart seemed to stop as he held his breath to minimize trigger jerk. He squeezed off two rounds, but it was when the second round left the chamber that he suddenly realized what he had done. What a horrible mistake he had made. The image his brain created, for reasons unknown, of the third suspect in a strange mask, changed back to reality. He blinked his eyes rapidly, trying to clear the photons and reset his brain.

The rustling sound came from a young Asian woman who had emerged from the restaurant's back doorway carrying a small black trash bag for the dumpster. She was no man at all. There was no mask. His aim was perfect this time, with both bullets ripping through her chest at 1,200 feet per second, no more than a half inch apart, taking her innocent life instantly.

His heart sank as he watched her drop to the filthy ground, knocking several wooden crates down with her. And when she did, the alley suddenly flooded with light, an ear piercing alarm rang out, and Pat ripped off his cold, hard plastic hearing protectors and shatterproof range glasses. Walls, buildings, dumpsters, and people in the alley dissolved, only to be replaced by a series of giant floor-to-ceiling green screens. The alarm stopped, and over a crackling loudspeaker he heard the range official announce, "Okay, Agent O'Donnell, looks like you just took out Lucy Liu. Good thing this is just practice!"

Pat could hear some people chuckling in the background of the loudspeakers. Embarrassed, Major O'Donnell, an Air Force Office of Special Investigations Special Agent, de-cocked his weapon with a soft *CLICK* and re-holstered it on his hip before walking back to the range official's platform. He had just completed testing out OSI's newly-installed Hogan's Alley simulated tactical range. It was a brand new facility using the latest in virtual reality technology to simulate three dimensional environments and targets. His weapon was a modified 9 mm Beretta that fired blank rounds synchronized with laser bursts at targets for precise feedback on his shooting acumen. But today was not his best shooting day, as evidenced by his quick trigger action in the range.

The back of the room was filled with spectators, literally dozens of agents from within the bowels of Headquarters OSI situated on Andrews Air Force Base in Maryland, just outside the nation's Capitol. They had come out to watch the thirty-six-year-old fellow agent perform in the Hogan's Alley range. Pat knew he was a legend of sorts within OSI because nearly one and a half years earlier he became the first agent in the organization's history to shoot and kill an FBI agent. Of course, no one in OSI, not even its one-star general commander, was privy to what really happened that fateful day when he rescued his five-year-old daughter from the clutches of the stark-raving mad FBI agent, Vicky Desantis. She had abducted little Erin in some sick and twisted desire to start a family with Pat. No one was privy to the fact that he was a certified psychic, a virtual telepathic savant with the ability to remotely sense events in the past, present, and future. And no one was privy to the TOP SECRET Special Access Program he belonged to, under the auspices of the now-deceased Agent Desantis and the Justice Department, a program that used his psychic powers to rescue abducted children. Rumors ran rampant, but only a few trusted souls within the mysterious and shadowy *black world* SAP knew exactly what had happened...and within the OSI, Pat was the only one allowed inside this tiny inner circle.

He sauntered back to the range management platform, smoothing back his dark brown hair, awkwardly conscious of the stares from the crowd of onlookers, but trying hard not to make it apparent. His mind raced to understand what just happened, unsure if the range officials inserted a demonic figure in the computer to play a joke on him. A couple of probationary agents in dark blue tactical raid jackets with "OSI" emblazoned on the front and back in large gold letters were whispering to each other as he approached. They were both young women, attractive blonds no more than twenty-two or twenty-three years old. Like two giddy schoolgirls passing the cute boy in the hallway between classes, their best efforts to study him without being obvious failed.

"Oh, he's real cute!" one squealed softly to the other.

Her friend nodded a broad smile of bright white teeth, half acknowledging her, but really hoping she would get Pat's attention.

"Uh huh, and I love those blue eyes," she giggled in muffled response.

Pat heard what she said and smiled to himself slightly. He briefly made eye contact with them, causing the two girls to blush with wide-eyed excitement over the small touch of attention he gave them.

"Looks like you have a fan club," the range official chuckled as Pat handed him his hearing and eye protection.

He was an older gentleman, a thin almost skeleton-looking civilian special agent with fingers stained yellow from decades of chain smoking. He took the equipment and placed it in a black steel cabinet behind the platform, then pulled a score sheet from a noisy, dinosaur of a dot matrix printer next to the podium where his microphone sat.

"Well, the good news is you passed both qualifying tests this morning before you entered Hogan's Alley, so you're good for another half year. You're cleared for your PCS to Korea next month."

Pat took the sheet and studied it carefully. Although he passed the firearms tests required to maintain his concealed weapons carrying authority, he did so barely. He typically qualified as an Expert Marksman, rarely letting even one errant round miss a target. But ever since killing Vicky, his concentration was off, and so was his aim. While he drew some comfort knowing he was approved to depart on a Permanent Change of Station, or PCS, move to the Far East, he wished his shooting ability were better. After all, in his line of work, it was a matter of survival.

"I shot like crap!" Pat cried as he examined his scores. "And look what I did to poor Lucy," he moaned using the nickname the agents had affectionately given the Asian actress in the virtual world machine. "Did you guys screw around with the program? I mean, like make Lucy look like Darth Maul to mess up my shooting?"

His buddy gave him a curious look. "Um, no. You suck on your own, we didn't need to make it any worse!" he taunted with a slap on Pat's back.

They both looked at a computer monitor which held in freeze-frame fashion the last scene in the alleyway. Pat stood over the woman's body which was soaked in a pool of rich red blood. Right behind him was the third ex-Soviet agent firing a round into the back of his head at point-blank range. On the screen the words, *You're Dead!* flashed as a cruel reminder to him that he failed this particular practice test.

"You'll get back to your usual proficiency, my friend," the range instructor smiled. "Just give it some time and relax when you shoot. Breathe deeply, hold it in, fire, then exhale," he said letting out a long breath that brought the heavy smell of tobacco to Pat's nostrils.

He knew his friend meant well, but it was hard to take him seriously when he looked so run down and ragged and smelled so foul.

"I hope so, Buddy," Pat smirked as he placed his signature on the official form certifying he had qualified as annotated.

By then most of the spectators had left the range, with just the two young women still loitering about, still whispering to each other, still trying to pretend like they were talking about anything *but* Pat.

"Better watch those young lieutenants, O'Donnell!" his friend chided as he took the form from him, nodding his head toward the two pretty blonds.

The girls made Pat think again about Vicky Desantis, a very hot, very sensual, crystal blue-eyed blond FBI agent who once even tried to seduce him during their days of working together in the CRYSTAL ROUNDUP psychic program.

"Uh, no problem with that! I'm happily married, thank you!" he smiled, knowing he needed to steer clear of even casual flirting after his bad experience with Vicky.

Just then a voice came over the loudspeaker, "Telephone call for Major O'Donnell. Sir, you can pick it up in the break room."

"I guess that's my cue," Pat said slipping his pen back into a side leg pocket of his khaki-colored tactical cargo pants. He gave his old friend a firm shake and departed.

The break room was dimly-lit when Pat entered, with two tall brass floor lamps in corners burning incandescent lights. The room was fairly well-apportioned, with a small brown leather sofa and matching side chairs lining a long paneled wall across from the doorway. The only thing that seemed out of place in the otherwise relaxing den-like break area was a large Coca-Cola machine in one corner that threw off a bright red and white glow, along with a soft humming sound from its compressor. Next to a side chair was a small end table with a lamp and telephone, one of its six button lights flashing. Pat sat down and flipped on the lamp, retrieved a notepad and pen from his pants pockets, grabbed the handset, and hit the flashing button.

"Hello, this is Pat O'Donnell," he announced, clearing his throat slightly, unsure who was calling him.

When Pat heard the voice at the other end of the line, his heart skipped a beat. He suddenly had a confused, conflicted mix of joy and fear, comfort and trepidation.

"Hey, Pat, it's John Helmsley. How have you been?"

Pat paused for a second and closed his eyes before responding, saying a nanosecond-like prayer in his head, already knowing what was coming.

"Sir, it's good to hear your voice," he said, sitting almost at attention in silent respect to his old friend and mentor.

He conjured up in his mind an image of the stocky, light brown-haired colonel with gold, wire-rimmed glasses and perpetually ruddy face.

"How's the Pentagon work been lately? I hear you've been busy outprocessing before your PCS to Osan Air Base," the colonel said.

"It's never slowed down since the terrorist attacks, and now the war in Iraq that began last month. It's a wonder I've been able to get as much done getting the family ready for the move."

"Well, don't pack out just yet, Pat. The Secretary of the Air Force is calling the IG right now to…" he began, but Pat cut him off.

"I guess I knew this call would come sooner or later, Boss," Pat said somberly.

He stared down at the notepad on his knee, hands jittering slightly. Although Pat couldn't see him on the other end of the line, at that same moment Colonel Helmsley tapped a pen on his desk and paused, already knowing this news would hit Pat hard. After all, it was precisely because Pat had become involved with the CRYSTAL ROUNDUP program in the months following the 9/11 terrorist attacks that his life changed forever. Not only had Vicky Desantis abducted Erin, but she also viciously attacked Pat's wife, Sara, and left her for dead, bleeding profusely with deep cuts to her arms and wrists. Even his dear friend, the family priest, was murdered because CRYSTAL ROUNDUP operatives thought he knew about the program.

"Can you meet me at Al's Garage tomorrow morning?" the colonel asked.

Pat understood the signal to visit the safe house in Arlington, Virginia, but he didn't immediately respond.

"Pat? Are you still there? It's time."

Pat gulped hard before responding. "Sir, do you remember how the movie, The Exorcist, begins? The old priest is on an archeological dig site and uncovers a relic of a demon he once battled."

"Yeah, Pat. I've seen it, so what about it?"

"Well, when he finds the object, he knows instantly that he's about to do battle with the demon once again. Boss, I think I just had a moment like that. I think I just stared in the face of evil. I guess your call isn't a coincidence."

He could hear the colonel sigh.

"You know I don't believe in coincidences, not in the freakish circles you and I run in. I don't know what it could mean, but I suppose things are about to come to a head."

"See you tomorrow, Boss."

~ 2 ~

Springtime in northern Virginia, in the suburbs of Washington, DC, was always a special time of year. Red robins, cardinals, and blue jays screamed and chirped noisily in the trees, finding sanctuary among the leaves made thick and green from an abundance of rain. Honeybees scrambled about finding the best sources of nectar and pollen to take back to their perennial wax nests. Cherry blossoms were everywhere, like giant bouquets, and as the sun rose and warmed the earth, it created gentle breezes that pushed the floral scent with it into the open windows of the O'Donnell home in Burke.

Pat yawned and stretched as the alarm went off, drawing in a deep breath and the cherry blossom treats along with it. Pat had synesthesia, a rare condition characterized by the blending and blurring of his senses. It was something he never thought about consciously until his journey began in the dark and mysterious world of the CRYSTAL ROUNDUP Special Access Program. Before the expedition started, it was all so natural for him. So automatic. He could hear with his eyes, and taste with his hands, and see with his ears, or some other bizarre sensory combination that occurred randomly. He grew up thinking everyone sensed the world the same way he did. It was not until he was tested, poked, and examined when he joined the CRYSTAL ROUNDUP family, that he learned just how unique he really was. The nexus between his synesthesia and his psychic abilities became apparent, and ultimately served as a venue through which he could focus on and better understand the paranormal signals he received.

Today the blossom fragrance was not just sweet and flowery, but it was also moist and dewy. He could even *see* the sweet aroma that teased his brain with images of white and pink shapes with soft round edges. In his mouth he could taste the scent as well, a gentle fruity flavor that made him hungry this morning for fresh apples, cantaloupe, and grapes. He smacked his dry lips together enjoying the orchestra of sensations God had arranged and softly delivered to him in three dimensional hints and flashes, bursts and pulses, sounds and scents and tastes. All this from a single whiff of flowers most people would experience as a quick, boring, bland bouquet and nothing more, something easily overlooked or dismissed by the nose.

"Wake up, Baby," Pat whispered to Sara as he gently shook her shoulder.

She roused slowly from her deep sleep, barely prying open one of her bright green eyes to look at him. She brushed her long red hair aside and rubbed her face.

"Today is our first day of freedom! No more need to pack out and fly off to Korea," he said with a giddy smile and much more energy and excitement than Sara had at the moment.

The night before Pat had broken the news to her about the cancelled assignment to Osan Air Base. She was beyond being thrilled since the prospect of leaving the home they loved was something she loathed.

"I just love Colonel Helmsley for saving us from the Korea tour!" she exclaimed as she pulled him in for a morning kiss. "Do you report in to your new job at the Pentagon today, Baby?" she asked.

"Er, not exactly," Pat began. "I have to meet up with Colonel Helmsley at a safe house this morning, and then I guess we go over the plans for how I'm going to support his ops."

He thought about the colonel's efficiency in making the new arrangements. The Secretary of the Air Force nixed the Korea assignment while the Secretary of Defense personally assigned Pat to the Joint Staff as Chief of Special Projects in the J39, the Global Operations Directorate where many hush-hush projects were undertaken. Of course, it was all a cut-out, a canard, a cover to allow Pat to work freely in the CRYSTAL ROUNDUP program while giving him a job on paper that enhanced his potential for promotion later in his career.

Sara gave him a worried, almost disappointed look. "Pat, I knew all this would start back up again someday, but please be careful. I don't want to go through another--" she started to protest, but he leaned in and kissed her lips.

"I know, Sorcha, it's gonna be alright," he reassured her, calling her by her Gaelic nickname.

He glanced awkwardly at her wrists and the scars Vicky left behind from her knife attack in their kitchen. He knew she had every right to be cautious considering his job almost got her killed.

Pat rose to get ready for the morning, looking back and giving Sara a wink as his feet touched the cool oak hardwood floor of their bedroom. He saw she had a wry smile on her face, like she wanted to say something.

"What is it, Baby?" he finally asked, his psychic powers betraying him at the moment.

"It's a good thing you killed Vicky, 'cause I would have killed that witch myself if I had the chance!"

He chuckled out loud, adoring her Irish wrath--much like his own--but hers was almost nurturing in how she channeled it toward protecting him and their family.

Following a hot steamy shower, Pat sauntered into the kitchen, only to be assaulted by his two children at the breakfast table. Sean jumped from his seat, a warm strawberry Pop Tart in his hand, and nearly tackled his father to the floor. The eleven-year-old giggled non-stop as Pat feinted a fall on his back, pulling Sean with him. Dry crusty crumbs fell everywhere, including dad's once neatly combed hair. Erin shrieked loudly, nearly slamming a glass of orange juice on the table as she bounded from her chair. She pounced on top of Pat, where she and Sean pinned him to the floor in fits of laughter. The six-year-old, first grader's long auburn hair spilled over Pat's face, tickling him. One by one, Pat managed to pry them free, laughing almost uncontrollably along with them. He looked at Sara who was snickering as she poured Pat a cup of piping hot coffee.

"I love you, Daddy!" Erin beamed, her bright hazel eyes sparkling as Pat lowered her down into her chair. Her tiny feet, nestled inside warm, pink-piggy slippers flailed about almost knocking over her cereal bowl before she was snugly back in her seat to resume drinking her juice.

"I love you guys so much!" he cried patting Sean's light

brown mop, trying his best to part and straighten it out. He shook the crumbs from his hair and used his strong fingers to comb his part back into some semblance of shape.

"I already told the kids about staying here and not going to--" Sara started, but Sean cut in.

"Yeah, we didn't want to go to Korea, Daddy. We want to stay here with our friends, right Erin?"

Erin nodded as she sipped her juice. Pat took a seat at the table across from them, stirring cream and sugar into his mug. "We're all happy guys," he grinned grabbing a bright red apple from a basket on the table, then taking a loud bite.

"I'll let the school know today that we're not pulling the kids out next month," Sara told him.

Pat stayed and chatted with his children while Sara went about getting ready to take them to school. He was in no real hurry today. He had no sense of urgency like he did most mornings making sure his uniform was perfect or watching the clock to ensure he didn't miss his Metro bus to the Pentagon. Today, instead of commuting in to his old job within the office of the Air Force Inspector General where he oversaw OSI counterterrorism operations in the Global War on Terror and Operation Iraqi Freedom, Pat would wear civilian clothing, pack his trusty handgun in a fanny pack, and drive over to the safe house. He was officially relieved of his former duties.

During the long, painfully slow commute from Burke to Arlington, he had a lot of time to think about the past. But these past thoughts also gave him some understandable angst about his pending future. Even though it had been almost eighteen months since Vicky's death, he and Colonel Helmsley barely spoke with one another. It was just as well, he surmised, since he knew the colonel wanted Pat to cool his heels and regroup with his family. Helmsley, once in charge of the Department of Defense side of the program, was now retired from the United States Air Force and made chief of the entire program at the Department of Justice. A long time friend of the Attorney General, he was given a clear mandate: clean up the CRYSTAL ROUNDUP program and make it legal and ethical.

Pat's battered, white Subaru Outback jerked and jostled, seemingly making inch-by-inch progress in getting to Arlington. A light morning drizzle only slowed traffic all the more. A normal thirty-minute drive took one and a half hours this morning. It was right about 0930 when he pulled up to the safe house, a four-year-old townhome tucked away on a quiet suburban street lined with mini-vans and SUVs. It was a stereotypical soccer mom community plucked from the screenplay of any modern day television sitcom about life in the suburbs.

Stepping inside Al's Garage brought back a flood of horrifying memories. It was the first time he had been there since Vicky attempted to seduce him, just before she went crazy and abducted Erin. He once literally stood in the safe house dining room, Vicky's half-naked body in his arms, her breasts bare and tempting, and their hungry mouths locked together in a forbidden kiss. It was an act of great conscience that he was able to break her seductive grip before things got too far out of hand, and head home faithfully to Sara.

But today his skin crawled, and his heart raced like a laboratory rat conditioned to anticipate pain. He wanted to be anywhere but there at that moment. His mental anguish was interrupted in an instant, however, when his peripheral vision caught a glimpse of a black man off to his right moving from the dining room toward him. When the man entered the kitchen, Pat rushed to him like he was a long lost friend. With his eyes filled with excitement, Pat grabbed him so tightly he picked him up and nearly spun him around. He was thrilled to see Dr. Woodrow Wilson Davis, the chief psychiatrist on the CRYSTAL ROUNDUP team and the man responsible for helping Pat unlock the secrets of his extraordinary psychic abilities and synesthesia.

"Woody!" he cried loudly, finally releasing the tall, thin, gray-haired man from his bear hug. "I am so happy to see you!" he exclaimed, forgetting all at once his earlier apprehension at being there.

"It's so good to see you, too!" Dr. Davis returned, this time grabbing Pat and initiating his own tight hug.

As the two old friends chatted and began to catch up on things since they last saw each other, they didn't realize Helmsley had walked in and was standing there, grinning. He finally snickered, then cleared his throat.

"Uh hum, anyone gonna invite me to this family reunion?" he teased.

Pat ran right up to him, thrusting his arms around the somewhat portly gentleman, nearly knocking his glasses right off his face. "Colonel, it's great to see you again," Pat said softly, patting his back.

He noted how much longer the colonel's hair was now in retirement, but it was still parted right down the middle as it always had been since they first met almost seven years ago.

"You too, Pat, you too. And you know, it's John now."

Pat smiled cynically. "Sir, it will never be John. You're

always going to be Colonel or Sir, so get used to it!"

Pat knew he could never view Colonel Helmsley through any lens except one formed of deep respect. And the colonel didn't seem to protest, either.

"Shall we chat a bit in the clear in the living room before going downstairs to the SCIF?" the colonel suggested, putting an arm around his shoulder and leading the way.

Pat was anxious to learn what Helmsley had done to revamp the CRYSTAL ROUNDUP program, but knew he had to wait a bit before they proceeded down to the safe house basement that had been transformed into a Sensitive Compartmented Information Facility where they could hold secure conversations up to the TOP SECRET level.

He noticed the safe house furnishings were all different from before, now much newer and even more elegant. The living room clearly had been professionally decorated--the entire house had been, for that matter. He found the change comforting; in some strange way, it made it seem like a different place, not the *house of horrors* as he had nicknamed it in his head.

"Pat? Hello, Pat?" the colonel called to him, breaking the obvious daydream that was distracting him. "I take it you like what we've done here?"

"I sure do, Boss. It looks great!" Pat smiled, taking a seat on the floral print Ethan Allen sofa next to Woody.

He was tempted to put his feet up on the highly-polished, dark brown maple coffee table, but he thought twice about it.

The three men talked for nearly an hour, each filling in the others on their families and lives, and sharing many good laughs. It all served to put Pat at ease and ready him for what he was sure would be new adventures in rescuing lost children.

He felt so comfortable, so warm inside being with them that he began to mentally posture himself for the new operations. Suddenly Helmsley looked at his watch.

"Dr. Jacobsen will be here in a few minutes. Pat, we need to introduce you to the newest team member, and Woody's recently-acquired personal assistant."

Woody jumped right in. "We hired Dr. Jacobsen late last year. He's a fresh graduate of UC Berkeley's psychology program, tops in his class. In fact he's a bit of a prodigy, the youngest in Berkeley's history to earn a PhD at the age of twenty."

Pat was stunned by the news, and a bit unsettled. His tight jaw and pursed lips conveyed his feelings clearly. "Wait a minute--I'm going to work with some kid who's not even old enough to drink beer? And he's from *Berserkly*? I mean, those people out there don't exactly seem to like the military."

Woody was about to speak when the doorbell rang. He walked over to answer it, leaving Helmsley and Pat alone for a moment. Pat glared at the colonel.

"Pat, give the kid a chance. He authored an amazing thesis about the paranormal, a paper that has generated a lot of interest in the psychology community."

Pat just shook his head, and was about to comment when Woody walked in with Dr. Jacobsen. Although Pat had imagined he'd be meeting a nerdy, thin, frail young man, he was surprised by his very-chiseled appearance. Jacobsen was nearly as tall as Pat and appeared quite physically fit, downright athletic. He had long black hair, almost to his shoulders, a deep California tan, and light, almost grayish colored eyes. Had it not been for the black hair, Pat thought he could be a poster boy for a surfer magazine. He extended his hand to greet him, surprising Pat by the firmness of his shake.

"Hello, Mr. O'Donnell. I'm Dr. Jasper Jacobsen, nice to meet you."

Upon hearing his first name--and the fact that he used the title *doctor*--Pat's impression instantly reversed back to what it was upon hearing the news about the newest team member. His jaw dropped, his eyes went bug-wide, and he nearly let out a muffled laugh he tried hard to suppress.

"It's Major O'Donnell, but you can call me, Pat. And please tell me you go by another name besides..."

"My friends call me, Jake," Dr. Jacobsen interrupted abruptly, something he apparently was accustomed to doing all his life in order to fend off teasing about his name, or so it appeared.

Pat smiled and nodded. "Good thing. 'Cause I gotta tell you, using a name like Jasper in some of the circles I run in will get your butt beat!"

"Gentlemen, shall we get started? We have a lot of work to do, lots of children to rescue, so shall we go to the SCIF and brief Pat up on things?" Colonel Helmsley prodded.

Pat insisted everyone walk ahead of him as they made their way to the basement stairs. He wanted to study Dr. Jacobsen in his own special, psychic way. He concentrated his thoughts on the back of Jake's head, attempting to penetrate, with laser-like precision, below the skull to unwrap whatever secrets he may hold. He couldn't pick up anything with enough clarity to validate his concern. First it was the Hogan's Alley satanic image that caused him to shoot an innocent, albeit virtual, woman…now it was a young kid about whose loyalties he was uncertain. One thing was for sure, however, Pat had a gnawing sense of distrust of him. He knew he was going to have to maintain his guard around Jake, keep his psychic radar running at full power, and constantly scan for any ominous blips on the screen. This guy was trouble.

~ 3 ~

Even the furnishings in the SCIF conference room were brand new. Its dark blue sunlight dampening drapes and medium beige carpeting were pristine clean, and it almost seemed to Pat as they entered, that theirs were the first shoes ever to touch the soft fabric. The formerly fluorescent overhead lights were gone, only to be replaced by stylish track lighting that made the room look much less like a government office, and much more like a cozy recreation room. In some way, he thought it was all intentional. He suspected the colonel had seen to it that the entire safe house was stripped down and made new and fresh, as if he knew the old place would haunt him. He took up a seat near the front of the long wood conference table, freshly polished and glistening, while Colonel Helmsley sat next to him, the others across from them. With a couple of flicks on a remote control unit, the colonel revealed a large plasma screen behind a retractable, wood-paneled wall that barely made a sound as it opened. The screen must have been six feet across, and it instantly lit brightly when powered up. He deftly worked the controls on the remote to move a small, arrow-shaped cursor across the screen before he opened up a presentation with the familiar banner, TOP SECRET CRYSTAL ROUNDUP.

Pat grimaced as he mentally tried to prepare himself for yet another nauseating briefing about young children who had been abducted and murdered. Although he was a master at what he could do with his psychic powers, each case was still revolting and disturbing. As a parent himself, he never could get used to the horrors of child crimes. He oftentimes thought that if he ever did, if he should ever find himself numb to the repulsive nature of such offenses, then it was time to turn in his badge and gun and find another line of work. But this time he was in for a surprise. Pleasantly so.

"Today we're going to brief you in on how the SAP has been redesigned to keep it in line with the Attorney General's intent that everything we do is above board and legal," Colonel Helmsley began as he stood up and walked to the screen, still holding the remote control. "The President rescinded the original Finding from the Kennedy administration that allowed us to fabricate witnesses or evidence in order to protect the program while ensuring the bad guys don't get away."

The colonel paused for a moment. Pat glanced at Woody and Jake who kept their attention on him for what he could only assume was to gauge his reaction to the developments. It seemed a bit rehearsed, however, as if they had huddled at some point and talked about how he might react.

"Six months ago he signed a new Presidential Finding, a copy of which is here," the colonel continued, pulling a TOP SECRET memo from a folder near his seat and handing it to him.

Pat read it while Colonel Helmsley resumed his briefing. He

scrunched up his face upon reading a key line in the new document, one he found intriguing.

"Sir, what's this Oversight Committee about?" he asked, uneasy with the prospect that the circle of insiders in the TOP SECRET program appeared to have expanded.

"Relax, Pat," Woody chimed in. "The Oversight Committee is an important new feature in the program. A bunch of attorneys from the Justice Department."

Pat rolled his eyes. "Great, lawyers! Now that's not gonna impede progress, will it?" he asked sarcastically.

"They work for the AG directly, but so do I. So if there are any disagreements between us, the AG has final decision authority," the colonel explained.

Pat was relieved at least to hear that--comforted that a reasonable set of checks and balances was now in place, lessening the chance that rogue operators in the program could once again hijack it for personal reasons. During the briefing he learned about an important change in venue for the operation--an element Colonel Helmsley personally added that Pat found to be brilliant. The team would operate out of a newly-built wing at the Justice Department's Child Crime Victim Center in Arlington, not far from the safe house.

"In October 2002, the President held the Conference on Missing, Exploited, and Runaway Children at the White House. He signed the new Finding at the conclusion of the meeting following a Special Access Program update from me. And when I proposed we run ops out of the CCVC, he had only one question for me: 'How much money do ya need?'" the colonel quoted with a Texas twang.

Pat was growing excited at the developments, and leaned

forward in his chair. "The CCVC gives us great operational cover as well as access to real-time information on abductions. I mean, we're right there at the hub for all related news and developments, as well as formal reach to the law enforcement community for rescues!"

"Yes, and the real beauty is in the simplicity of how we plan to operate," Jake began to say, for the first time offering any input in the discussion.

Pat shot him a skeptical glance, actually slightly amused that the *newbie* would have any meaningful input. "How so?" he asked with a smirk.

The young man stood up and joined Colonel Helmsley at the front of the room near the screen.

"Well, you see, our thinking is that when you develop psychic details about missing children, we can flow that information to the CCVC's tipline. Once in the system as an anonymous lead, it will alert the appropriate law enforcement agency who will act to rescue the kids accordingly."

Major O'Donnell rubbed his eyes for a moment letting the process sink into his brain a little deeper. He looked at Colonel Helmsley.

"So, Boss, no high tech gadgets this time around? Like the minivan with the satellite links and all?" he asked, slightly disappointed.

The colonel chuckled. "Don't worry, Pat. We have plenty of super secret spy stuff to augment what we do, only this time I think you will find we will travel a bit lighter than in the past."

For the next two hours the team briefed Pat about how the CRYSTAL ROUNDUP program would operate out of the CCVC. He learned about a series of strict rules put in place following the debacle in operations from a year and a half before. They were affectionately called the *Three Commandments* of the Special Access Program and were considered inviolable. For starters, all new cases Pat worked had to be approved by the Oversight Committee unless there were exigent circumstances. The only exceptions were bona fide Amber Alerts. These had blanket pre-approval. Second, they would only take on cases of probable stranger abductions. Without exception, they were not to work kidnappings by likely family members. The rationale was simple. Stranger cases represented the greatest threat of molestation or murder, where harm was done to victims in the narrowest of windows, so a necessary rapid response always made these incidents a higher priority. Finally, under no circumstances at all was Pat to directly engage in operational work. In other words, he was not to be a trigger puller. Although Colonel Helmsley did his best to assuage his concerns, this particular rule riled Pat up fiercely.

"Sir, I'm a badge-carrying federal agent! What do you mean I can't take part in any take downs? You know I'm much more seasoned than most others out there, what with my counterintelligence and counterterrorism operational experience and all!"

He was getting angrier as he spoke, downright disrespectful toward the retired colonel. And he knew this. He tried to calm himself down as he listened to his mentor explain the reasoning, though he knew his cherry red face and tight jaw were hard to miss.

"It's just that there are a lot of people on the CRYSTAL ROUNDUP team now, Pat. I've got more than a dozen FBI agents with badges and guns locked and loaded. But I've only got one Pat O'Donnell. Just one. I think you know from our last set of operations, especially when we went after Usama bin Laden, that your stock is high. Extremely high! We cannot afford to have anything happen to you. Without you, there is no CRYSTAL ROUNDUP."

Pat leaned back in his chair and closed his eyes. He knew the colonel was right, but he hated the thought of being relegated to functioning as a virtual administrative clerk, with at most a role in gathering intelligence. He was an operator, after all. He had spent years chasing not only spies and terrorists around the globe, but he was also a seasoned criminal investigator with hundreds of felony arrests and complex cases solved in his portfolio. Within the OSI he was considered one of the finest the organization ever produced, with arguably the best record at interrogations to top it off. He hated the unfairness in it all. But he also understood the value of being the sole node in this psychic intelligence platform, likened to a single satellite with a particular imaging capability. Take that one satellite down, and the intelligence community goes blind. If he were killed or injured, thousands of children might never be saved.

"Sir, I am willing to give it a try, but understand that I will continue to always carry my gun just in case."

As Pat said this he patted his fanny pack which drew Dr. Jacobsen's attention like a powerful magnet. "Is there a gun in your bag right now?" Jake asked, clearly astonished and suddenly overtly nervous.

Pat tilted his head sideways and slowly shook it. "Yeah, why Jake?"

"Oh, I just hate guns. I wish they were banned completely. I don't want to be near them at all," he insisted flippantly.

Pat let his head drop and hit the table in front of him hard, startling Woody and the colonel. He let out a muffled cry, his face pressed against the cool hard wood surface. Then his cries turned to small fits of laughter. When he lifted his head he was grinning, face redder than before.

"Maybe I *should* call you Jasper. Let me tell you something, Buddy, get used to it. Either you fit in with this team, or you don't belong on it! We're not going to adapt operations--and possibly risk lives--just to accommodate your anti-Second Amendment view of the world!"

Pat nearly shouted out his words causing Jake to take a step back, almost ducking behind Colonel Helmsley, as if he thought Pat was coming right over the table at him. Although he wanted to rip into Dr. Jacobsen some more, to tear him up, he thought it was best to control his Celtic anger. In an uncharacteristic huff, he rose and left the room briskly, heading up the stairs to the kitchen, not saying another word. Colonel Helmsley was right behind him.

Pat stood in front of the gray marble counter top and quickly poured himself a cup of coffee from a pot that had been sitting and warming for more than two hours. The aroma was powerful, and he knew the taste would be worse. He sipped the now-bitter brew and made a face. He turned to see Colonel Helmsley standing by the doorway, hands on his hips, looking much like a dad trying to talk with his unruly teenage son. Pat felt bad about his outburst, but his convictions were strong. Cops were an insular sort of people, after all. It was bad enough allowing an outsider to come inside the inner circle, but an outsider who seemed to be clearly at odds with the law enforcement business model...badges, cuffs, and GUNS. That was over the top to Pat. He gave the colonel an almost apologetic look, knowing he had crossed an invisible line of courtesy with his rage. In the privacy of the kitchen, with Woody and Jake still downstairs, the two men talked.

"Sir, this guy's dangerous. Didn't we vet him properly before hiring him?"

"Look, Pat, he's the best out there, one of the brightest young minds in this arena to have come along in decades. I agree he's going to have to adapt to us, but you need to lighten up a bit yourself."

Pat shook his head in disgust. "Boss, I don't care what his views are, so long as he keeps them to himself and doesn't let them impact our ops. That's what's really important. He could get one of us killed!"

The colonel smiled and put an arm around his shoulder. "In case your complex paranormal brain hasn't picked up the clues yet, Jake respects you tremendously!"

"He does?" Pat asked, somewhat surprised.

"Yes! Look, over the last few months as he read about your capabilities during his indoctrination, he hasn't stopped talking about you. You represent the epitome of all he has researched the last several years at Berkeley. You two may disagree about politics and gun laws and all that, but you both share the same goal. You both want to rescue kids."

The colonel made a fist with his right hand and gave him a gentle punch in the jaw. Pat slowly nodded. He had been trying to peer inside Jake's brain the last hour or so, and could only pick up innocuous signals. Although Pat detected nothing untoward about him, he felt certain deep down Jake was a ticking time bomb, and it was only a matter of time before Berkeley-boy got him hurt. He knew he should not let their political differences overshadow their work together, but it was going to be hard.

"I dunno, Boss, I--"

The colonel stopped him mid-protest. "Like I said, give him a chance. We'll start operations first thing Monday morning at the CCVC center on Wilson Boulevard."

He looked at the clock in the kitchen. "Look, Pat, It's almost four o'clock, and it's a Friday. Let's say we wrap things up in the next hour and go get a pint of ale?"

He imitated an Irish brogue with his suggestion, looking up at the tall major as if offering an olive branch.

Pat smiled and nodded. "Okay, but just you, me, and Woody. Surfer dude down there ain't old enough!"

Colonel Helmsley laughed out loud and smacked him hard on the back. "Not to worry. He told us this morning he needs to leave early, has a date with his fiancée."

"A girlfriend? That's encouraging," was all Pat said, smirking as the two headed back downstairs to finish the orientation.

~ 4 ~

Palm Sunday in 2003 fell on April 13th, and this year, like so many Pat could remember, the weather was perfect. It was as if God wanted to guarantee all good Catholics would find it in their hearts to attend Mass that He painted a bright golden sun in the sky, erased all but a few clouds, and waved gentle warm breezes that pushed and pulled celebrants from bed. But Pat didn't need any prodding. He enjoyed this time of year, arguably the most important holiday week in the Catholic calendar. He went about getting himself and his family up and ready for the 1000 Mass at Our Lady of La Salette church, right there in their hometown of Burke.

He stood in front of his bedroom bureau mirror and slowly brushed his hair. Bright sunlight squeaked through the mini-blinds and cast a bothersome glare on the mirror's glass surface, making the task more challenging than usual. As he did, he thought about their former parish priest, Father Mike Reynolds, who was murdered in the fall of 2001 by Vicky Desantis's henchmen. He died a martyr as far as Pat was concerned, staunchly resisting every effort by Desantis's thugs to pry from him the secrets of the confessional, the sacrosanct communication Pat had with him before he died. They drugged the priest to death with an overdose of the mind-altering chemicals they used to loosen up his lips. In some absurd way, Vicky had become so consumed with the TOP SECRET program that protecting its existence became more important to her than protecting the children for which the operation was originally designed. Things had gotten so out of hand back then.

He shook his head as he finished tying his red and blue striped tie that looked decidedly patriotic against his starched, white dress shirt. Sara and the children were ready several minutes later, despite Pat's best efforts to move them along so they could arrive early and get a parking space. He was always amazed at how the casual Catholics came out in droves for Palm Sunday, Easter, and Christmas Masses, but seemingly were in hibernation the rest of the year. They always arrived early and took the best parking spaces, leaving the more consistently faithful, like the O'Donnells, to fend for themselves and park miles away.

"You look beautiful, Honey!" Pat exclaimed seeing Sara standing in the bedroom doorway, neatly decked out in a conservative blue dress, her sparkling red hair shimmering and bouncing off her shoulders. His heart skipped a beat as he stared at his bride, generating for a moment the same kind of fluttering feelings he had when they first met almost fifteen years earlier.

"Thanks, Sweetheart, and I have a surprise for you," she said, stepping to the side to reveal Erin standing behind her, smiling from ear to ear.

She wore a dress that matched Sara's, and her long, auburn hair was combed the same as mom's, save for two light blue, silky ribbons on either side. Pat gasped seeing her like this. It suddenly hit him how she was morphing into a young lady, practically growing an inch or two overnight. Tears filled his eyes as he swept her up in his arms for endless tummy tickles. Finally, he let her down, straightened her dress, and took another long look at mom and daughter standing side by side, looking increasingly like each other day by day.

"Hey what about me?" came a soft voice behind Sara and Erin.

Each of the ladies took a step to the side, and there in between them stood Sean, dressed almost like Pat in a dark blue pin-striped suit. Pat beamed, called him over, and grabbed a brush to fix his hair while mom and sister giggled at the resemblance.

"Did Mommy tell you about my progress report from school, Daddy?" Sean asked, obviously excited about something.

"I forgot to tell you, Pat," Sara began with a huge smile. "He got straight A's again, like last semester. I'm so proud of you, Sean; you have improved so much over the B's and C's you got last year!" Sara cried giving him a big encouraging hug.

Straight A's? Pat wondered. *That boy's up to something.*

"Well, we better get moving so we get a pew we can all sit in!" Pat exclaimed, ushering his family along with both hands.

During the ride to church in the family minivan, Pat thought about Sean's sudden superb performance in school. He had always been a B student, rarely getting A's. He didn't think too much of it when Sean came home with straight A's the first semester of fifth grade, but twice in a row was suspicious. But there was something else about Sean--a very deep secret--that only he and his son knew about. Although Pat abhorred family secrets, this one he kept to himself and cautioned Sean to do the same, for genuine fear over his safety.

During the course of CRYSTAL ROUNDUP operations following the 9/11 terrorist attacks in America, it became apparent Sean also had a psychic gift, although Pat was slow at first to realize it. It was Sean who gave the initial, vague warnings about a threat to Erin, describing it as an *evil man who wanted to kidnap the princess*. Pat realized later that his son's perception of the threat was fuzzy because Sean's psychic abilities were immature and undeveloped.

I wonder, I just wonder, Pat thought as he drove the family to church in silence. He suddenly became worried that Sean was cheating in school, somehow using his powers to gain an edge on tests and homework assignments. He knew he would need to have a talk with him soonest, lest someone else begin to question the surprising improvement in class and stumble across Sean's abilities. Outing his extrasensory talents could put his life at risk. That was a risk Pat was not ready to face.

Although they arrived at Our Lady of La Salette at 0920, the parking lot was already crammed with cars, minivans, and SUVs, many parked crudely in an obvious mad dash to get good seats. He circled around the lot a few times, eventually working his way to the rear parking lot where he found one last slot far and away from the walkway. Pat hustled them all along and was fortunate enough to find a pew near the rear of the church with enough space for the four of them. He looked around at all the new faces, so many of them unfamiliar. When Pat knelt down and blessed himself, he called upon the Blessed Virgin to be with him in prayer this morning.

Mary, I am so worried about my life right now. Once again I find myself ready to start a new journey in this special program. Help me to succeed in the mission the Father has for me, so that I can rescue as many children as I can from the clutches of certain evil. Amen.

All the while he prayed, Pat could not help but feel the presence of the Mother of God next to him, kneeling similarly, prayerfully. When he thought about his fear, he believed he felt a gentle, warm hand caress his, and with it came a surge of great power and strength. Jolts of spiritual energy, tingly and electrified, surged through him in subtle spasms. He knew deeply now that he was primed spiritually, postured to once again fight evil in the name of God. It was a confidence-granting sense of empowerment placed personally in his soul by Christ's mother with whom he had always felt a sense of special bonding.

That evening, following a scrumptious dinner of baked halibut, long grain wild rice, and asparagus, Pat took Sean by the hand and discreetly tugged him downstairs to the recreation room for a little chat. He pulled the wooden six-paneled door to a close once inside, and quickly turned on the overhead lights, adjusting the brightness to a medium glow. He gave Sean a scowl as he waded through a pile of toys parked inconveniently in the middle of the room.

"Come on, Buddy, sit here with me," Pat motioned, patting an empty seat cushion on the long, beige fabric sofa next to where he sat.

Sean cautiously approached his father, clearly unsure if he had done something wrong and was about to be scolded. Pat wrapped a loving, firm arm around his son's shoulder and pulled him in for a hug. He could feel his boy relax instantly.

"Sean, do you remember a long time ago when Mommy was in the hospital and we played a little game? I asked you to guess the number I was thinking."

"Yes, Daddy, but you tricked me. You weren't thinking of a number, it was like a bunch of them all green and sticky," Sean replied, recalling the time his father had actually thought about a field of green shamrocks instead.

"Right. Do you sometimes know what people are thinking?"

Pat almost hesitated when he asked the question. He knew that if Sean was not yet aware of his gift, revealing it to him might be like giving him an empty shopping cart in a Toys "R" Us store and telling him to fill it up with anything he wants! Sean looked down at his feet as they hung over the seat, too short to reach the floor. He had a sad, almost worried look on his face.

"Yes, Daddy, is it okay that I do? Am I in trouble because of it?" he asked, his eyes like two saucers now, slightly red and moist with tears.

Pat smiled and pulled him in even tighter, then caressed his hair. "No, Buddy. You're not in trouble. You have a gift that almost no one else in the world has. It's not a bad thing to have it, but you need to be careful with how you use it. The most important thing about it is you must keep it a secret."

Sean gave him a peculiar look. "Why? I mean it's kinda cool to know what people are thinking."

"It is, but if people--and I mean bad people--find out you have this ability, well they, they...they might hurt you," Pat stammered. He didn't want to scare his son, but he knew he had to impart upon him the seriousness of the matter. "Look, please promise me you won't ever tell anyone, not even Mommy or Erin about this ability. And never show off to anyone that you can read minds, okay?"

Sean looked down at his hands, then up at his father. "Okay, Daddy, I promise."

"And one more thing Sean, you cannot use your gift to get straight A's!"

A little smile danced across his son's face before he put on a puppy dog expression. "I'm sorry, but it's just that the smartest girl in my class, Jessie Owens, sits right in front of me, and it was easy to listen to her thinking about the answers."

Pat snickered, although he did his best to stifle his admiration of Sean's ingenuity. He reached across his lap with his right hand. "Shake?"

"It's a deal, Dad!" Sean said grabbing his father's hand and giving an exaggerated shake that turned into mock fighting as the two of them fell together to the soft carpet below, wrestling.

That night, as Pat nestled in among the cool, soft silky sheets with Sara, his mind was preoccupied with thoughts about his first day at the CCVC. He had trouble falling asleep, tossing and turning, wondering what horrors lay ahead, what brutal abductions were waiting there to greet him upon his arrival. Without even realizing it, he eventually drifted off into sleep sometime close to morning.

In his dream, Pat found himself sitting Indian style on a

throw rug in a tiny bedroom. It was dark, but a small amount of light from a streetlamp came through a window over a twin-sized bed draped in a Barbie doll comforter that looked old, vintage, faded. The light scarcely pierced through a cheap pair of torn, light blue curtains with a blueberry design. His synesthesia kicked into gear, creating in his mind a mosaic of senses...there was a constant clinking metal sound, like a chain somewhere nearby, probably outside the house. It was a sharp sound that had an aura of light-blue sparks surrounded by soft black velvet, and a dizzying, overpowering smell he couldn't quite catalogue. He was so busy trying to process the senses he received, that he nearly jumped out of his skin when he heard a soft voice come from atop the bed, barely at eye level to where he sat.

"Who are you?" she whispered in a soft, angelic voice.

He got up on his knees and leaned in close enough to see her face, barely three inches away. The little girl was about nine years old and was dressed in a pretty pink sundress and pink sandals. Tears streamed from light brown eyes down to the sides of her face, almost dripping into her ears. He realized at that moment that the frail brunette, terrified with hands tied with plastic lock ties to the bedposts, hadn't spoken to him with words, but somehow conveyed her thoughts to him. Pat also realized this dream represented a first for him as well--it was the first time ever that he interacted with someone in a dream, had a conversation of sorts.

Mentally he whispered back to her, "I'm a friend, and I want to help rescue you. Can you hear my voice?"

She nodded.

"What is your name, Honey, and do you know where you are?"

"Emily. Emily Parker. Some man took me from the mall parking lot when my mom turned around to put my baby brother in his car seat. Are you my guardian angel?" she asked innocently.

He was not prepared for the question because he was much more focused on her rescue, certain now he had stumbled upon his first fresh case in the new-and-improved CRYSTAL ROUNDUP operation.

"Well, sort of, Honey. Where do you live, Emily? Do you know the name of the mall?"

She sobbed as she spoke with her thoughts.

"Dayton, we were at the Dayton Mall after church. Please take me home now!" she began to cry out loud, slipping out of her telepathic bond with Pat for a moment to wail in the physical world.

"Shhhh. You have to be very quiet. We don't want to make the man mad at you. Do you know where he took you?"

"To a trailer park someplace. I think it's near the mall. We didn't drive real long."

"It's gonna be alright, Emily, I'm going to make sure…" he started to say but suddenly found himself riveted from the dream and back in his bed, alarm clock screaming for his attention.

Sara dove across him to grab it and fumbled with the buttons to shut it off.

"Are you okay, Pat?" she asked, setting the silenced clock back on the nightstand.

He looked at her, pursed his lips, and shook his head. "I'm not sure, Sorcha. The dreams about missing kids have started back up again," he cried burying his face in his hands.

~ 5 ~

Wearing just his light brown sleep pants and an old black T-shirt with a Led Zeppelin logo, Pat leapt from bed and headed straight to his den. He knew Emily had precious little time to wait, and he needed to act fast. He opened a small safe in the back of the room and retrieved a special key to the Secure Telephone Unit on his desk. He hit the speed dial number to Colonel Helmsley's secure cell phone and prayed quietly the colonel would be near it and pick up. It rang six times before he got a voice mail prompt, and with each unanswered ring his angst grew tenfold.

"Crap!" he stammered. "Boss, Pat here. Had another one of those episodes like in the past. We need to act fast. Call me ASAP!"

Pat had to talk around the subject so as not to reveal any Special Access Program proprietary information over an unsecured line. He was certain his panicked-voice message alone would be signal enough to his former boss that things had suddenly moved up an order of magnitude in the program.

He paced the soft, reddish Persian rug in his den for several minutes, waiting for Helmsley to call back, but he never did.

The wait was excruciating. A gut-wrenching sense of helplessness came over him, and ultimately he decided he was not going to be able to do much more from home.

He knew he had better get ready and drive straight to the CCVC, so he hurried about showering and dressing in casual business attire…a pair of gray dress pants, crisp white shirt, dark blue sport jacket, but no tie. He grabbed his Beretta from the den safe and slapped one of three magazines filled with copper ball rounds in the stock, placing the other two in a Bianchi leather dual magazine pouch. After chambering a round, he strapped the semi-automatic pistol in his black leather belt holster and bolted from his garage, catching but a glimpse of his light brown brick colonial home in the rear view mirror as he raced against traffic over to Arlington.

Although he had been in the law enforcement business for more than fourteen years, Pat never visited the world-renowned CCVC--the clearinghouse for crimes against children that included its own television program, *Lost Innocence,* which aired weekly over broadcast and cable television stations across the country. Since its inception in the early 1980s the center and its television program were responsible for repatriating with their parents over 60,000 children who were missing, exploited, or abducted.

He pulled up to the CCVC headquarters building just a few minutes past 0700, marveling at the modern architecture of the facility. The three-story structure featured strange angles, making the top two floors appear to hang precariously over the ones below. It looked like a giant pyramid turned upside down with its peak buried halfway into the ground. The light brown and white marble building seemed to be held together by toothpick-thin supports that Pat surmised was probably nothing more than an illusion created by the sharp angular levels and giant plates of reflective windows all around. The sun was coming up as he arrived, shooting streaks of bright golden rays off the building and lighting up Wilson Boulevard.

He found parking in a pay lot on the north side of the campus and walked around to the front to two large, smoky-gray glass doors that were at least twelve feet high each. Once inside the lobby, he spied an information kiosk with no attendant, beyond which were a security cordon complete with metal detectors and two typical rent-a-cop contractor guards, both a bit pudgy in ill-fitting uniforms. He immediately could sense the passive-aggressive attitudes of the man and woman, and decided it would be best for him to avoid confrontation with them on his first day. He pulled his cell phone from his jacket and was about to call Colonel Helmsley, when it rang.

"Sir, it's great to hear from you, did you get my message?"

"Sure did, Pat, and I called your house, but Sara said you left early. Where are you right now?"

"I'm at the CCVC lobby...how about you?"

"I'm on Wilson Boulevard, about to turn into the lot. Stay put, and I'll be there in a few minutes. Out here," the colonel said just before hanging up.

Pat nervously paced the front of the lobby, all the while conscious of the occasional stares from the two security guards. But in a matter of moments he broke out into a bright smile upon seeing Colonel Helmsley walking up the marble-tiled walkway in front of the center, just a few feet from the entrance. The auto-sensing doors sprung open producing a wind rushing sound as he greeted him.

"Pat, let's not talk here, we'll go up to the new wing on the third floor where we can chat in safety," he cautioned as they walked to the security area.

Colonel Helmsley displayed his CCVC building pass to the guards. "I'm escorting this gentleman," he informed them.

"I still need some ID!" the woman barked, rolling her eyes at the colonel.

Pat pulled a small black leather case from his jacket pocket, first displaying his bright gold OSI badge on the outside, then unfolding it to reveal his credentials on the inside. "I'm carrying," he told the guards to ensure they knew his gun was about to set off the metal detector.

He whisked past them, not out of disrespect, but because it was plain to see they could care less. A robot could perform their jobs better. They did as they were trained—demanded to see identification, but it was clear they had never grasped the concept of why they needed to see it. They barely glanced at his credentials, casually waved him through, and made no effort to verify he was authorized to be there and to be armed.

He and the colonel rode an elevator alone. "Security sucks here, Boss. I mean no offense and all, but those two clowns will let anyone in!"

"Sorry, Pat, I know. I wish I had some control over them, but the Justice Department doesn't own the building. You may already know that the CCVC started out as a private venture by a group of parents who lost children to pedophiles many years back. It wasn't until the early nineties when it partnered with DoJ for added leverage. It's a quasi-governmental entity now, and we only lease space here in our partnership with the founders."

Just then the elevator bell rang, and the doors opened to the third floor. The colonel put a finger to his lips as Pat was about to speak. "Our wing is down the end of this hall, so everything up to our door is not SCIF'd and therefore out of bounds for our work."

They walked up to a dark wood door with a simple lever-style opener made of shiny brass. Just to the left was a placard that read, *Special Projects Division,* causing Pat to snicker at its non-descript name. On the other side of the wooden door was a small entry-way, not much larger than six by eight feet. At the far end of this foyer-like space was a large steel vault door painted off-white, with an electronic cipher lock to the right of it. Colonel Helmsley slid his CCVC badge through a reader next to the cipher lock keypad, causing the device to *BEEP.* After a half-second or so, a green light appeared on top of the keypad upon which Colonel Helmsley entered a six digit code. Then, with a heavy *CLUNK* sound, the vault locking pins retracted, and the door swung open freely.

Waiting to greet Pat on the other side were Doctors Davis and Jacobsen. Pat was surprised to see them both there so early. "Hey Woody, morning Jake," he said giving them both shakes. "We need to work on something ASAP. I had a dream last night that I know is real-time."

"Well, I'm staying at a hotel a block from here, and Jake's apartment is around the corner, so it was easy for us to rush over when we got the call from John. But please, let's go into your new office and go over the dream," Woody suggested with an arm over Pat's shoulder.

My new office? he thought, wondering if he was being led to a typical cubicle graveyard arrangement to which he was accustomed, something straight out of a Dilbert comic strip. But nothing could have prepared him for the opulence that awaited him. At the far end of the Special Projects Division wing was an enormous office, at least fifteen by twenty feet, with a gigantic cherry wood desk in the center, on a plush beige carpet. Behind it was nothing but glass--and an impressive view of the Pentagon and the Capitol Mall area. Pat could tell as he glanced out to take in the view, that it was one of those weird angle floors and end offices he had admired from the street just moments before.

Off to the left of the desk were a small sofa and three side chairs that Pat immediately knew were there for his special purpose--his *psychic state* sofa upon which he could rest and draw up impressions about child victims.

"Well, Pat, lay it on us. What happened in your dream last night?" the colonel asked as he sat in one of the side chairs, motioning for Pat to lie down.

Woody and Jake took up positions near him as well. Although the colonel and Dr. Davis were old hands at this, Jake was not. He clearly was eager and excited to jump into Pat's world, something he had studied extensively, but with which he had no practical, firsthand experience.

Pat related the details of the dream and how it was apparent to him from his "conversations" with Emily Parker that she was abducted Palm Sunday afternoon in Dayton, Ohio. Woody appeared stunned by the revelation that Pat had conversed with a dream subject who was able to give him enough clues to home in on who she was and to where she likely was taken. He looked at Dr. Jacobsen.

"We've never seen this before, Jake; this type of interaction is unprecedented for us!"

The colonel interrupted. "Jake, did you get the morning Amber Alert reports? Anything from Dayton?"

"Yes, John, here they are," he replied grabbing a small stack of papers from Pat's inbox on top of his desk. "There were six alerts nationwide in the last twenty-four hours. And there's one from Dayton, and, and..." his jaw dropped and hands shook as he scanned the report. "It was a ten-year-old girl named Emily Parker. She was taken from the Dayton Mall around three o'clock yesterday afternoon, but no one saw the abduction!"

He handed the report to Pat, affixed to which was a photograph of Emily supplied by her mother.

"That's her! That's the girl from my dream last night. Look, we need to alert the Ohio authorities that she is probably in a trailer park near the mall, in a trailer with torn blueberry curtains in a bedroom window!"

Colonel Helmsley ran to Pat's desk and grabbed his computer keyboard, nearly knocking the monitor off the desk with his sudden bustle of energy. He did a search for trailer parks in the Dayton area, finding twelve. Although he grimaced when he told the team there were a dozen parks, he broke out into a bright smile seeing them displayed on a map with the Dayton Mall in the center.

"Only one park is near the mall, about two miles away. The others are all at least fifteen miles out, really out in the surrounding suburbs!" he cried out. Next he grabbed Pat's telephone.

"Boss, who are you calling?" Pat asked somewhat stunned by the pace of things on his first day.

"We have a CRYSTAL ROUNDUP Bureau agent downstairs

in the CCVC Operations Center. He will ensure an anonymous call comes in to the OC that will be traced back to a pay phone in Dayton. He will have to say he saw the little girl's face in the window of a trailer with those torn blueberry curtains. It's a tough story to sell, but they will still act on it. There's no doubt in my mind they will."

Pat listened intently as Colonel Helmsley passed along the information and instructions to the FBI agent over a secure line. When he hung up, he crossed his fingers.

"Look, our guy in the OC will call me the moment he has any news. How about we get you in-processed Pat, so you can park in your reserved slot tomorrow, and get into the building with your own pass."

"Okay, Sir, but I'm literally on pins and needles right now. Emily is in danger, and I sure hope these guys act fast!"

A Dayton police cruiser and two Ohio State Trooper vehicles were the first to arrive at the Sunridge Trailer Park just off Paragon Road, near Grant Park. Within seconds, seven other city police and state police vehicles closed in on the park and cut off all ingress and egress points. It was a small complex, with four paved roads and about forty trailers of all shapes and sizes. The officers swarmed the area, running quickly from unit to unit, glancing at the windows for the reported blueberry design curtains. They made quick work of it, and within three minutes of arrival, one of the troopers keyed his radio.

"This is Sergeant Cooper, I'm outside of trailer number thirty-four on the west end road of the park. It has the curtains we're looking for, the right design and torn and all."

"Stand-by for back-up," came the male voice of the senior officer in charge of the hastily-arranged command center at the park entrance.

By now local news reporters had begun to converge on the scene, having picked up the radio transmissions on their police scanners. The police blocked the road and would not let the media within ten feet of the park. The commotion of the growing operation was loud and tumultuous, something Cooper could hear over his radio.

"Roger that," Cooper replied. "Aw shoot!" he screamed into his microphone seeing the trailer door swing open swiftly.

The five foot, ten inch husky state trooper jumped to his left taking cover on the side of the trailer. He aimed his gun at the door and yelled, "Police, drop any weapons and come out slowly with hands in the air!"

But there was no immediate response. Twenty or so fellow police officers arrived and began taking up positions around the double-wide. They had no idea how many suspects they might have to deal with, and didn't need anyone fleeing with Emily from a rear door or side window.

Sergeant Cooper shouted again, "Come out now! Hands up!"

A frail, very old voice came crackling from the trailer door. "Please, don't shoot me. I didn't mean any harm."

Cooper and his back-up watched as a wretchedly skinny man in his seventies stepped out with empty hands held high and trembling. He was incredibly unkempt, with straggles of gray hair, white undershirt peppered with dark stains, and bare feet. He had on boxer shorts that awkwardly reached down to his knees. Old bruises and age spots covered his arms and legs, and on his right wrist was a plastic hospital identification band.

Sergeant Cooper cautiously walked toward him, and when he was certain he was unarmed, he re-holstered his gun while his fellow officers kept theirs trained on the old man. As he quickly handcuffed him, the man spoke in a hoarse voice accompanied by sniffles.

"Please, don't take my Susan away from me again," he cried.

Cooper gave him a curious look, worried now that the anonymous caller was a false lead or a hoax. "Who's Susan?" he asked him while two other state troopers entered the trailer to clear it.

"My daughter, Susan, of course! Please, don't take her away again," he repeated sobbing.

Two officers who had entered the trailer emerged with a little girl whose hands were now free from their plastic zip locks. The little, pink-sundress-wearing beauty in her matching pink sandals let out a cry when she stepped down from the trailer and spied the old man in handcuffs. She stood with her hands on her hips at first; then she wagged a finger at him while shouting sternly to the old man, "I'm not Susan! I'm Emily, Emily Parker!"

It was as if she had become exasperated at some point trying to explain it to him many times over the course of her near twenty-four hour ordeal.

"No!" he stammered. "No! Don't go away, Susan. Please not again!" the old man cried loudly now, clearly emotionally spent and disturbed.

Two police officers escorted Emily to the front of the park where an ambulance was situated, while Sergeant Cooper waited with the old man in front of the trailer for a forensics team to arrive and process the residence for evidence.

When Emily and her escorts arrived at the park entrance, dozens of news reporters rushed the line trying to get pictures of her and a chance to talk with her. The police did their best to keep them at bay, but one determined journalist with a live news team got through and ran up to Emily with camera rolling and microphone extended.

"Emily! Emily! How does it feel to be rescued?" shouted the pretty and perky blond reporter, tossing her hair back so the camera would capture her face on live television.

"I just want to go home and see my mom," the precocious pre-teen replied, matter-of-factly, seemingly unfazed by the hubbub.

"Did the man hurt you in any way, Honey?" she asked.

One of the troopers pushed her back with a stern warning. "Get out of her face! How dare you ask such an insensitive question?"

Suddenly, Emily stopped and looked right at the camera.

"I really want to thank my guardian angel. He came to see me last night in the trailer and told me everything was going to be okay. And he was right."

~ 6 ~

Pat sat in front of the camera and half-smiled as the flash went off, his preoccupation with Emily Parker and her pending rescue tormenting him.

"Your building pass will be ready in just a few minutes, Mr. O'Donnell," the clerk said, handing him a form for his signature to complete the task.

It was his last stop of the morning, having already picked up his magnetic card for entry to the private parking lot where he had a reserved space. Colonel Helmsley's Secure Telephone Equipment cell phone rang out loudly just as the young bushy-haired male clerk, a local college intern, handed Pat his building pass, still warm from the printing machine.

He listened intently as the colonel spoke. "Uh huh. Yes. That's great news!" he exclaimed before disconnecting and putting the phone back in his jacket pocket.

Pat was anxious to learn the details, although it was obvious to him and the others that Emily had been rescued, and that even before he had completed in-processing at the CCVC on his first day, he had found another child.

"I guess we'll get the dump from you upstairs?" Pat asked

excitedly, knowing full-well Helmsley wouldn't talk about a sensitive operation in the open. The colonel nodded, smiling.

Once back in the Special Projects Division, Colonel Helmsley switched on a large screen, flat-panel television and pulled up a curious-looking channel guide. He gave the men a quick run-down of the call about Emily's rescue he had received from the Operations Center as he fumbled about the controls. Pat noticed Jake's eyes were practically bugged out as the colonel relayed the good news, along with the details about how his dream matched the facts of the crime, resulting in the little girl's recovery.

"We can access every television station in the world on this system. I'm trying to locate a local channel from the Dayton area. Okay, here we go," Colonel Helmsley said settling in on Channel 2312.

It had live, continuous coverage of the breaking news about Emily Parker's successful rescue. They sat in silence, watching the scene from a news helicopter over the park. An Ohio State Police Crime Scene Investigations mobile unit was parked in front of a trailer, and it was from this overhead vantage point that Pat saw something that made details from his dream suddenly make more sense. Behind the trailer where Emily was held, was a large black Labrador Retriever chained to a huge metal pole. Dusty dirt, mixed with the dog's feces, made an almost perfect circle around the pole as the dog paced about, nervously clanking its chain leash. Pat's synesthetic senses bombarded him again at this moment. Each time the chain clanked, he heard the metallic sound and saw light-blue sparks in his mind, the same sparks he had seen in his dream. They seemed to dance off the dog's black fur, and as it kicked up the earth and excrement, the pungent stench flowed into his brain.

His heart raced when the scene suddenly switched to a replay of the live interview the reporter had done barely one hour before when Emily was escorted to the ambulance. For the first time outside of his dream, he was able to see the little beauty, free now from her confines and about to be repatriated with her parents. They all watched the local news reporter barge her way through to speak with Emily, the only journalist bold enough to succeed in getting an exclusive scoop on the big news of the day. His mouth was agape--as were the others--when Emily spoke those haunting words about a guardian angel visiting her and comforting her the night before her rescue. She stared straight at the camera, her young, sweet confidence brimming. To Pat she seemed to be speaking directly to him, eerily looking right at him. To him and the others in the room there was no escaping the obvious...Emily had her own psychic connection to Pat, just as he had to her the night before.

"Shit!" Woody said aloud, astonishing them all with his uncharacteristic word choice. "Shit," he repeated without taking his eyes off the television. Finally he looked at Pat. "You realize what this means? Not only did you interact with her, but she interacted with you last night. This is huge."

Jake was sitting by taking it all in it seemed. "Dr. Davis, as you may recall from my work, we've had case studies where people with reported psychic abilities are able to communicate with each other over great distances."

Woody opened his mouth and was about to speak when Colonel Helmsley chimed in.

"I know, Jake, and I don't doubt for a moment that our little

Emily has such powers. We may have to someday bring her into the CRYSTAL ROUNDUP family. It would be safer for her to be on our side looking out, than outside looking in--and potentially tipping off the public to the existence of the program."

Pat was taking the entire conversation in, all the while thinking about his son and his abilities. Emily was about the same age as Sean, and he just couldn't imagine her or him drawn into the secret Special Access Program black world. It troubled him that the colonel was suggesting something as draconian as pulling children into the program before they were old enough to make such decisions for themselves!

"Boss, isn't she a little young for this stuff?" Pat asked, finally unsticking his thoughts of Sean from his mind.

The colonel chuckled, his eyes twinkling a bit. "I'm talking about way in the future. Of course she is too young now, but we may have to keep tabs on that young lady in the meantime. If the day comes, and she's ready, she can make that call."

Pat looked over at Dr. Davis who seemed to be trying to get his thoughts together.

"You know, Pat. We may be able to use your abilities to help us find others with extrasensory powers. Perhaps we can build a group of psychics for the CR program to help the interagency group in its other operational missions!" Woody practically shouted as his thoughts tumbled out.

Pat could tell he had never really given this possibility much consideration; the apparent scarcity of assets like him kept the program's focus so narrow over the years. He nodded at Woody. In one respect he was actually relieved to think about the prospect of having others available to lend support to the

CR program, to help out agencies like the CIA, Defense Intelligence Agency, National Security Agency, and others. It could mean he would have more time to concentrate on finding children, the spiritual mission he came to realize after 9/11 was his true calling, the special purpose God preprogrammed him to do…his Supreme Truism as he liked to call it.

"Gents, I'd like to get to work on the five other Amber Alerts you have this morning."

"Here you go," Jake answered, handing Pat one of the files.

"No, I need all of them, Jake. All at once. I can't predict which one will come to me first, so I need to absorb them in one shot, then lie back and see where they take me."

He sat at his desk and read through the five files in silence...four girls and one boy, all between six and twelve years of age. All were taken within the last twenty-four hours, and all were believed to be stranger abductions. He strolled over to the sofa, reclined back on it, and closed his eyes. The three others sat quietly in the side seats. Although the colonel and Woody were familiar with the routine, it was Dr. Jacobsen's first exposure to Pat's daytime reveries and psychic states. Jake had a microcassette recorder in his hand that made a loud *POP!* sound when he pressed the record button.

Pat opened his eyes and scowled at him over the disruption. But a second later, when he closed them again, he was swept away in a rushing sensation akin to a subway train careening through a station without stopping. He could even feel a gust of wind it seemed, just like the pressure from the train as it coursed through the narrow tunnel before the platform, pushing cooler air ahead of it. When the sensation of the train blasting past him stopped, Pat found himself standing on a platform beneath an escalator, holding onto a metal railing to keep him from rocking too far forward. While he was present in this scene, watching the sleek silver train whiz by, he was simultaneously alert and present in his office with his team, describing to them everything he witnessed.

About ten yards ahead he saw the little girl, one of the faces from the stack of Amber Alerts. She was Rosario Gutierrez, a seven-year-old Mexican-American girl reported last night to have been abducted by a white woman in a beat-up pickup truck from her front yard in Compton, California. She was still wearing the yellow shorts and white and yellow blouse her mother tearfully described to the police when she reported the abduction. She did not appear to Pat to be abused or traumatized at all, for which he gave a momentary thanks to God. He watched as the woman stood near the platform, continually checking her watch, and looking toward the escalator where Pat stood. She seemed to be waiting for someone, and never once boarded one of the Red Line trains that stopped nearly every five minutes.

The woman was in her mid-fifties or so and had an East European look to Pat. He didn't know why he ascribed this ethnicity to her, but there was something about her straight, short brown hair, her slightly hunched shoulders, and her rough hands and face, that all seemed to suggest to him a tough Slavic life. One where she spent much of her youth tilling soil in long dresses and scarves, hands calloused over from years of toiling on a farm. Over the cackling loudspeaker Pat heard a public safety announcement for Union Station, and he knew then that he was in the heart of Los Angeles.

"She just seemed to have made eye contact with someone on

the escalator. I'm going to walk over there since no one seems to see me. I feel like a ghost," Pat whispered to the others in his office.

"Be careful, Buddy!" Colonel Helmsley cautioned. "We had a close call with Emily Parker thinking you were her guardian angel. We seem to be in uncharted territory right now!"

He watched as a white male in his mid-forties walked over to the woman and Rosario. The sick pervert eyed the little girl up and down as if examining a piece of merchandise in a store. Pat stood barely two feet away from them and nearly fell forward when a commuter walked right through him from behind, as if he were a spirit. It felt like his vital organs were pulled out of his chest as the man passed right through him. Pat scrambled with flailing arms and hands to grasp the air, pulling at his imaginary heart and lungs to tuck them safely back inside his body.

"Nice lil' one for me this time, Ilka," the creep nastily said while caressing Rosario's long black hair. The girl looked up at him with worried, chestnut-colored eyes. The business professional, well-dressed in a conservative suit, silk red tie, and expensive Italian shoes, sickened Pat so much that he lunged at him and swung his fists hard, attempting to deliver two powerful blows to his face. But he just caught empty air and nearly tumbled through them both as if they were holographic images made merely of photons.

Ilka obviously knew how much the man valued his new purchase.

"I vant zix dousand dollas for dis vun, Mister Harris," she demanded in a thick, Slavic accent.

The man was startled. "That's robbery!" he protested.

"Dake it, or leeb it. I lots of odder men to sell to," she said pulling Rosario's tiny, caramel hand as if ready to walk away.

"Okay, okay, six it is!" he said gruffly, pulling his wallet out and counting out ten one hundred dollar bills, then adding them to a larger stack of bills in a thick envelope he had in his jacket pocket.

The woman took the cash and released Rosario's hand. She leaned down and looked at her. "¡Haz lo que este gentil hombre te diga!" she cautioned, instructing her to do whatever the man wanted.

Rosario nodded just before the monster whisked her onto a train that had stopped with the destination, *North Hollywood,* displayed on its front and side. When the train whooshed away, Pat was deposited back in his office, eyes open and blinking to adjust to the sudden change in light.

"Boss, we need to--" he started to say but noticed Colonel Helmsley was sitting at his desk on the phone with the Bureau agent in the Operations Center. Since Pat had given them real-time information about everything he witnessed, the colonel was one step ahead of him relaying the details to the CRYSTAL ROUNDUP agent.

"Okay, sounds good. Yeah sure, shoot. I'm gonna put you on speaker phone," the colonel said as he pressed a button.

The agent's voice filled the room. "Hello, team, I was just giving John an update on the Emily Parker case from Dayton. The old guy that abducted her thought she was his daughter, Susan. It seems she was kidnapped and murdered thirty years ago in Missouri when she was nine, and apparently Emily looks an awful lot like her. The old guy had just been released from a VA mental health clinic a few days ago. It's kinda sad, but it doesn't appear he was going to harm her at all."

"That's great to know. This is Pat O'Donnell, by the way. Thanks for the update, but I don't think Rosario is going to be as lucky, have you got that one energized?"

"No worries, while John was relating your info I was submitting an anonymous call into the Amber Alert system, and an urgent BOLO went out immediately to the LAPD."

Pat smiled and clasped his hands in prayer. "Thanks man, appreciate what you're doing."

He heard a slight chuckle over the speaker phone. "Hey Pat, none of this would be possible without you. I look forward to meeting you someday. Thanks, Buddy!"

For the next two hours, without a single break, Pat and the team worked to unlock information about the remaining four Amber Alert victims. Each time, Pat was able to lie back and receive psychic impressions about the abductions and current whereabouts of the three remaining abducted little girls, taking them in whatever order they flowed into his brain, apparently saving for last the one missing boy. Frequently his synesthesia was in full operational mode, giving him an extra set of clues about each crime to add a finer level of detail to his psychic images. He would smell flowers, fast food, sewage, and garbage. He tasted juice and tears, and he felt the sting of a belt across one of the victim's faces. As he spoke out loud about all that he saw, felt, tasted, and sniffed, Colonel Helmsley was on the phone with the Operations Center relaying the information. His psychic tips were converted into anonymous calls that resulted in a handful of hostage rescue teams put into action to liberate the girls from the four corners of the United States.

"Sir, I gotta pee!" Pat said suddenly after working through

the details of the last girl who was abducted. "Let's take a quick break, and when I come back maybe we can jump in on the last kid, the little boy from St. Louis."

The colonel nodded. "I agree. I think we could all use a break. That's some amazing work you've done today, Pat! Maybe Woody and I can go visit the Operations Center and check on the progress in rescuing the four girls. Jake, you wanna stay behind and work with Pat?"

"Sure, John! I would love to. This is so fascinating for me!" he eagerly agreed, tape recorder in hand with a fresh tape for the last session.

When Pat returned from his break, he grabbed a can of Coke from his office refrigerator and offered the same to Jake. But the Berkeley graduate cringed and asked instead if there was any organic tea or bottled water. Pat smirked handing him the water, then took up his position on the couch.

He closed his eyes and let his mind relax, thinking with his senses and not with his mind as Woody had trained him long ago. Typically, when he let his thoughts fade, he found his synesthesia was most pronounced, and the impressions he received oftentimes were a confused confluence of sight and sound. Taste and touch. And once they settled in his brain, a mosaic would emerge that morphed from the chaotic to the clear to orient him to his goal.

The last missing child --Ricky Sullivan, an eight-year-old, blue-eyed blond boy, was last seen walking to a convenience store barely half a block from his home in Ladue, Missouri, just west of St. Louis. No one saw him abducted, and surveillance video from the store showed he never arrived. He simply vanished from the earth.

Pat let the facts he had read in the Amber Alert report sink into the background of his mind, as he drifted slowly into that obscure place somewhere between real dreams and daydreams, where he knew his paranormal attention was most focused. As he did, he found himself pressed firmly against a solid surface. Standing upright, with arms open wide, his body clung to the giant object. His eyes were closed, and his face was turned to the right as his left cheek scraped against the surface. It was cool to the touch, and rough like sandpaper or gravel. Pat could smell the touch itself. It presented like a bag of potatoes, brown and earthy. The object's smell was not just brown, but reddish in spots, and the only visual image he received was of something dense and opaque. He opened his eyes slowly, trying to focus, but because he was so close to it, the object was difficult to see clearly. It was huge. Pat looked up and saw no end to it, no sky at all even though he knew it was daytime in this vision. He pried himself away from the object carefully, not sure what it was or if he was in any immediate danger.

He stepped back and realized it was a brick wall...the tallest he had ever seen. He looked to his right, then to his left, and saw the wall went off in both directions as endlessly as it towered upward. He ran to his left, hoping to see some end to the structure, but the image never changed; it never seemed to have any boundaries. He stopped and turned immediately to his right with a leap, only to strike a new brick wall that just a moment before wasn't there. He turned to run to his left again, but found a similar new wall blocking that direction. He turned left once more, only to find a wall there as well, trapping him in a confine no larger than an old-fashioned telephone booth. He looked up once more and saw the wall had completed itself into a low ceiling above, forcing him to lower his head lest he scrape it. He was now in a small coffin of sorts, made of harsh red and brown brick all around him. Dark and frightening.

Pat came out of the vision in a panic attack. He sat up abruptly, grasped his chest tightly, and sucked in air as fast as he could. Jake grabbed his arm to keep him from falling off the sofa.

"What happened, Pat? What did you see? You never said a word during this episode."

"I don't know. I was trapped, in, in, in, in a brick wall like room, I mean tiny like I could barely stand up. Christ! I hope Ricky's not been buried alive!"

The colonel and Woody walked back in as Pat was describing the horrifying vision he had, scant as it was on details.

"Maybe you're just a bit burned out right now, Pat," Woody offered. "After all, you solved five crimes in your first day! Perhaps you need to back off for now. We'll come back to this all tomorrow. You can't save everyone in one day!"

But Pat wasn't so easily convinced. He maintained a blank stare as he tried to comprehend what the mini-nightmare might have meant. One thing was for sure in his tortured mind…Ricky Sullivan was in grave danger. The lack of clues to finding him troubled him greatly. Never before had he experienced an obstacle to his psychic quests.

Colonel Helmsley had a big grin on his face as he opened a small black notebook.

"Pat, you're going to love this. All of the girls have been recovered safely. The LAPD descended on the Metro system, stopping the Red Line, going from train to train until they found

Rosario and this Harris guy. Apparently he's singing like a bird right now, giving up all he knows about the Polish woman and a ring of other pedophiles. The other three girls were found unharmed as well, though in one case the perp was pretty close to assaulting one of them."

"Thank God!" Pat said aloud, drawing a nod from Woody.

He made the sign of the cross and prayed silently to himself. A gush of warm emotion filled his heart at that moment, the same kind of joy he had felt since he was a child whenever he connected with God on a deep, personal level. But it didn't last long. Suddenly, his head began to hurt fiercely, like a migraine was forming, though he had never had one before in his life.

"I've got a splitting headache right now. Maybe you're right, Woody. Maybe it's too much in one shot. Let me head home, and we can pick it up early tomorrow. Let's find Ricky in the morning, along with any new cases."

But he was still unsettled. There was just something about this case with its brick wall image that was vastly different from every other psychic impression he had ever experienced. He couldn't put his finger on it, but the disparity bothered him, and a sickening, menacing sensation suddenly flooded his gut.

~ 7 ~

He fell into a deep sleep that night following a heavy dose of Motrin for his migraine…*Vitamin M*, as he sometimes called it. A pint of Irish stout to swallow it down didn't hurt either, although it was certainly not something he did often. With Sara snuggled in close, his arm around her shoulder, he peacefully surrendered to his cocoon-like slumber. For the first several hours his sleep was uneventful, but as morning drew near, his dreams became nightmarish. He had a foreboding sense of being in an evil place, with forces, dark and demonic, taunting him from deep inside. He sometimes dreamt of this place, several times really since childhood. It was typically a forest of some kind whose deep and mysterious foliage seemingly provided cover and concealment to the proprietors of hell who roamed it freely, attempting to draw him in.

Despite the thick-as-pea soup force of evil that emanated from it, magnetically trying to coax him closer, he always felt a parallel, competing force that repelled him away. Little did he know, but Saint Michael, the Archangel who once cast Satan into hell, stood in silent sentry and gently pushed Pat away whenever he would venture too near the gates of the underworld. Saint Michael--also the Patron Saint of Law Enforcement Officers—was permanently attached to Pat on a silver medallion around his neck that he never removed. More significantly, Michael was eternally by his side spiritually, something he never, ever realized. Michael, under the direction of the Virgin Mary, was stuck to Pat like glue to, "ensure Pat succeeds in his Supreme Truism," as she told the Archangel.

Courtesy of his invisible bodyguard, Pat always kept a safe distance from this place whenever it surfaced in a dream. He had long-since come to believe it was not an actual place on the planet, but a symbolic location. A representation of evil perhaps, if not Hades itself. In the instant dream, the malevolent location from his childhood nightmares was now juxtaposed with current events, and weaved together in some strange fashion. This time, on direct orders from God, Saint Michael was told to stand down. Tonight, God needed Pat to enter hell.

Once again he found himself hugging the giant brick wall from his vision of the day before. This time, however, he ran to his right, never daring to turn around lest he find another wall blocking his path. Up ahead he saw what appeared to be a small opening. Although it looked to be no more than fifty yards away, he ran and ran and ran at breakneck speed, seemingly never making any progress in reaching it. He stopped to catch his breath, looking down at his drenched shirt. Sweat poured down his sinewy biceps to his forearms. He looked back at the wall once more, only to see he now was suddenly standing at the mysterious opening, as if all along what he needed to do was to relax and automatically transport himself to it. He crouched down and peered into the waist-high square cavity, but saw only darkness on the other side. Slowly, gingerly, he stepped in with his right foot, then he swung his head and torso inside, followed by his left foot. He stood up cautiously, not sure if he would bump his head on another brick ceiling. He saw in the dim glow of stars and a half moon that he was in a forest…the evil woods of his youthful bad dreams. He heard noises through the trees, muffled somewhat by a thick abundance of fresh green spring leaves. He tiptoed to the source of the noise, and as he got closer, he could hear suppressed cries.

A young boy was sitting on the ground amongst a clump of small, immature trees. His feet and hands were bound. Pat knew instantly this little cherub was Ricky Sullivan...there was no mistaking him from his Amber Alert poster. A tall, burly man stood in front of the boy. He wore black pants and boots, a black jacket of some kind, and from the rear Pat could see he had on a dark hood. He believed he had stumbled upon the pair just after the man set Ricky down, and now the abductor simply stood and stared at the boy.

All the while Pat watched the man, he knew he was simply dreaming the vision. And although he was aware he was in a dream, he was certain what he was witnessing was occurring in real-time somewhere. He looked around for clues...street lights, road signs, a monument of some kind in the distance, but there was nothing. Nothing but trees, the boy, and his abductor. He even tried to catalogue the scents, sounds, and touch of the forest, but it was if his synesthesia was strangely shut off and out of commission.

Pat crept forward, trying to get a closer look at the man, and when he did he stepped on a brittle twig that made a loud,

SNAP! The man turned instantly and looked toward him. Pat gasped, realizing immediately that, like his dream of Emily Parker, in this dream the hooded man knew he was there. And just like the episode in the Hogan's Alley simulator, the man's face appeared for a brief second as dark red, evil, and demonic. Pat had to blink to make the hideous visage disappear. The man ran straight up to him, and through a face-covering black shroud, that only let Pat see his sick green eyes, he could tell the man was both startled and intrigued at the interruption.

In a deep, booming voice he screamed at Pat, "Who the hell are you? How did you get in here?"

But Pat thought the man almost seemed to be looking beyond him, as if through him. He took a step back, and the man didn't seem to notice. He realized the kidnapper couldn't see him clearly, if at all.

"Who are you? Let that boy go, you sick bastard!" Pat screamed.

When Pat spoke the man's eyes sparkled in the moon's glow. Pat's voice had helped the maniac triangulate his position. He leapt forward with his right fist pulled back and pummeled Pat in the face, knocking him to the ground.

Wow! This isn't right! I'm in a dream, but that hurt like hell! Pat thought, attempting to get up, but the man jumped on top of him swinging wildly.

The man delivered two more solid punches, one more to his face, the other to his chest. Pat managed to roll him off to his left. He jumped on top and tried to pin him down, but the man was powerful. Pat stayed on top of him for no more than five seconds before the man pushed him up and off. Pat lunged at him again, managing to smash a fist into his face. He swung two more times, but the psycho successfully blocked both attempts with his forearms. The man kicked upward with his knee and almost struck Pat in the groin, but he managed to veer off to his right quickly and avoid the crippling injury. Pat spied a large rock and grabbed it, ready to crush the madman's skull, but the kidnapper was fast and moved his head to the side before getting hit. The twenty pound stone came crashing down into the cool moist earth with a loud *THUD!* right next to the sicko's head. Pat was crouched down, trying to maintain some semblance of control. He swung his right knee into the side of the man's head, driving his skull sharply against the cold rough rock. It was an intense double smack that stunned the man long enough for Pat to move in and lock him down.

He grabbed the man's right arm to control the punches and quickly pulled him into a cross-arm lock, part of his self-defense training as an OSI agent. He tried several times to undo the tight hold Pat had on him, but it was fruitless. Each time the kidnapper struggled, Pat would put reverse pressure on the man's elbow joint, forcing it backwards and inducing severe pain in him. When the man finally relaxed, Pat asked him again who he was.

"Screw you! You're a cop aren't you?" he asked, his voice suggesting he was proud of his ability to read people.

"Something like that. Now who are you!?" Pat demanded, once again sharply pulling back on the man's arm, stretching his tendons severely.

"Go to hell!" he sneered loudly.

"I kinda think I'm already there."

"You ain't seen nothin' yet, pig," the man spat out with a snicker.

Pat reached down with his right hand, slipping two fingers under the man's cloth shroud. He was about to yank it off, to get a good look at the face of evil, when the man began laughing.

"You don't get it, do you? I'm in control here. Go back to your bed and wake up!"

At those words, Pat screamed out loud in anguish, finding himself wide awake in his bed. Sara dove across him to turn on the nightstand lamp.

"Pat!" she shrieked. "Oh, Baby, are you okay?" She caressed his face, then suddenly pulled her hand back. "Your nose is bleeding. Let me get a tissue."

She handed him one before she went to wash her hands.

"That was the worst nightmare I've ever had, Sorcha," he said as he sopped up the dark red blood oozing from his nose.

He suddenly became aware that his chest hurt, too. When he unbuttoned his pajama top there was a fist-sized red mark right in the spot where the hooded man had punched him in the dream. It was dead center on his Saint Michael medallion, and it left a deep outline of the round pendant in his flesh. He looked at both hands and saw his knuckles were red and scraped from his sleep-time fistfight. Sara grabbed both hands and kissed his wounds.

"Jesus, Pat! What happened?"

"I don't know, Honey, but I don't like the way things are turning right now," he said as she nestled her head on his shoulder, sitting up with him in the bed.

He held her close, the two of them in silence contemplating the new dangers. Pat thought in terms of deep secrets and mysteries, of paranormal forces and evil, of God-inspired mission and purpose. Sara's thoughts were more earthly and immediate. She worried about stalkers and killers, about threats to her, to her husband, and to their children. She continued to kiss his hands softly as they said not another word to each other for several minutes. Finally, Pat interrupted their quiet, comforting moment.

"I need to go make a phone call."

He slipped out of bed and blew her a nervous kiss, seeing a fearful expression on her face just before trotting off to his den.

He fired up his STU secure phone. Ordinarily he would call Colonel Helmsley, but he knew he had to call Dr. Davis to discuss the portentous dream. Only he would be able to help Pat make sense of it. He woke him up in his hotel room at 0400 in the morning. Although groggy, Woody perked up instantly when Pat related what he just experienced.

"I'm afraid I have few clues to go on at this point to try to find Ricky," Pat said sadly after giving Dr. Davis a replay of events.

"It's okay, Pat, we'll find him. Right now, I am very concerned about you. The fact that this guy interacted with you in the dream is alarming. Obviously he is another psychic, and he is very powerful since he was able to create a physical effect on you with the bloody nose and all."

"I suspected as much. And once he discovered I was there, he controlled the dream--MY dream--letting me go on *his* time, not mine, scares the daylights out of me!"

"Well, one good thing is, there appear to be limits on his abilities. He couldn't see your face. We don't need him figuring out who you are! Look, I'll see you at the office in a few hours. Let's discuss as a team and see where we go."

Pat hung up and shuffled into his kitchen where he made a large pot of Starbucks French Roast coffee, savoring the aroma from the freshly-opened bag as he carefully measured the scoops and set the pot to brew. His migraine had subsided, but his brain was still racked from the frightful dream. He sat at his kitchen table in total silence sipping one, two, three cups of hot coffee before he heard the alarm clock way upstairs in his bedroom go off, beckoning him to get ready for the day.

Sara gave him a long kiss when he sauntered back to the bedroom. He knew she was once again feeling troubled about his work. Although she was not privy to the precise details of his job, of the fact that he was a certified psychic, he knew she had her concerns and shared as much with him. After all, his work nearly killed her the last time around.

"Pat, be careful. I, I mean we, can't go through another spell like a year and a half ago."

"I know, Honey. It'll be okay," he said pulling her in close, wrapping two strong arms around her waist.

"Well, let me go get breakfast ready for the munchkins," she said with a peck on his cheek before departing.

He was about to step into his bathroom when he heard Sean's wispy voice from the doorway.

"Daddy, I saw the man in the woods."

Pat's blood drained from his body at that moment, and when combined with the surging caffeine buzz he had going on, he suddenly felt faint. He tumbled forward to sweep Sean up, and at the same time pull him to the bed to keep himself from falling down. Knees wobbly, he managed to sit with Sean in his lap.

"Christ, Buddy, what man? What did you see?"

"In the woods, in the black clothes, but I couldn't see his face. Daddy, he's real mad at you. He wants to kill you," his son replied, glancing up at his face with a worried look.

Pat stared at him for a few moments. There was no way he could be making this up, and if there was one thing Pat learned from the debacle with Vicky Desantis and her abduction of Erin, it was to trust his son. To listen to him. After all, Sean tried to warn him many times that someone wanted to kidnap Erin.

"What else did you see in the woods?" he asked, hoping Sean had not seen Ricky Sullivan tied up.

"Nothing, just you two, fighting. In my dream last night."

He pulled Sean in tight and hugged him. "Listen. I love you very much, and nothing bad is going to happen to me, okay? I want you to tell me anytime you have any dreams like this or if you see things even in the daytime. Deal?"

"Deal!" Sean said wrapping his arms around Pat's shoulders and giving him a bear hug.

He scooted his boy off to the kitchen and thought about the implications of everything at this moment. His greatest fear was that if Sean could tap into the psychic fabric of this twisted man's mind, then it stood to reason the opposite was true. A psychic child-kidnapper stalking his psychic son, was the worst possibility he could have ever imagined.

~ 8 ~

"Hey, Pat, come on in!" Colonel Helmsley beckoned with his hands when he came through the vault door at the CCVC. "Woody gave us the run-down on things this morning bright and early. How are you holding up?"

The normally jolly, retired colonel had a frightened look on his face.

"I'm hanging in there, Sir. But pretty scared right now. We have to find the Sullivan boy right away," he said as they walked into Pat's office together.

Colonel Helmsley grimaced. Pat could tell there was something he already knew--terrible news--he was about to deliver.

"Pat, have a seat. Ricky was found early this morning, in Babler Memorial State Park, about twenty miles west of his home."

He sat down at his new desk for the very first time, running his hand across the pristine hard wood surface, thinking to himself how unfair it all seemed…how unjust it was that he couldn't save the boy. He was certain God had chosen him for the express purpose of finding children, but he never could comprehend how God sorted them out. Which ones Pat could save, and which ones were meant to die, were distinctions he didn't understand.

"Tell me how, Sir." He was dour and almost inconsolable at this moment.

"A search team combed the park beginning at daylight. He was found tied to a tree, beaten. We're waiting on the formal autopsy, but it does not appear he was sexually molested."

Pat felt the last tidbit was a consolation prize of sorts, like God, in some twisted way, had tossed him a bone. It was as if the Creator was saying cynically to him, "Hey, I didn't stop the murder, but at least the kid wasn't raped!" But deep inside Pat knew better than this. He knew He never did things for evil or sarcastic purpose. God was not like man.

"Christ!" was all he could utter.

"There's more," Woody offered. "The killer left a message on the ground beneath him, in twigs." He showed Pat a photograph from the crime scene. Clumsily assembled in splits of dried twigs and brush, was the sinister taunt, SWEET DREAMS PIG.

Jake had been flipping through a stack of papers on his lap as the others spoke. "We think the warning was meant for you. Because, you know, he knew you were in law enforcement and all. And that you entered the scene through a dream."

"Yeah, I get all that, Jake, but where do we begin with this guy?" Pat snapped at him, the lack of sleep and abundance of coffee synergistically making him grouchy.

"Well, there are two important points we cannot lose sight of. First, he is obviously a person with great psychic power. He controlled your dream once he realized you were there watching him. The second point is that he knows you are also a person with tremendous extrasensory abilities, otherwise you would not have penetrated through to witness the scene."

Pat mulled it all over in his head. There was a third point to which no one else was privy...the fact that Sean saw part of the scene, too. He only hoped, and prayed, that the killer had no awareness of his son.

Colonel Helmsley picked up a large manila file folder from the top of Pat's desk. "We think we've seen this guy's work before. FBI profilers have been cataloging old cold cases for years in an effort to help solve serial crimes. Over the past twenty-three years there have been eighteen similar abductions of pre-teen boys throughout the country. He never sexually assaults them, but he always beats and murders them. All have been found tied to trees in either state or national parks. It's all in here," he said handing the heavy folder to him.

"I take it you want me to concentrate on finding this guy--all approved by the Oversight Committee?"

The colonel nodded. "And we have two more Amber Alerts this morning. Thankfully a slow day compared to your first."

Pat flipped through the file folder containing police reports from various municipalities, newspaper clippings of local news stories about the abductions and murders, FBI profile reports--six of them--all with fairly different psychological depictions of the suspect. He smirked to himself about the profile business being more art than science, with a little wishful thinking and voodoo thrown in. It was no wonder they never caught this guy, he realized, since they seemed to be chasing a half dozen different people. Over the course of three hours that morning he read and reread, and studied and analyzed, every scrap of information about the killer and his victims. There was nary a scrape of physical evidence left behind…no hairs or fibers or bodily fluids. His new nemesis was a phantom, as much a mysterious shadow in the real world as he was the hooded, faceless man in his dream.

Once he had digested all he could, he read through the two Amber Alerts from the morning. One was a little ten-year-old girl named, ironically, Amber. She was last seen playing in her front yard in Houston the day before, her mother discovering her missing when she called her for supper. The other was a little boy, Darius Johnson, a black child of eight last seen by his mother on the sidewalk in front of his Detroit brownstone tenement last night.

With his right hand on the picture of Amber, and his left hand on Darius's photograph, Pat closed his eyes for a moment. The others looked on in curiosity because Pat had never worked cases at a desk like this before. He concentrated on the two reports simultaneously. There was something about them both that made him realize they were not in danger at all. He began to smile.

"Amber is with her father in his apartment. I guess he and mom are separated. When the police talked with him last night, he denied seeing her, but she was hiding in a bedroom. She's fine. Darius is at a friend's house two doors down from his home. Some kid named, TJ. I guess it's a nickname. TJ sneaked Darius in the house, and not even TJ's parents know he's there."

Woody walked up and put an arm around his shoulder. "Great work, Pat! We'll make sure this gets into the system so the proper cover is placed on how the information was generated. You know, there's something about your abilities this time around that I noticed yesterday and now today. Something quite extraordinary."

Pat gave him a cross-eyed look. "Like what?"

"Well, a year and a half ago you had to be physically close to an event if it was recent, but the older the event was, the further away you could be and still pick up psychic impressions."

He nodded, recalling the dangerous special operations mission he, Woody, and the colonel flew in Pakistan and Afghanistan in the hunt for Usama bin Laden following the 9/11 terror attacks.

"Yeah, I remember that."

"But now you seem to be able to quickly gather clues about very recent events right here in Virginia, no matter where they occur!" he grinned, smoothing back his gray hair with one hand.

"Huh, I see that now that you mention it."

He thought about the past day and a half and realized how right Dr. Davis was. In some way, too difficult to grasp, his abilities had matured during the hiatus in his work with CRYSTAL ROUNDUP. It almost seemed that during the year and a half gap in operations, his synapses had a chance to form strong links and bonds to better enable him to tap into his psychic abilities.

"Well, I better hit the couch and try to home in on this psycho," he said taking the thick file folder with him to the sofa.

As Pat reclined back, he let the flow of information about the serial killer sink into his brain. Earlier, when he read the entire file, he tried to sort and inventory each case, placing facts and pictures into a kind of mental database or filing cabinet. *Eighteen little boys savagely beaten and murdered,* were his last thoughts just before he slipped softly into one of his trance-like states again. He kept his eyes wide open, and pupils automatically remained fixed, something he often experienced when he was just learning about his abilities a year and a half ago.

Once again he found himself pressed hard against an enormous brick wall. He pried himself free and took a step back, trying to assess the size of it. Immediately to his left he saw the edge of the wall, a boundary that hadn't ever been there before. He inched close to it and saw a huge void beyond it, and well below it, a chasm that made him feel dizzy. When he examined the wall from its left edge, straining his vision in the process, he saw that it went endlessly to the right, but this time he saw small openings dotting it for what looked like miles of wall. From this position he counted them, twenty-one openings in all, and each appearing to be the same waist-high square portals like in his dream. Pat decided to run to them, to peek inside, or even to enter them to see what clues he could find.

When he reached the first opening and squatted to look, a loud crashing sound startled him. He watched as red and brown brick quickly filled the opening, blocking his view. He had to jerk his fingers back abruptly to keep them from being crushed by the closing, bone-crushing wall. He ran to the next one. Peering inside, he caught a glimpse of a forest just as a heavy wooden door slammed it shut from the other side, nearly knocking him backwards. Off he went, jogging to the third door, only to be met this time by a giant metal grate that dropped rapidly from the top, the mesh of which was so tight, no trace of light could pass through in either direction. On and on he ran, and each time he reached a new opening, a different barrier abruptly appeared to block his access.

Panting hard now, having reached opening number twenty-one, Pat stopped and sat down with his back to the wall. He was overwhelmed with frustration at being unable to pick up any clues. He buried his face in his hands, wanting to just fall to sleep in his vision and rest. This particular psychic episode was mentally and physically demanding. In his vision he began to pray out loud, tears streaming from his eyes.

"Oh Mary, Mother of God, please guide me, please aid me, please comfort me, please show me how to find this man!"

"Pat? Pat? Can you hear me?" Jake asked, shaking him by the shoulders on his sofa.

He bolted from the vision at that instant, his eyes painfully sore from being wide open for several minutes. Woody handed him a bottle of Visine which he gratefully took, practically squirting half a bottle of the soothing substance into each eye.

"We had to wake you Pat. You started crying and praying out loud, only you had no tears coming out," Woody explained handing him a tissue to sop up the excess soothing liquid.

"This is intense!" Pat said clutching his head. His migraine from the day before had returned. "I think this guy has killed more than the eighteen kids we know about. It looks like at least twenty-one of them, but what do you make of the brick wall I keep running into?"

Jake smiled a proud grin that suggested he had just broken the equivalent of Imperial Japan's WW II Purple Code. "I think I understand. This guy knows you are trying to peer into his world, into his past murders. He is putting the brick wall up to block you from seeing inside, and every time you see an opening, like today, he has to cut your access off at the last moment. A door, a grate, bricks. I bet he is sitting out there somewhere sensing your attempts, and he is in real-time mode throwing more barriers up."

Although Pat nodded, even smiled at Jake because his theory made a lot of sense, he had no idea how right Jake was.

In a dark blue Toyota pickup truck, on a quiet and deserted road in Youctangee Park, in Chillicothe, Ohio, the sick and twisted child killer sat. He gripped both hands tightly into fists, his flesh turning bright red, making the whitish scars on the back of each hand stand out even more. They were long diagonal blemishes…permanent remnants of the cuts he suffered when he first went to prison several years before. He dared to fight the toughest convict in the jailhouse, el Demonio…the Demon, as he was known. But after an impressive go at it, the killer lost. When it was over, he lay on the floor in a pool of his own blood, his face resembling ground beef from the severe beating he sustained. Several of el Demonio's surrogates, members of a Latino prison gang, held the killer down and carved up the back of each hand with shanks. For the rest of his life, whenever he would put both hands together, the diagonal scars lined up perfectly with each other.

As he sat in his truck, the man suppressed his screams, but he was enraged. He knew someone was probing him, trying to unlock his dark secrets and stop him. He had to work feverishly to block the spy's view, to keep at bay the interloper as he ran from opening to opening. He wanted nothing more at this moment than to kill him, to gut him, or to slit his throat. His eyes were squeezed shut so tight they began to ache, and he had an accompanying dizzying sensation.

But then his intense focus and effort began to pay off. Inside his sick brain flashes of light, like a high intensity strobe, began to slow. It was almost like an old film projector that was slightly out of sync. As each frame slipped in front of the bright projection bulb it would jerk before moving on. There was one errant frame, however, a kind of subliminal message inserted awkwardly in an otherwise bland film. When it flashed on the mental screen in his brain, he saw it. It registered.

Suddenly a smile danced across the freak's face. "Arlington," he whispered. "Arlington, Virginia."

A sick grin traced across his lips as he realized now that he had a journey to make.

He let his hands relax and the blood to flow once more into them. Opening his eyes, he spotted a young boy playing on the park slides all by himself. He watched him for nearly twenty minutes, wanting to ensure he was really alone. The ten-year-old lad was dressed in a bright red and black sweater with a monogram resembling a private school uniform. A backpack sat nearby the slides. The hooky-playing elementary-schooler was unaware of it, but he was hopelessly stuck to a spider's web…a web spun by a hungry killer about to pounce.

The serial murderer shut his engine off and listened to the chirping of nearby birds. It was otherwise silent. He licked his lips, quietly pulled the silver handle on his truck door upward, and stepped outside. *My journey can wait a little longer,* he thought. *Right now I have a craving to take care of.*

~ 9 ~

The sudden, loud ringing of his newly-acquired secure cell phone made him jump from bed. Its accompanying vibration made it wobble, dance, and buzz on the nightstand. He really was not completely asleep anyway, still very much wound up over the serial killer he was on the hunt for. His thoughts had been racing in between cat naps of five or ten minutes at best.

"Hullo," he mumbled after his clumsy hands nearly knocked the phone to the floor.

"Pat, John Helmsley here. We had another abduction and murder, this time in Ohio. Same M.O. and all."

The colonel's tone was serious and sobering. Pat rubbed his eyes as he strained to see the clock on his nightstand.

"That sucks, Boss. I'm, I'm really trying hard on this one, but not much is coming through as you know."

He looked at Sara, hoping he had not awakened her. Her eyes were closed, and she was breathing slowly and steadily.

"I take it no more dreams tonight?" the colonel prodded, hoping for the slightest morsel of information to track down the murderer.

"Hell, I don't think I ever really fell asleep, Sir."

There was an awkward pause. "Pat, he left another message, this time in the kid's blood, on his chest. It read, C U SOON PIG. I think he's coming after you, better be armed at all times."

"I am, Sir. Christ, here we go again," he muttered before he hung up, glancing down at Sara's scarred wrists. "Here we go again!"

He closed his eyes and tried to drift into a psychic state wherein he could finally—hopefully--breach the killer's brick wall and see his face, or his car, or his house...something, anything. But instead, he fell into a deep sleep completely disconnected from his work. His lack of quality rest in recent nights, and the news about another killing, and his desperate yet unsuccessful attempts to find clues, literally caused his brain and body to shut down. To try to cope.

Although he felt like he had been asleep for at least a few hours, it was really only mere minutes when he was suddenly awakened by a pulling sensation on his arm. In that enigmatic state of consciousness, where chemicals in the brain essentially sever a person from reality, Pat immediately assessed danger.

He instinctively reached out, grabbed the encroacher, and placed him in a Judo choke hold. His right arm bore down against his neck, cutting off blood flow to his carotid artery. With his left arm up under the man's armpit, he forced his hand against the back of his head, creating a fulcrum to choke and crush his throat. Pat was not sure if he was awake or asleep. And if asleep, he was not sure if he was once again locked in a physical-dream battle with the killer. He couldn't take any chances, so his instinct was to crush and kill, to break his neck.

"PAT! STOP!" Sara screamed leaping across him, trying to

pry Sean free.

His son made a feeble gurgling sound and was within seconds of passing out. Pat instantly came to his senses and released his grip when Sara pounced on him. Sean fell to the floor clutching his neck and coughing furiously, face red, tears rolling down his face. Pat jumped down, scooped him up, and placed him on the bed.

"Sean? Sean? Can you hear me, Buddy?" he asked, beginning gentle chest compressions over his soft red pajamas to keep his heart pumping, just to be safe.

"Daddy, Da—Da—Da—Daddy," he labored in between taking deep choking breaths.

"I'm so sorry, Buddy," Pat cried leaning down to hug him. "I'm so sorry, Pal."

He lovingly caressed Sean's hair.

"What is going on, Pat?" Sara demanded, her Irish fury practically shooting sparks from her lips.

"I'm sorry, Baby, can you go get Sean some cold water?"

She stormed out of the bedroom. When father and son were alone, Pat asked him if he had had another dream about the man in the woods.

"Uh huh, Daddy. And he's driving a pickup truck. It's dark colored, and he has lots of scars on his hands."

Sean held his hands out and turned the back of them toward his father.

"This side, Daddy. On the back."

Pat was intrigued. "Go on, Sean, can you see any more, like a license plate number or what the man or his scars look like?"

He shook his head.

"Okay, listen, make sure when you have these dreams you

stay in the background and don't make a sound. I think this guy can see us at the other end of the vision if that makes any sense. Don't let him know you are watching!" Pat whispered out his words not wanting Sara to hear him.

He nodded understanding just as Sara walked back with a tall glass of ice cold water, still scowling at Pat. Sean gulped it down eagerly, soothing his sore, slightly swollen throat. Once he seemed to have settled down, and his coughing spasms had subsided, Sara trotted him back off to bed. She grumbled to Pat that she would sleep with Sean in his bed to comfort him. It was probably a good thing, Pat thought, since she was furious with him at that moment. In his utter exhaustion, he was back asleep in minutes, and didn't wake until dawn.

"Morning, Pat, you look like crap!" Colonel Helmsley teased, seeing him drag his feet as he walked into his office.

But Pat knew he was right. His eyes were bloodshot with large dark circles underneath. He was pale and drawn, the stress from trying to find the serial killer taking its toll physically on him now. Mentally, he was exhausted and tortured, and he was particularly angry with himself for having assaulted Sean, thinking he was an intruder--THE intruder.

Dr. Davis had been looking him over, and Pat could sense he was worried about him.

"Jake has an idea, something he worked on at UC Berkeley, that helped enhance psychic impressions in his test subjects," Woody suggested, throwing out a line to see if he would grab it.

Pat squinted and turned his head sideways, not sure if he

liked where this was heading. He did not immediately respond.

"We want to hypnotize you. I've seen a definite correlation between hypnosis and extrasensory abilities," Jake offered, holding his tape recorder in one hand and a small gold medallion attached to a chain in the other.

Pat looked at the colonel, hoping for some guidance. While he trusted Dr. Davis implicitly, this was, after all, Jake's idea--Jake...the Birkenstock clog-wearing, gun-hating tree hugger's idea. And to top it off, the whole visual of the moment seemed like a cheap magician's nightclub trick, complete with a silly gold medallion and chain. It certainly lacked an air of credibility to him. Helmsley nodded at him. Pat sighed heavily, having wished secretly his mentor would have vetoed it.

"Guys, look. My brain is fried. We can give it a try, but how much more refined can my impressions get?"

Pat was getting cranky now, and he practically shouted the question out. He kicked off his shoes with a jerk, removed his sport coat and tossed it crudely on his desk, and reclined on the sofa in a semi-defiant plop.

Jake sneered seeing the Beretta secured in his belt holster. Pat thought he almost seemed to avoid getting anywhere near the handgun, taking a position up behind his head after moving one of the side chairs to a new position.

Frickin' pansy! he thought.

Jake began the process by explaining how hypnosis works, although Pat was quite familiar with it from his undergraduate days in psychology class, as well as having used it throughout his career to support OSI investigations. He was definitely not a big believer in it, and he felt it stood an inch behind the line between reality and witchcraft, and clearly on the witchcraft side. But he reasoned it was worth a try, although he pretended to be uninterested.

Positioning the gold medallion above his head, forcing his eyes to look upward and become fatigued, Dr. Jacobsen slowly lulled him into a hypnotic trance. Despite Pat's skepticism about hypnosis, the process of succumbing him to its trancelike magic was relatively quick. It was probably because he was just plain tired. Once he was completely in a deep, soothing state, Dr. Jacobsen regressed him back in time to the first psychic event about the killer...when he dreamt about him in the woods with the Sullivan boy.

"Christ! I don't want to be here!" he cried out, flailing his arms a bit. "He just heard me, and he's coming at me!" he nearly screamed in terror.

His breathing was heavy and labored, and he felt panicky despite his awareness that he was under hypnosis. He tried hard to remain focused on the vision of his recalled dream, knowing at a deep level of consciousness, and in part because Jake had given him the hypnotic suggestion, that he had to report back to them on any new details that emerged.

As he was trying to look beyond the attacker for clues nearby--like his truck that Sean told him about, a brick wall suddenly appeared between him and the man. This was unquestionably odd because in his original dream such a wall did not exist once he penetrated the evil woods. Within seconds the wall had become several walls. All around him, and closing in on him like a tomb. The bricks made sick, heavy scraping sounds as they rapidly slid together. Small chunks of brittle red brick fell from the coffin-like lid and down his shirt, causing him to brush and swat at them in his office. Inside the confines of this death trap, he could smell the sparse stale air as it rapidly disappeared, almost like it was being suctioned out. He found himself heaving deeply, as if his head were stuck inside a tight plastic bag. His body began to crave oxygen-rich air, but found none. He started to breathe harder and faster, gasping and choking for air, trying to tell the others what was going on. His voice actually changed, much to the shock of the three men. When he cried out, it had a muffled sound as if he were physically trapped inside a coffin trying to get out.

Jake panicked at that moment. "Pat, Pat, when I count to three you will awaken in your office and everything will be fine!"

But Pat was almost out of breath, in a panic over how long it seemed to be taking to rescue him. He choked once more, then went limp and lifeless.

His face was bright blue when Jake shouted, "One, two, three!"

He snapped his fingers, but Pat didn't respond. Dr. Davis grabbed his wrist.

"His pulse is rapid but shallow. We need to start CPR!"

The thin, old African-American doctor straddled Pat's chest and began frantic chest compressions, alternating with mouth-to-mouth resuscitations. This went on for two full minutes, but he was unresponsive.

"John, call nine-one-one, we need to get him to a hospital."

Colonel Helmsley practically ripped the phone on Pat's desk out of its socket as he yanked the receiver hard.

"Wait! Wait!" Woody suddenly uttered just as the colonel was about to hit the buttons. "He's breathing."

Pat made a strained, choking, sputtering sound, then opened his eyes, looking straight up at Dr. Davis who was still on his chest inches from his mouth. He realized quickly what had happened.

Looking up at him he said aloud, "Geez, Woody, is this what you do to me every time I'm knocked out in one of my psychic states? I mean, you could at least buy me a drink first!"

Woody leaned down and hugged him tightly.

"Damn, Son! You had us all scared! You okay? Wanna go to the hospital?" He grabbed Pat's face with both hands, leaned down and planted a loud kiss on his forehead. "Thank you, God!" he said, looking upward toward Heaven.

"I'm okay Woody, really," he said, sitting up and feeling his tight chest with both hands.

He gulped down a bottle of water Dr. Jacobsen handed him, while giving the young man a glare. He wasn't shy at all about telegraphing how unhappy he was with Jake. His original skepticism about the whole hypnosis idea seemed validated in his mind now.

"Let me tell you, that was powerful," he moaned as he wiped cold water drops from his lips with his sleeve. "That was insane."

For the next half hour he gave them a full report on the strange experience he had while under hypnosis. Jake kept his distance while he took meticulous notes, and along with the colonel and Woody, sat in astonished silence as they all took in Pat's ominous words. But there was one white lie he inserted in his account. He knew he had to relay the information Sean developed about the killer, but he had to do it in a way that provided cover for his son.

"I got two brief flashes while I was being crushed in that brick pile. I saw a dark colored pickup truck, and a pair of hands. The back of them, really. This guy's got scars on the back of each hand."

But more than two hundred miles away, things were not alright. The killer sat in his truck, parked at a rest stop along Interstate 80 in Bloomsburg, Pennsylvania. A wretched, pelting rain prompted him to keep his windows rolled up, the interior of which became foggy from his breath. His muscular arms were bare in his light blue polo shirt. With his eyes closed, he had built in his mind the wall around Pat, not knowing who he was or what he even looked like, but hoping to encase him in rubble and kill him with his mental powers. He was disappointed, angry, that he survived. The only image he received before his connection to the event was broken, was Dr. Davis looking down at him.

The deviant smiled, finally able to see the face of his nemesis, or so he thought.

"You old black bastard!" he cackled. "You don't look much like a cop to me. It's gonna be like shooting fish in a barrel!"

He fired his engine up, and entered the highway heading east. With Woody's features burned in his mind and tagged as his enemy, he now had a renewed sense of energy.

~ 10 ~

Pat finished telling his intrigued colleagues all about the psychic journey that nearly killed him moments before. He could almost read their tormented minds just from their body language alone. Colonel Helmsley slowly wiped his brow and stood up. He walked to the small office refrigerator, retrieved a second bottle of ice cold water, and handed it to him with slightly trembling hands. He could see the colonel was distraught over the power of the psychic killer and his nearly successful attempt to suffocate him.

"Listen, I think we've done enough for one day. We had a handful of Amber Alerts, and the good news is all but one of the kids was recovered safely," Colonel Helmsley finally said.

It was as if he feared pressing their luck at the moment might have dire consequences.

"I appreciate that, Sir. I'm wiped out and--" Pat began to say, but Jake abruptly interrupted.

"I'm sorry, Pat. I thought the hypnosis would help us out. I never imagined any of this happening!"

He was looking halfway down at the carpeted floor, with an

almost shamed expression. Pat smiled crookedly at him. He saw how much the event had upset him, and how genuinely concerned Jake was over his welfare. It was suddenly hard for Pat to be angry with him.

"It's okay, Jake. I'm alright now. You did your best."

And with those words, Pat made a fist with his right hand and smacked Jake hard in his left bicep. It felt like hitting a solid door.

"Damn, Jake, you work out?"

"I keep in shape, yeah." Jake looked up at Pat with a warm smile.

"Well remind me not to mess with you!" he teased.

For a moment Pat thought, rather awkwardly, that the two men had begun to form a bond. It was an almost unimaginable turn of events considering their polar opposite views of things like gun control.

"I hate to be the bearer of bad tidings, gentlemen," Colonel Helmsley said with a smirk. "But tomorrow we are going to have our first interagency meeting for CRYSTAL ROUNDUP."

Pat's eyes grew wide with an immediate jumble of fear and loathing. "No! No! No!" he stammered. "Not again, Boss!"

The colonel tried to allay his concerns, but to no appreciable avail. "Look, we're going to have a short meeting to bring the group up to speed on current ops. And yes, Pat, they need your help again on other projects."

Pat walked over to the crazy angled window in his office and peered out to the Pentagon where renovation efforts were still underway following the 9/11 terrorist attack there.

Jake had a puzzled look on his face seeing the interaction between them. "What's an interagency meeting?" he asked, hesitantly.

"It's all the trusted people in the CRYSTAL ROUNDUP program, from all the beltway three letter agencies," the colonel explained.

"They want me to do more than find children!" Pat stammered without even looking back, never taking his eyes off the Pentagon in the distance.

"Like what," Jake asked, still very much a novice to the Intelligence Community.

"Like find bin Laden," Pat replied, turning around and facing them now. "I guess that's what they want, huh, Boss? The last time we tried that, we almost got our asses blown away in that Apache helo over Tora Bora."

"Well that's a possi--" the colonel began before Dr. Davis cut him off.

"Keep in mind, Pat, that we probably don't need to go in theater again this time. Like I said yesterday, your powers have matured to the point that the whole time and space component thing seems moot anymore. I think you can find UBL from right here!"

Pat began to nod, but then his demeanor changed abruptly. He had a worried look now. "Is General Swank still a focal point member?"

Colonel Helmsley nodded. "He sure is. Sorry, I know how much you love him!" he chuckled.

"Love him like a cobra, Sir." He looked at Jake and saw how clueless he still was. "Let's just say Major General Swank is the meanest guy on the planet. He's the Air Force Director of Intelligence. Just wait, you'll see for yourself. This guy could make the Pope cuss."

"We need to be at the Headquarters FBI conference room, same as last time. Look on the bright side, after tomorrow it will be Good Friday, and I'm calling an official day off. I think you can use the rest," the colonel said, offering Pat a peace prize of sorts.

Dr. Jacobsen rolled his eyes. "Oh great, I thought we had a separation of church and state? Now you declare a Christian holiday a federal holiday?"

The other three were taken aback by his comments.

"You know Jasper, I was just starting to like you…" Pat said, heading straight toward him with steam practically coming out of both ears.

"Look, no offense, but this whole Christian myth is so over the top!" Jake said smugly.

Pat stood inches away and angrily looked at him.

"My Catholic faith is everything to me, everything!" he growled so furiously, a bright blue vein sprung up on his forehead.

"Oh great, a Catholic! I was raised Catholic, the looniest of all the faiths!" Jake said, derisively rolling his eyes.

Pat was ready to slug him in the face but held back, not wanting to give him the satisfaction since it appeared Jake delighted in egging him on. Colonel Helmsley had been silent, but he finally intervened, giving Woody a slight smile in advance which Pat caught from the corner of his eye.

"Okay, kiddos, let's save the debate for another time! I think we've all been through one helluva crucible today! Woody, why don't you and Jake head out for the day. I want to give Pat a tour of this place, the Operations Center and all."

After Dr. Davis and Dr. Jacobsen left, Colonel Helmsley gave

Pat a stern eye.

"Chill out and cut Jake some slack. He is new to our world--the black world--and is just now finding his way."

"Sir, I can appreciate someone being new to what we do, but that's not what bothers me. Like I said that day back at the safe house, he can be dangerous if he hates guns and all. Heck, now I have doubts that he really cares about saving innocent kids! How am I to be sure when we catch that sick sonabitch killer out there that he won't want to defend the guy, call in the ACLU?"

"I know, Pat. I know. But don't misjudge his personal, political beliefs as a lack of support for what we do. I have no reason to doubt his loyalty or intentions at all."

He nodded his head slowly, and then with a sarcastic grin he mumbled, "Okay, Sir. I'll give him enough rope to hang himself, I guess!"

Colonel Helmsley let out a loud roar and smacked Pat's back hard. "C'mon, let's go take a tour!"

The Child Crime Victim's Center's Operations Center was located in the basement of the peculiar building on Wilson Boulevard, in the tip of the buried, upside down pyramid. When they stepped inside, it reminded Pat of the many military operations centers he had been in over the course of his fourteen years as an Air Force OSI Special Agent. There were the familiar giant, wide screen monitors in the front of the room tracking whatever was of interest to the center at the time. But instead of the things he was accustomed to in such settings:

aircraft sorties, enemy order of battle information, battle damage assessments, missile warnings, and so on—what he saw were things of interest to the CCVC. On one screen was a running tally of missing and exploited children whose whereabouts were still unknown. Although he couldn't add them up in his head, Pat surmised there were thousands. That fact alone was a sobering reminder of the work he had cut out for him.

How could they expect me to work non-missing child cases when there are so many of God's little souls still lost out there? he thought, reminding himself of the interagency meeting coming up the next day.

On another screen he saw a list of solved cases, where either the child was recovered safely, or a crime had been solved with the arrest of a perpetrator. This one contained some statistical data. Since the CCVC's inception in the early 1980s, it had been responsible for the recovery of more than 60,000 children. Pat was strangely comforted by this...he felt in some small way that a large stone had been lifted from his back, that he was not alone in this effort, and that many good, decent people were engaged in what he considered one of the most profoundly important duties in the country. Finding children.

In the middle of the Ops Center there was a huge bullpen with four rows of open tables arranged in a semi-circle facing the large screens in the front. He counted twenty or more stations in all, each with a flat screen monitor, a computer desktop system, and a telephone with dozens of buttons for multiple lines. In the first row, centered in front of the main screen that tracked current news, he saw three high-back leather chairs that stood out from the rest. He walked over close enough to read the name placards. The center seat was for the Attorney General, Colonel Helmsley's good friend; to its right was a seat for the FBI Director, and to its left was a place for the CCVC Director.

"Pat, this is Jim Connors, the Bureau rep who works our programs down here," the colonel said introducing him to the tall, slightly balding FBI agent, dressed rather casually considering his line of work.

He was in a pair of tan tactical cargo pants, dark blue polo shirt, and dark brown hiking boots. On his belt he wore his gold FBI badge with his Glock semi-automatic pistol secured in a holster on his right hip.

"It's a real honor meeting you, Pat!" the middle-aged man said, shaking his hand vigorously. "You are amazing! Look, no one else down here is briefed into the program, so we have to be careful what we say," he cautioned in a low, deep whisper while tapping the STU telephone on his desk.

Pat realized then it was the only secure phone in the room.

"Look at this," he said as he played with his computer keyboard. "We track data on not just our case resolutions, but the time it takes to resolve them."

Pat and the colonel looked at a chart that showed a spike in the last three days.

"Wow! It looks like you skewed the data, Pat" the colonel said tapping the line chart on the monitor.

"That's a good thing, but it could also generate a lot of interest if we're not careful. I mean, if like the press or someone started to notice the sudden surge in recoveries and all," Pat said, somewhat concerned and ever mindful of operational security.

"Well, it's not lost on the rest of the folks here. They are all pumped up about the results from this week," Connors added, beaming.

"Jim, show Pat how a case gets processed from his information into a rescue."

Agent Connors was excited to do just that. For several minutes he took them through the conversion of CRYSTAL ROUNDUP information into SWAT team recoveries and arrests. Pat learned that when Colonel Helmsley relayed his psychic data in real-time mode over a secure line to Connors, the latter used technology in the Special Access Program world that would dial the 911 center nearest to the abduction or sighting, giving the appearance of coming from the local area. Related technology allowed him to alter his voice to sound like anyone he wanted--male, female, young, old, local accent, foreign accent…whatever fit the scenario. He could add background noise to mimic the conditions he wanted to portray, like when the "caller" in the sighting of Rosario Gutierrez phoned the LAPD from a cell phone in the subway station. Conveniently, the roaring sound of a train entering a station could be heard in the background, adding bona fides to the caller. Connors would simply call it in and hang up. Emergency responders would take it from there. It was an untraceable process that worked each and every time it was tried.

"That's pretty impressive," Pat said as he listened. "I especially like the simplicity of it all. Listen, thanks for the briefing and thanks for flowing this information into the right channels. Without you none of these kids would be rescued."

Connors looked at him strangely. "Without *me*? Pat, my job wouldn't exist if it were not for you."

He smiled, absorbing the compliment. "Well, Boss, mind if I kick off early? I need to catch up on some sleep before our meeting tomorrow."

"Go ahead, Buddy. See you at ten in the morning at the Bureau tomorrow."

Pat left the center and drove home doing his best to keep his eyes opened to avoid a crash. He desperately needed sleep, but he had no idea then what his dreams had in store for him that night. Genuine, restful sleep would prove to be an absent commodity that evening.

~ 11 ~

When he returned home, Sara was there to greet him with a scowl, still grousing over what he did to Sean earlier that morning…his sleep-induced choke-hold. He did his best to explain to her that he had had a bad dream and lashed out at his son thinking he was in imminent danger, but she hardly bought it.

"Just be careful, Pat. I know that whenever you start working in these sensitive operations you get extra-stressed, but remember what reality is, and that our son is just an innocent little boy!" She uncharacteristically wagged a finger in his face, causing him to take a step back.

He simply whispered out the words, "I'm sorry."

She was right, and he knew it, but at that moment, what he needed most was sleep. He went to his bed, closed the blinds and the drapes, and fell on top of the soft quilt comforter…face first. He didn't even bother to remove his gun, or his tie, or even his shoes. Within seconds, he was fast asleep.

Instantly, he was transported to eight different places all at once. He had never experienced this before; each preceding dream or vision was always to a single, solitary place…one place at a time. His brain felt ready to explode as his neurons fired away at the scenes, busily trying to process one at a time before moving on to the next. He was in such a mad whirl that he was unable to dedicate sufficient time or energy to any particular dream place. At best, he was able to glean mere tidbits of data from each scene's surface, scooping up handfuls of information like water while running from one to the next.

He felt like a circus performer spinning ceramic plates on long flimsy sticks, trying to keep each one from crashing to the floor and shattering. Each vision was like a plate unto itself...no sooner had he focused on one scene, when he would find himself running frantically to two or three scenes ahead--spinning the plates--then on to the next. Back and forth for hours and hours, endlessly spinning plates, scooping gems of evidence, and running, running, running.

There were five little girls and three small boys. Each was the victim of a stranger abduction from throughout the country. The one and only consoling fact he gleaned from the terabytes of information his overworked mind tried desperately to process, was that not one of them was a victim of the serial killer he hunted. Despite the frenzied pace at which his brain cells churned the flotsam and jetsam of data, he found this bit of intelligence strangely consoling. He felt these kids at least had a chance.

His synesthesia was in overdrive as well. There were shackles that one little blond cutie had on her wrists that had a cold and crunchy texture, like cereal in a bowl before the milk was added. It was dark there. It felt like she was in a small closet or similar confine. He hated this particular scene because it reminded him of the cruel, tight, suffocating brick coffin the serial killer had stuffed him in.

Another girl had a cloth sack over her head that smelled purple and tasted like dust. There was a commotion around her, but she couldn't see its source because of the scratchy burlap blindfold. People were arguing, several of them, about the girl. The language was strange and foreign. Butter-flavored words melted into his thoughts, and sparkles of colorful light accompanied each syllable. Before Pat could peer outside the bag, he was jolted to the next scene.

One of the stolen boys was strapped to a hard object in a dark place. It was cool and tight inside, another tiny enclosure like the closet in which he found the first blond girl. Inside the pitch black confines, the boy's trembling hands made a squeaking sound in Pat's synesthetic mind. He felt he was in the trunk of a car, so he forced himself to step back and capture the license plate. His brain granted him one second to pull it off, but he burned the image into his mind before being pulled to the next scene.

He stood by a fast-moving river in the night. A chilly breeze caused him to shudder. He turned around and saw a park pavilion, complete with picnic tables, built-in barbeque grill, and bike rack. A light colored sedan sat in a parking space near a walkway that led to the river by which he stood. He ran to the car and saw a middle-aged man in the driver's seat, slumped over the wheel with blood flowing from a gunshot wound to his head. His side window was coated with chunks of brain matter and skull, and bright red blood ran like fresh wet paint down the glass and into the doorframe. Pat spied a young boy about ten years old in the back seat. He was tied up and moving. Thankfully alive. For a split-second, he thought he may have stumbled upon the serial killer and a suicide scene, but when he looked at the man's right hand in which he clutched a Smith and Wesson .357 magnum revolver, he did not see the giveaway scars he hoped for.

He raced from scene to scene, gathering clues and doing his best to catalog them in the right mental file so as not to jumble them up, otherwise rendering the information useless at best, or at worst, causing SWAT teams to descend upon the wrong place at the wrong time. He tried talking to each child, but none responded. Not one had any psychic abilities. He tried to discern as much as possible about each abductor to add this data to the collection he was assembling on each case. He was harried and exhausted, quickly running back and forth, tossing some morsels into each file, keeping the fragile circus plates spinning, until suddenly he began to slow down. It seemed he had pulled from each scene all the information he could, plucked every shred of available data, and tucked it all away for the time being.

He was severely dizzy. He felt as if he had been on a spinning amusement park ride for several hours, left alone with no attendant to stop the attraction. As he stepped off the platform to terra firma, he wanted to do nothing more than to throw up as the world continued to spin like a centrifuge all about him. He fell to the ground in his dream, hoping to stop the twirling torture he was forced to endure.

He woke slowly to find a small amount of light coming through the blinds and drapes. The sickly rotation had begun to subside. It was one of those waking moments where he had no sense of date or time, nor any sense of how long he had been asleep. He assumed it had only been a few hours, but when he looked at the clock, he realized it was 0600 the next morning. Pat had slept more than fourteen hours straight, without moving, tossing, or turning from the position he first created when he hit the bed. Sara was asleep next to him, snoring loudly. When he got up and looked in the bathroom mirror, he saw deep, red sleep lines across his face, and it even seemed to him that his nose was slightly askew. It had been pushed to the side for such a long time--to allow him to breathe--that now it appeared crooked. He grabbed it with his right hand and tried to push it back to the center, but that only made it feel sorer. Despite being out like a light for over half a day, Pat was more exhausted than before he hit the bed. He was physically drained, and his legs ached terribly, as if he had actually run the miles he only dreamt about as he sprinted from scene to scene.

Stumbling from the bed to the bathroom, he showered and got ready for his morning at FBI headquarters. He decided to put a call in to Colonel Helmsley once he had put on a new dark blue pin-striped suit, replacing the horribly wrinkled one he wore to bed.

"Boss, can we meet up at the office before we go to the meeting? I had a horrible night. We have lots of work to do."

"Sure thing, Pat. Judging from the ops reports I read this morning on my computer, we have a bunch of new cases."

There was a long pause before Pat spoke again. He stared at his own reflection in the bedroom mirror, noting his nose was much closer now to its normal centerline appearance. But there was something much more important he had on his mind, a sense of something wicked that had been developing slowly in his brain over the past several days, beginning with the malevolent face he saw in the simulated firing range.

"Sir, is it just me, or have you ever noticed that so much evil precedes Christian holidays?"

The colonel was silent for a few seconds. Pat could hear him breathing.

"I know what you mean. I have sensed that myself for years. See you soon. God bless."

Jake was poring over the stack of new Amber Alerts that arrived that morning. There were eight new missing children reports from over the last twenty-four hours. Pat, of course, was way ahead of him, having dreamt about each of them, and armed now with the clues needed to recover them. Jake started to hand the heavy batch of documents to him, but Pat put his hand up dismissively.

"I don't need to read them, let me run you through how each was abducted, by whom, and where they are right now."

His display of overconfidence caught Colonel Helmsley off guard. Normally Pat was reserved and quite humble about his skills, but today he seemed to teem with certainty, with an uncharacteristic tinge of arrogance.

Jake positioned himself by the sofa with his tape recorder rolling, while the colonel sat at Pat's desk and called agent Connors. Woody sat across from Jake to take clinical notes of the session as he always did. Once the team was readied, Pat related the details he had from his marathon dream. One by one, he opened the mental files he had created the night before, one for each of the eight abductions. Although he had spent only a few seconds at a time with each scene during the dream, before he rushed to the next to spin its plate, he actually had visited each place hundreds of times over the course of fourteen hours. With each visit he would toss a gem or a pearl of information into the respective mental file. This accumulation of data paid off. He had assembled huge portfolios for each crime, so detailed and complete, that it took over two hours of tape to record this particular session.

"Unbelievable!" Woody exclaimed when he finished his last case. "Pat, I am amazed, but I'm also worried about you. You need to take it easy. You are going to burn out fast. Maybe it's this place. Maybe there's just too much of a concentration here of information about lost children that is pinging your senses."

The colonel nodded in agreement, but he also seemed mindful of the time. Tapping his watch he announced, "Look, gang, we need to head out now to attend the interagency meeting. Pat, great job--all your info is now in the hands of the Operations Center, and the right emergency calls are being made as we speak. Shall we go?"

The colonel insisted on driving them all over in his new, sleek, black Mercedes sedan. Pat sat in the rear right, tilted back in the exquisite soft leather reclining seat. In seconds he was fast asleep. The other three dared not wake him following his incredible journey from the night before, knowing he lacked any meaningful sleep at the moment. In the thirty minutes or so of driving across town to downtown Washington, DC, Pat managed to rack out enough to refresh him somewhat for the meeting. Although a bit groggy-eyed, he perked up when they pulled into the underground parking lot beneath the FBI Headquarters building, to a space reserved for the colonel because of his privileged status as the Attorney General's special projects man.

The conference room door was wide open when they entered a few minutes past 1000. Instantly, Pat's eyes riveted on Major General Robert D. Swank, the six-foot-something, bald, two-star general who never seemed to smile. Pat was convinced the good Lord forgot to add a drop or two of liquid from the happiness beaker when He stirred the solution used to create the general's DNA. This guy gave junkyard dogs a good reputation.

Swank gave him a smirk upon seeing him--which Pat found slightly entertaining. In the pre-CRYSTAL ROUNDUP era, when Pat worked for the Air Force Inspector General at the Pentagon, they saw each other at least twice a week, but Swank hardly ever acknowledged him. Today was different. Pat was back in his rock star status as the hub of everything going on in the CRYSTAL ROUNDUP world. And Swank clearly did not like being upstaged by a mere field grade officer.

"Ladies and gentlemen, let me make a few introductions before we begin our program update," Colonel Helmsley said standing at the front of the room, pulling Pat to his right side. "Most of you were in the Focal Point System the last time Special Agent O'Donnell was here in October 2001. Some of you are new. This is Pat O'Donnell, our program's chief operative. And this is Dr. Woodrow Wilson Davis and his assistant Dr. Jake Jacobsen."

There was a murmur as the room of fifteen or so senior Intelligence Community representatives digested what Helmsley had said. Most eyes were on Pat, but a few stayed on Jake who, upon hearing his name, shook his head slightly from left to right to push his long black locks from his eyes. Pat just knew they were trying to figure out how young he was.

"Let me give you an update by telling you about the incredible work Pat has done this week alone!"

The colonel proceeded to outline the first series of cases Pat cracked, followed by the two non-abduction cases he rapidly solved involving Darius Johnson from Detroit and Amber from Houston. But the thing they found most intriguing was his work that morning, from his plate-spinning, Olympic-style vision. While it was too early to know about its results, there was no doubt in the room when the colonel spoke that these eight children, too, would be found very soon.

"Finally, I need to brief you on a very serious matter Pat is pursuing. A serial killer we've been hunting for over a generation already."

He brought them up to date on the search for the phantom killer, the scarred man who enjoyed torturing and murdering young boys. No one said a word as he described the sinister depravity of the man they hunted, and when he mentioned their theory—that the madman was a powerful psychic—it seemed like the air had been sucked out of the room.

As soon as Colonel Helmsley spoke those words, a spark lit up inside the mind of the killer. He drove through the streets of Arlington in his older-model pickup truck, trying to home in on signals from his psychic enemy. He knew instantly that someone connected to his enemy was talking about him, so he pulled into the parking lot of a strip mall, and closed his eyes. He saw Woody's face again—his misperceived nemesis--

nodding as someone else spoke. He saw no one else in the room, but he knew it was across the river in Washington. He knew he was close, and getting closer by the day.

"So, as you can tell gentlemen, the CCVC is working this case hard. We need to stop this bastard before he kills another young child," the colonel said as he wrapped up his briefing.

Pat never took his eyes off General Swank during the presentation. He was so conditioned to abuse from him, like a dog that fears a rolled newspaper, that he didn't want to miss the signal the general was about to inflict some new pain on him.

Suddenly Swank spoke, his deep intimidating voice shaking Pat up fiercely, "This is all nice and everything, but CRYSTAL ROUNDUP needs to be focused on more than finding children! I knew it was a mistake to operate out of the CCVC."

When Swank spoke, his words managed to transmit themselves via some invisible form of energy from the room…and straight to the ears of the killer. Perhaps it was Swank's intensity. Perhaps it was the fact that Pat, the psychic with whom the killer maintained a crude link, feared him more than most people he dealt with over the years. Whatever it was, at that moment in time the killer not only heard Swank's words, but he caught a quick mental glimpse of his face, his two stars, the ton of colorful ribbons on his Air Force blue service dress jacket, and his name tag. The killer scribbled down, *major general swank USAF* on a notepad. Next to it he wrote, *crystal roundup*? And next to that he wrote, *CCVC?* He opened his eyes, the vision having evaporated from his mind in a mental puff of smoke. Then he broke out into a hearty laugh that quickly began sounding sick and evil. To a couple of passersby he looked like a man enjoying a joke he heard on his truck's radio. But in his twisted mind, the joy he felt at the moment was hardly innocent. He had just advanced the ball further down the field and achieved another first down. The home team was losing.

"We know Pat is capable of much more Bob," the colonel said answering Swank's demand that Pat turn his talents in another direction. "But right now he needs to be kept focused on finding this serial killer."

The tension in the room was thick. Pat could tell this group of senior and experienced Intelligence Community members, while sympathetic to what he was doing, was much more concerned about the issue or threat of the day. And that, of course, was bin Laden and Saddam Hussein. These two madmen were still at large, creating a political mess for the President. Finally, he broke into the conversation.

"Look, I know you want me to try to find UBL. Let me rephrase that. I found UBL once before, but CENTCOM didn't act fast enough, and he got away. I *can* find him again. It just may take some time. The good news is I don't have to fly to the theater again to find these jerks. I have to tell you, though, that this serial killer is consuming my time and energy."

"You need to get on board and support the war, O'Donnell!" Swank boomed.

"Bob, Pat will get to it when he can. You need to sit tight and leave the CRYSTAL ROUNDUP reins in my hands!"

In his new civilian job, Colonel Helmsley was a member of the Senior Executive Service of government, and a four-star general equivalent. Two-star general Swank hated being put in his place. He was used to it being the other way around. He stood up and strutted from the room without saying another word. Everyone rolled their eyes, and a few even let out an audible sigh of relief when he exited--in particular Pat. He knew that while they agreed with Swank's ideas, they hated his bullying demeanor and intimidation tactics.

Once he was gone, the colonel continued the meeting which lasted for an additional two hours. Each of the agency representatives—the National Security Agency, Central Intelligence Agency, National Reconnaissance Office, Defense Intelligence Agency, and all the others had a handful of questions for Pat. Although he was tired, he delighted in sitting through and answering their questions like a celebrity doing a television interview.

While Pat held court with his fan club, the colonel left to take a call on his secure cell phone. He was gone twenty minutes before returning with a grim face.

"Excuse me ladies and gentlemen, I need to hold a separate meeting with my team. Please excuse us while I speak with them. We were done for the day anyway."

With that the group began to disassemble, leaving Pat, Woody, and Jake alone with the colonel.

"Guys, I just got off the phone with Jim Connors. Six children were safely rescued from the eight in this morning's list. The other two are pending right now."

"That's great, Boss!" Pat said excitedly. "But you don't look like it's good news. What happened?"

"Although six were rescued so far, two of them were all mixed up. The information you gave us on the boy in the trunk of the car led to the rescue of the little blond girl in shackles. She was in the car, not him! And the information you had about her, led to the rescue of the boy in an apartment closet, not a car trunk!"

Pat had a worried look. He knew the implication was potentially devastating to the SAP. In his frenzy to capture and catalog the information from his maddening dream, he horribly mixed up some of the facts. Although both children were rescued, they were found with incorrect leads. If the media caught wind of this huge disparity, they would demand answers. It was going to be hard to explain.

"We cannot afford this kind of error, Pat! I only hope--no, I pray, that the remaining two kids are found based upon correct leads. If we have four mix ups in one day, no amount of tap dancing is going to ameliorate this."

To say the colonel was very upset with him at this moment was an understatement. That much was clear to Pat, who didn't particularly enjoy the dressing down from his red-faced mentor.

"Oh, man. I'm sorry, Boss. I did the best I could with this info. It came at me so fast and furious."

He sat down at the end of the long conference table and held his head in his hands.

"How could I have been so stupid!" he chastised himself out loud.

The colonel sighed. Pat knew he felt bad for the verbal butt-chewing he had just given him. The colonel walked over and put a hand on his back.

"Hang in there…sorry I snapped at you. We just have to be extra careful."

"I need to say something here," Woody interrupted sternly. "I've been holding back the last day or two, but given what happened today, I need to weigh in. Pat, you are getting too confident in your abilities. I can see it. Don't let this stuff go to your head. This morning when Jake wanted you to read the stack of Amber Alerts, and you refused—well, that was a mistake. Perhaps buried down in those reports was a nugget or two of info you needed to keep these cases sorted out properly. Never refuse additional help. Never think you know enough!"

Woody's spontaneous admonition caught him off guard. Pat buried his face in his hands, rubbing his baggy eyes.

"You're right, Woody. I needed to hear that. I'm sorry I let you guys down like that."

Like a father who just corrected his son, Woody put an arm around Pat's shoulder to console him.

"Tomorrow's a day off for all of us. Get some rest, and we'll regroup again on Monday. Try not to think about any of this stuff."

Suddenly the colonel's cell phone rang again.

"Hello, Jim. Uh huh? Really? That's great news. I'll let the gang know. Out here."

He gave them a smile.

"Well, the last two kids were rescued moments ago--no mix up at all, and a boatload of suspects are in custody, plus one dead guy in his car like you saw. You dun good!" the colonel beamed.

Dr. Davis chimed in. "Hey, Sunday is Easter, the

resurrection of our Lord. Pat--looks like you've resurrected CRYSTAL ROUNDUP. It's kinda fitting isn't it?"

Pat returned a nervous smile and nodded. But deep, deep down inside, that gnawing feeling of resurgent evil was still very much in his stomach. He harbored fears greater than he had ever felt before in his life. While he was joyful about the long, important Christian weekend that was upon them, and excited about CRYSTAL ROUNDUP's renewal, he was deeply troubled he had awakened a sleeping beast…a form of wickedness so vile, that it would make the legend of Pandora's Box seem like a birthday party.

~ 12 ~

On this Good Friday morning, Pat woke feeling spiritually refreshed and renewed. The weather was splendid indeed, but it didn't matter to him--it was the day itself that was most important. It was arguably the most schizophrenic Christian holiday because of the mix of grief over the Lord's death and the anticipated joy over His resurrection in just three days.

"Let's get you guys moving!" Pat urged his family, swooping Erin up for a kiss.

Although she was an adorable little girl, her white dress, black glossy shoes, and the little white ribbons in her hair made her even more beautiful today. With her arms wrapped firmly around Pat's neck, face nuzzled in close to his neck, he could smell her sweet auburn hair that flowed halfway down her back.

"God, I love you so much!" he gushed squeezing her tightly.

"She has you wrapped around her fingers. Better watch out!" Sara teased as she grabbed Sean's hand.

The family of four, all decked out neatly in springtime clothing, bolted for the minivan and the ride to Our Lady of La Salette.

The church was not so full for the midday Mass, so finding an empty pew for the entire family was not nearly as difficult as Pat knew it was going to be in just a few days on Easter Sunday. Just as he had consistently done at every Mass all his life, Pat knelt down, blessed himself, and prayed. He prayed for the successful conduct of the CRYSTAL ROUNDUP program, in particular for the arrest of the serial killer before he could kill again. He prayed for his own health and sanity, knowing that the colonel and Woody were right, that in the space of just a few days the toll it was taking on him was severe. Finally, he called on the Mother of God to be with him in prayer.

Oh Blessed Virgin Mary, I pray that you will help protect not just me, but my family and all those for whom I care deeply. Please keep them safe and away from the clutches of evil. Amen.

A soft, warm sensation flowed through him as he prayed, sending surges of spiritual strength throughout his entire body. Deep within his mind he heard a woman's voice whisper to him, "Patrick , I will be with you as before, as I am every day. Guard yourself because evil is nearby, but know that no matter what happens, God has a plan, and He loves you dearly."

He wiped small tears from his eyes with a fresh, clean white hanky, something his children noticed as they fidgeted in their seats. Erin clutched his arm tightly, not knowing why her father was weeping, but wanting to comfort him in his silence. But Sean knew. Sitting on his dad's immediate left, he took his father's hand in his own and gave it a squeeze.

He looked up at him and whispered, "The lady is right, Daddy. It's gonna be okay."

Although not an official holiday by any means, Colonel Helmsley's decision to give Good Friday off to his small staff was greeted with enthusiastic cheers the day before. Even Jake, who previously expressed displeasure at the informal holiday, took advantage of a free day off to go downtown and visit the Capitol Mall area. No one showed up for work in the Special Projects Division of the CCVC except for Dr. Davis, a young office administrative clerk named Suzanne, and Jim Connors down in the Operations Center.

"Suzanne, I came in to get caught up on some paperwork, but you have no reason to be here today!" he gently chastised her for showing up.

In reality, he didn't mind. He admired the young George Mason University student's dedication to work. She was a part-time hire who managed to pass the rigid background investigation required for access to the CRYSTAL ROUNDUP program. At nineteen years of age, just one year younger than Dr. Jacobsen, the stunning, slender, hazel-eyed, brunette gave him a warm smile and waved off his mild scowling.

"Oh, Dr. Davis, don't be such an old fuddy!" she teased, removing a stack of reports from his desk for filing in the huge black GSA-approved safe in her office two doors down the hall. "I plan to leave early anyway. Maybe in about an hour, unless you need me."

"No. You've done more today than I could have ever asked for. I'm just finishing up some of my clinical notes on the computer, so thanks for clearing off my desk of all the official papers."

She disappeared with the stack and left him alone to finish his work.

The deranged killer sat and studied the odd-shaped building, concentrating hard on the structure in an attempt to locate the only two faces he knew had any connection to him...the old black man he mistakenly believed was the psychic cop currently pursuing him, and Major General Swank.

He examined the peculiar angles and windows, working in his mind from right to left, searching for clues of any kind to where either of the two men might be. He slowly formed an impression of the interior layout of the building, moving from floor to floor, adding walls and corridors to complete the scene…creating an impressive mental blueprint of sorts. When he reached the third floor, and the far left oblique windows, he knew he had hit the jackpot. He saw Dr. Davis sitting at his desk, typing steadfastly by himself.

"Got you now, old man!" he whispered out loud.

Dressed in business attire of dark blue dress slacks, light blue shirt and red tie, and a blue sport coat with gold buttons, he pulled a .45 caliber Sig Sauer P220 semi-automatic handgun from a black leather holster on his left hip. Reaching into his glove box, he retrieved a stubby, homemade-looking silencer and screwed it into the gun's barrel. He smiled with each twist as it made a faint squeak. After he re-holstered his weapon, he shuffled through some old papers in the rear of his glove compartment and fished out a leather case with a gold badge on the front. He opened it and looked at the counterfeit, generic police credentials, in particular examining the picture under the crudely laminated surface. It had been made years ago, and was one of the props he used to lure young boys into his clutches. He held it up to the mirror and compared the photograph to his current face. Although the years had created some wrinkles, and he had lost some hair, he was satisfied he still looked close enough to the image to get through the doors to his intended target. Besides, he didn't plan to give anyone enough time to look closely at the photograph to even matter.

He left his truck parked on the boulevard and headed to the tall glass doors of the lobby. Standing in the entryway, just like Pat had done on his first day, he pretended to be waiting for someone as he patiently observed security operations. The same dayshift rotund man and woman security team was in position, casually inspecting building passes as people entered. Their indifference was obvious, and to the killer it presented a wonderful opportunity. Checking his watch a few times to play the role, he observed a couple of federal agents walk up, flash their badges, and gain instant access with no challenge at all. That was the break he was looking for.

He walked up to the pair and smiled broadly, "Good afternoon! I guess my partner's gonna be late as usual."

Unaccustomed to a friendly law enforcement officer, the pair laughed and waved for him to pass through, barely glancing at his credentials. When the metal detector screamed, they didn't even look behind them. Neither did the killer. He kept walking and headed straight to the elevators.

The sicko traced through the mental sketch he made moments earlier of the CCVC's interior. Walking like he knew where he was going, he headed directly to the new wing, to the heavy wooden door with the placard that read, Special Projects Division. When he stepped through it and into the small foyer, he saw the inner steel vault door. He was about to pick up the handset to announce his arrival when Suzanne popped the door open on her way home.

"Oops, sorry, I almost knocked you over!" she apologized seeing him jump back and away.

He had a certain air of authority about him that signaled to Suzanne he was legitimate. He also possessed what most serial killers somehow manage to exude...an abundance of cunning and charm. The ruggedly-handsome murderer grinned a warm smile when he briefly flashed his phony credentials case. Suzanne barely caught a glimpse of the badge because his smile was much more mesmerizing to her.

"I'm sorry, I'm here to work on a crystal roundup matter," he announced in a deep, low voice, once he knew he had her stare fixed on him instead of his counterfeit identification.

He really had no idea what he was saying when he uttered the program's nickname, but he was clever enough to know it was probably prudent to use the only buzzwords he knew were connected to his new psychic nemesis.

Suzanne was stunned by his sudden appearance, and a bit too flustered to challenge him or ask him to redisplay his credentials. While protocol and security procedure dictated she had to verify by name that he was on the Special Access Program control list, he seemed to be the real deal. He said the right thing. Besides, she was now in a hurry having promised her parents in Baltimore that she would be home for the Easter weekend before dinner.

"Um, okay. You can go on in. Dr. Davis is the only one

working right now; shall I let him know you are here?"

"Nah, we're good friends! He's always told me to stop by any time to discuss our business."

She smiled as he walked past her, and with a huge crunch, the vault door shut behind him. Dr. Davis and the killer were now sealed together in the soundproof confines of the CRYSTAL ROUNDUP nerve center. He walked slowly down the hallway, admiring the fairly plush interior decorator touches and furnishings. He knew exactly which room Dr. Davis was in, and he stood in the doorway for a few moments observing him typing away in silence, unaware of the killer's presence.

Suddenly Woody looked up, startled at the intrusion. "Who are you? How did you get in here?"

"Relax, Dr. Davis, you and I are going to have a chat about crystal roundup and your dreams."

When he said those words Woody stood up, and the hair on his neck bristled. He glanced at the man's hands and saw the scars Pat had described. He realized now he was standing face-to-face with the brutal killer they had been chasing all week. But he didn't want to let on that he knew this. He also didn't want the killer to realize that he had mistaken him for Pat O'Donnell...*he called them my dreams,* he thought.

"What agency are you with?" Dr. Davis asked, trying to throw him off the scent.

But the killer was far too intelligent and insightful, and he sensed immediately that Dr. Davis knew exactly who he was. He pulled his handgun out and pointed it at him in his left hand.

"Sit down!" he barked.

The flat screen television in his office was on with the volume set down low. On the Fox News channel was a banner that read, *Recent Spate of Child Rescues Raises Questions*. The madman laughed.

"Turn up the volume. I take it this is about you!"

Woody grabbed the remote and complied. The pretty, blond news anchor was updating the current headlines.

"We're following an unusual story today, one with many joyful endings, but also one that is shrouded in mystery. It seems there has been an unprecedented series of recoveries of children who have been abducted this week, all within relatively short timeframes. According to the CCVC, that's the Child Crime Victim Center in Arlington, Virginia more than a dozen children were rescued after anonymous tips poured in to local law enforcement agencies following their disappearances. A CCVC spokesman this morning told Fox News that while it is not unusual for anonymous tips to lead to rescues, what is unusual is the high number of successful recoveries in one week. The CCVC had no immediate explanation, but chalked it off to an alert public and a robust Amber Alert system. The CCVC had no comment, however, on a pair of rescues that seem to have gotten mixed up. On the east coast, two children disappeared around the same time, a little girl in Nashville, and a little boy in Atlanta. One anonymous caller phoned in a tip that he saw the boy placed inside the trunk of a car in Chattanooga, but when police went to the scene they found the Nashville girl. While that raid was underway, an anonymous caller in Dalton, Georgia said she saw the Nashville girl with a man in an apartment complex, but police found the Atlanta boy there instead. We are going to continue to follow this bizarre story to see if we can figure out just what went on."

"Well, looks like you're not perfect after all, Dr. Davis. So tell me, what do you know about my activities?"

"Go to hell you freak!" Woody responded, reaching for the phone on his desk.

He tried to dial 911, but managed only to hit the first number. A nearly silent bullet ripped through the barrel of the killer's Sig Sauer, through the silencer, and into Woody's left shoulder. The pain was searing, and flashes of hot, red light appeared in his mind as he looked down at the blood seeping through and soaking his white dress shirt. His strength waning, Woody struck the second number on his phone, only to be rewarded with another bullet, this time to his right arm. The killer almost seemed to be taunting him; there was no doubt in Woody's mind that he was a much better shot. He wanted to injure him, torture him. His right arm now twitching in sheer pain, Woody reached to strike the last number of the 911 emergency services line. He never made it. One last round from the killer's handgun screamed its way to Woody's forehead, dead center, punching a neat, round hole in his skull. Dr. Davis's eyes closed, and his mind, his thoughts, his brain…all shut down.

The killer sauntered over to his desk, strapping the warm-barreled handgun back into his holster, and with a Kleenex from Woody's desk in his hand, he placed the receiver back on the hook. He looked at the computer screen, at what he had been typing. He saw a large banner at the top of the page that, in bold, red block letters read, TOP SECRET CRYSTAL ROUNDUP LEVEL III. At the bottom right in smaller block print there was a curious set of phrases. One said, CLASSIFIED

BY: PRESIDENTIAL FINDING 03-005, and just below that, DECLASSIFY ON: EXEMPT.

Fortunately for Pat, Dr. Davis never used his real name in his reports, always referring to him as Operations Officer, or typically just, OPSO. He carefully sanitized his official documents to remove any trace of identifying who the key players were in the SAP program. The killer read the first paragraph aloud.

"OPSO described a dream he had where SUBJECT was in the woods with VICTIM (Ricky SULLIVAN). SUBJECT had VICTIM tied up and sitting on the ground when he first tumbled into the dream. OPSO could not identify SUBJECT, nor did he believe SUBJECT could see him."

The killer knew instantly that Dr. Davis was not the person who dreamed about him. He had disappointingly killed the wrong man. It wasn't that he was particularly upset about killing Dr. Davis. It was that he wasted his time going after the wrong person. He knew he still had some more hunting to do, but he also loved the delicious pursuit he was in. The next stop in his mind...General Swank. He realized Swank wasn't the OPSO because at the interagency meeting he talked about refocusing the program's efforts, as if someone else was doing the grunt work. But Swank would know who OPSO was. He printed a crisp, clean copy of the report and rolled it, complete with its classification markings and its White House "Presidential Finding" authority, into a tube shape and slid it into an inner jacket pocket.

"Fox News will love to receive this in the mail," he chuckled.

He was just about to leave when he noticed a memento on the desk near the phone. It was a small, black marble globe, the symbol of the super secret black world community within which the CRYSTAL ROUNDUP program resided, but of course the killer missed its significance. What he did note, however, was the brass placard glued to its black marble slab base. Etched in old English letters he read the three new strict rules, the *Three Commandments* of the CRYSTAL ROUNDUP program. And he snickered to himself. While he didn't immediately grasp the meaning behind the rules, he knew intuitively they were important. He was savvy enough to know they would play an important part in a new and twisted plan he was to devise. He departed the vault, letting the heavy steel door slam behind him, and leaving Woody's body behind.

~ 13 ~

Ever since CRYSTAL ROUNDUP thugs murdered Father Mike Reynolds, the parish was in utter turmoil. Our Lady of La Salette struggled to serve its community, sometimes borrowing substitute priests from neighboring churches to pitch in and cover the Masses. There were even plenty of times when no one was available, and no Mass was performed. Many parishioners simply left in frustration for other churches. But not the O'Donnells. They were as loyal to the parish today as they had been when their dear friend Father Reynolds served there. The "new priest," as he was fondly called by most of the celebrants, had arrived barely six months ago from New Delhi. He was a gangly young man with jet black hair, and traces of pock marks on his dark-skinned face from years of struggling with acne as a teen. He was formally known as Father Ravinandan Muthupalaniappan, but that was a mouthful for anyone. Most folks just called him Father Bob. Pat liked him a great deal. He was not Mike Reynolds, for sure, but he was an energetic new priest with a heart of gold who promised to care for La Salette as much as Father Reynolds, and that was good enough for Pat.

He approached Father Bob, bowed as the priest held up the Host, and then stuck out his tongue to receive the Body of Christ.

"Amen, Father," he stated as the thin, dry, perfectly-round wafer touched his mouth.

A profound gush of warm energy shot through him when the Eucharist reached his tongue, just like it did every time in the past. He approached the next server holding a gold chalice with the Blood of Christ. When the cool liquid swished around in his mouth, another rush of spiritual energy enveloped him. But the greatest jolt was yet to come. At precisely the same moment in time when the killer sent the third bullet from his gun into Woody's head, Pat had just received the Eucharist in both forms, and was headed back to his pew to kneel and pray. On his return down the center aisle, with hundreds of parishioners there to witness it, Pat fell to the ground, on his knees, clutching his head in agony. It felt as if his own head had exploded right there in the church. A searing, excruciating pain tore through his skull and brain like a fireball.

"NO!" he stammered out loud. "NO!" he cried as several people rushed to help him up, not sure if he was having a fit of some kind.

Sara had been ahead of him in the procession and ran back to help him, with Sean and Erin in between them.

"Baby, what's going on? Are you okay?" she asked, grabbing an arm and helping him walk back.

She realized at that moment how horrible he looked, how tired and stressed he appeared. His children were aghast seeing their father double over like that, frightened and not sure what to do.

"We need to go now, Sorcha. I think something awful just happened!"

The O'Donnells scurried from the church amidst startled stares from dozens of the parish members. Frankly, Pat looked like he was hung over, and many of those who saw him stumble that way obviously thought as much, judging from the handful of snickers he heard. Sara drove the van while Pat, not telling her much of anything, mumbling really, grabbed his secure cell phone and called the colonel.

"Sir! Something's happened to Woody. I think the killer got to him at the office. I think he's dead! We need to get there ASAP!"

"Calm down, Pat, let me head over there right now. I'm only a few miles from the Center. Sit tight, and I'll call you back!" he assured him, but Pat found the worry in his voice unmistakable. If there was one thing for sure, it was that Colonel Helmsley knew to trust Pat's instincts.

The O'Donnells drove in silence for the next few moments. Pat knew Sara was frightened by what he had related to the colonel, but she was also a bit gun shy about his work given what happened to her a year and a half before.

"You gonna tell me what's going on?" Sara finally asked with a look of confusion.

He didn't respond. Instead, he sat silently looking out the window, or so it seemed. In reality he was saying a rapid Hail Mary, literally at breakneck speed in his mind, over and over and over. Like a broken record. In some neurotic way, he hoped his prayers would reverse the past – if indeed Dr. Davis was now dead as he feared – and bring him back to life.

"Pat? What's really happening? Talk to me," Sara pleaded,

raising her voice and tearing him away from his prayer.

"When we get home, Baby. Let's discuss this in the bedroom."

She took his hand and held it tightly for the next few seconds as they drove. The children sat quietly, wide-eyed and genuinely afraid about what was happening to their father. He turned his head around and saw the terrified look on their faces and hated himself for bringing them such grief.

Once inside the quiet inner sanctum of their bedroom, Pat decided it was finally time to open up to Sara. There was little about his work that she knew for sure, so he made a quick mental tally of it. She was aware he was working on some sensitive projects with his old mentor, Colonel Helmsley. She knew he sometimes dabbled in counterintelligence and counterterrorism, and likely figured this all had something to do with it. And she believed he had been working with the FBI in the last year or two on profiling serial killers. But he knew she was unprepared to discover the central secret to his work, his psychic powers. And he knew that telling her all this would put her life at risk, not to mention that he was breaching security regulations that could land him in jail. But he also thought about how she was almost killed a year and a half ago when Vicky tried to stab her to death...and that was for knowing nothing at all! He reasoned he owed her at least this much. It was time to come clean.

He looked out the bedroom window to the large wooden playground set he built years ago in their fenced-in rear yard. In small flower boxes along the fence line, Sara had planted dozens of wildflowers that bloomed and blossomed, throwing color all around, contrasting beautifully against the rich dark green carpet of grass. The sweet and gentle scene also stood in stark disparity to the anguish he felt at that moment, angst over his special abilities and the danger they presented. He turned and looked into her green eyes, which had widened with anticipation, as if she had prepared herself mentally for the worst possible news he could deliver.

"I'm a psychic, Sara. And I've been working in a TOP SECRET government program that uses my powers to find children who have been abducted. And back in 2001 I flew to Pakistan to find Usama bin Laden."

He stopped and waited for a reaction. Her mouth was opened wide in disbelief, and those two, giant green saucers for eyes grew even larger. He looked down and saw her hands trembling. He stared at her for several seconds…seconds that seemed like a millennium, knowing full well her mind was busy assessing what she just heard. She started to nod her head.

"Oh…my…God. I never put it together, but those dreams you have and the kids that were rescued. Pat, just how gifted are you?"

"Apparently the best the government has ever seen. Not bragging here, in fact I wish I wasn't given this gift, but it is what it is. But there's more, Honey. Remember Dr. Davis, the member of my team I told you about years back? I think he was murdered today. That's what the episode in church and the call to Helmsley were about."

"Oh, no! Last time it was Father Reynolds who was killed, now Woody Davis?"

He sat down next to her on the bed, and she leaned her head on his shoulder. He explained to her all about the past week and his work at the CCVC, and how he was now on the hunt for a serial killer. He told her about the fact that the killer apparently was a gifted psychic as well, only he turned his powers to the dark side for torture and murder. And that right now, it was quite evident the killer was after members of his team.

"So, you're not the only one out there with this ability?"

"Honey, listen. I wasn't ever going to tell you this, but you need to know. Sean has this ability, too."

"WHAT!" she practically screamed, jerking her head from his shoulder to look him in the eyes.

Her pale skin face had turned crimson red, along with her neck. He could almost feel her temperature rise like a stovetop burner.

"How long have you known this? Does he help the government, too?"

"Calm down, Sweetie. No one knows but you, me, and Sean. He and I have talked about it, and I've warned him not to abuse his skills. Ever wonder how he suddenly starting getting straight As?"

A slight smile crept across her face.

"That little bugger! I thought he was just working extra hard!"

She grabbed his right hand and held it tightly in both of hers.

"What about Erin, does she have ESP as well?"

"No. It doesn't appear so. Thank God for that!"

With a look of tremendous relief, she let out a long sigh. Her eyes began to shrink back to their normal size as she continued to squeeze his hand harder. Pat continued when he felt her relax more.

"Sean has had visions about the killer at times when I've been blocked. It has been his information I've fed into the program at work, along with mine, that has helped us learn more about this sicko. Only no one at work is clued in to Sean's abilities."

"Baby, if the killer knows you--well, if he knows someone out there has this power, do you think he will come after Sean or you?"

"I don't know. That's why I'm telling you all this now, with the possibility that Woody is dead... No! I'm sure of it. You need to be alert. Maybe you should carry a firearm. I have a backup gun in the safe you could--"

She shook her head vigorously.

"No way, Pat. I'm not going to carry a gun. I've never handled one, and I'm not about to learn!"

"Alright, listen. At least carry some pepper spray in your purse. It will give you some protection."

For the next several minutes they talked and talked, and Pat opened up more and more to her about the CRYSTAL ROUNDUP program and his abilities, not just as a psychic but as a synesthete, as well. Sara was amazed with it all, if not a bit intrigued, but naturally troubled by the sinister world Pat was knee-deep in at the moment. Suddenly his cell phone rang causing them both to jump. He looked at the caller ID and saw it was the colonel. He gulped loudly and hesitated to answer, afraid of the bad news he was certain he was about to receive. On the fifth ring Sara poked him in the arm and insisted he answer.

"Hello? NO! Oh God, this can't be happening! I'm on my way!"

He dropped the phone to the floor without even closing it and broke out in a loud wailing cry, letting loose a flood of tears and emotion, magnified exponentially by his tired, exhausted physical and mental state.

"What happened?" she asked.

"Woody's been shot, in the head. They rushed him to the hospital, but it doesn't look good. He's barely holding on right now."

His body jerked in near spasms as he tried to control his reaction, but he was inconsolable. Tears flooded his face, and Sara dabbed tissue after tissue on his cheeks to wipe them up, leaving his face puffy red and swollen.

"Shhhhh, Baby, shhhhh," she whispered letting him rock in her arms on the bed like a small child at the moment. "It's going to be alright."

Still sobbing, Pat cleaned himself up quickly in the bathroom, then headed out to Arlington in his Subaru Outback. He drove there in record time, oblivious to traffic around him, gliding along as if angels had lifted his car up and flew him to the CCVC. Upon arrival he found a group of police cars and an ambulance with lights flashing in front of the center. He rushed inside and up to the third floor where he ran into a crowd of police and EMT personnel huddled in the hallway outside the vault door.

"Excuse me, gentlemen," he said wading through them.

"They won't let you in there," one of the Arlington Police Department officers said, a tone of frustration in his voice.

"I work here," he replied sliding his ID through the cipher lock and unbolting the door.

Colonel Helmsley was waiting just on the other side for him, while between eight and ten men he had never seen before, wearing FBI tactical gear, were walking back and forth between the hallway and Woody's office. He saw an occasional flash from a camera come through the open office doorway.

"Who are these guys?" Pat asked.

"That's most of my special team from the Bureau that I mentioned to you at the start of ops this week. I have my own crime scene specialists because we thought we'd need them in some of the child cases. Never thought we'd need them for one of our own."

"I need to see Woody's office."

"Pat, no. Look, it's a mess in there."

He didn't wait for the colonel to finish. He pushed right past him, stood in the doorway, and looked at Dr. Davis's desk and chair, and at the massive pool of blood on the seat and floor. Normally he was not very squeamish because of the fair share of crime scenes and autopsies he had experienced in his career, but seeing the blood of someone for whom he cared deeply, spilled and sprayed as it was, made him sick to his stomach. Pat ran to his own office and vomited into the trash can next to his desk. The colonel followed him in, handing him a box of Kleenex and a bottle of water.

"Here you go, Buddy. I know this is tough. I'm so sorry, Pat."

He sniffled, taking a tissue and wiping his mouth. The taste of heavy, bile-rich puke was nasty in his mouth. After an initial swish and rinse which he spit into the waste bucket, he took a gulp of water and sat back in his chair.

"We need to track this guy down now!" Pat said gritting his teeth. "Do they have surveillance video that maybe could show him entering the building?"

The colonel shook his head. "We've looked into that. Apparently Mr. and Mrs. Apathy downstairs haven't been too diligent about cueing up the digital recorders like they should every day. We have nothing to go on, except we're trying to locate Suzanne. She clocked out on the cipher system around half past noon today. We still don't know how or when the guy entered the vault."

"How about video from nearby businesses or traffic cams that maybe show him driving around in his pickup truck today?"

"I've got a couple of Bureau guys on the street right now looking into that. Don't worry Pat, we'll get this guy. You don't need to get involved. Remember the Three Commandments…no ops work for you!"

"I am involved! Hell, I'm practically responsible for this attack."

"It's not your fault, Pat. Let my FBI team go after this nutjob. You need to sit tight back here and work your magic to make their job easier."

"That's gonna be tough. I owe it to Woody to--"

"We're running down some leads right now, to include a forensic exam on Woody's computer to see if he accessed any files when he was here. Good thing our OPSEC is pretty tight, so your name won't be in any reports."

Just then Dr. Jacobsen walked in looking ashen and disheveled. He had no firsthand experience with violent crimes or gruesome crime scenes. He was shaking as he spoke.

"I can't believe this has happened. Pat, do you think he mistook Woody for you, thinking he was the real psychic?"

That thought hadn't occurred to Pat before. He just assumed the madman was on a killing spree going after anyone he worked with to eliminate the psychic threat to him.

Maybe I am all he wants. Maybe Sean was right when he told me this guy was coming after me!

"I don't know, Jake, but you may be right," he said nodding as the meaning of what Jake said began to make more and more sense to him.

They were interrupted by a voice from the doorway. An FBI crime scene examiner stood there holding a computer printout.

"John, not sure if this means anything, but the last activity on Dr. Davis's computer was a batch print job. He printed the report that's up on his screen currently."

"Well, what do you think is significant about that? Perhaps Woody printed a copy for Suzanne to file?" the colonel offered.

"Nope, I don't think so. It was printed at twelve forty-two today, but Suzanne left at twelve thirty. There's no printout to be found in his office."

"Crap!" Colonel Helmsley moaned, his mouth wide open.

"Crap!" Pat added, knowing full well that the killer not only had penetrated their physical inner sanctum to shoot Woody, but he had violated their OPSEC. He was now armed with information potentially devastating to the program and its continued success. Information that could potentially expose Pat and his family to public scrutiny.

~ 14 ~

Easter Sunday came, bringing with it the promise of a new life, a resurrection…not just in terms of the Christian faith, but the Special Access Program had been resurrected, as well. Pat stood in front of the church with his family and recalled the last words Woody spoke to him about restarting CRYSTAL ROUNDUP. He realized how insightful Woody had been when he compared the program's resurrection to Good Friday and Holy Week, making the innocuous connection just a few days before. But there was one more resurrection of sorts that he wanted right at that moment more than anything else—he wanted Dr. Davis to recover completely and quickly.

Pat prayed hard for his dear friend, but the prognosis in the three days since the shooting was not good. He was in a coma following nearly fifteen hours of surgery to remove the killer's bullets. The ones to his arms were relatively easy to remove, but the one in his head was not. The only saving grace to come from it all was the way the bullet entered his skull. It penetrated his forehead at a sharp angle, and instead of continuing in a straight line through his brain, it curved upward and back along the arc of his skull, only grazing his cerebellum.

The bullet rode the boney structure of his cranium like a bobsled on a curved track, until it came to rest midway in the very rear of his head. Although the surgeons found no major damage to his brain, nothing could be for certain until Woody regained consciousness. For now, everyone had to wait.

It's not fair, God. Why did Woody have to suffer for me? I'm the guy the killer wants...please help him to recover.

The O'Donnells trudged into the crowded chapel, unable to find a single pew empty enough for them to sit together. Pat led them to two pews, a row apart, with enough room for two people in each. They were forced to split up as a family, with Pat and Sean in front of Sara and Erin. He was awkwardly conscious of the stares and whispers from a few fellow churchgoers. People who had been there to witness his meltdown on Good Friday. He looked back at Sara and gave her a smile. He concentrated for a second on his wife's thoughts, and discovered, to his surprise, that Sara felt empowered in knowing his secrets. He had never spied on her mind before, had never considered it, really. But he saw the door was slightly ajar, and he peeked inside. She had a new sense of invincibility; her confidence and pride in her husband swelled within her. That made him feel wonderful.

A small group of musicians next to the altar warmed up their instruments while the choir practiced the entrance hymn. It was loud at first, but when Pat knelt down, blessed himself, and began his opening prayers, the music and singing faded into the background. Suddenly, that familiar warm sensation of the Virgin Mary's presence reappeared and filled his being. Her sweet voice whispered in soft echoes inside his head.

"Patrick, you were right to tell Sara what you did. Her

support to you is vital now. Love your wife. Love your family. We are all God's children, even those with whom we squabble."

Pat snickered inside. *Mary, you just had to throw Jake in there, didn't you? May I ask that you touch his soul, too?*

He never got a response, just a sensation when he prayed, that the Virgin Mary smiled a little wider at him from heaven.

Easter Mass was intensely long, even for Pat who enjoyed it more than most. But his children were horribly bored and fidgety. They played little tapping games with their feet, trying to signal each other between the rows, giggling suppressed laughs when their mom or dad fussed at them to stop. A few of the nearby parishioners gave the family disgusted stares and glares. The long, long service finally ended close to 1230, and he didn't look forward to the upcoming competition he faced leaving the parking lot. It was almost as if the moment people left the threshold of the church their civility vaporized. It was every family to itself in the frenzy to get out fast, outmaneuver each other in their vehicles, and joust for nose position.

"Let's go to Sunday brunch!" Pat suggested as they strolled slowly down the walkway to the parking lot. "I have reservations already at the Fort Belvoir Officers' Club."

"That sounds wonderful, Sweetie!" Sara agreed, clutching his hand in hers.

Taking the family to Easter brunch was his way of trying to regain some semblance--no matter how small--of a normal family life. It had become an O'Donnell tradition over the years, and each time Pat tried to surprise them with a different venue. He was also doing his best to keep his mind off Woody's attempted murder, but that was nearly impossible. He was frustrated because Woody had been in intensive care following surgery, and no one was allowed to visit with him since the shooting. Colonel Helmsley arranged for continuous FBI security outside the ICU, much to the chagrin of the hospital staff, but given the killer's unpredictable behavior, it was a prudent measure. Pat was slightly reassured by this.

Erin and Sean walked behind, holding hands like mom and dad, pushing and shoving each other playfully, giggling and chattering. Pat glanced back and gave them a wink, knowing deep inside they were happy to see mom and dad so much in love. Not to mention the fact that their father had made it through Mass without having another embarrassing episode, like falling to his knees and screaming.

Fort Belvoir was one of the oldest military bases in northern Virginia. It maintained many of its original brick colonial structures going back to the early 1900s when it was first built. The road leading to the O'Club took them along a scenic route that passed in front of the most beautiful colonials of them all. In most front yards were fresh, colorful spring flowers, while affixed to many of the front porch frames were flags representing the state of residence from which the occupant hailed. He slowed as they drove past the last row of homes upon approach to the club complex.

He smiled when the children squealed with delight upon seeing they were seated right next to the dessert tables, four of them to be precise, arranged as one long twenty-four foot station covered in gold cloth. Pat and Sara were more interested in the view, with a window by their table that overlooked the Potomac River. They sat next to each other and held hands, allowing Sean and Erin to get their food first. The kids made a beeline to the hot entrees, piling their plates with stacks of baked chicken, fried chicken, freshly carved roast beef, baked ham, baked turkey, baked fish, and fried fish. Mom and dad shook their heads over the absence of anything resembling a vegetable on either of their plates. Once the kids were seated, hungrily gobbling down their high fat and protein meals, their parents got up to serve themselves.

The brunch area was actually quite a sight to behold. There were huge, separate sections with several tables just for salads, with bins holding every conceivable topping on earth. There was another sizeable station for breads...french, sourdough, pumpernickel, rye, wheat…in slices, in rolls, in buns, and in loaves. In the center was the hot entrée station that the children had practically raided, next to which was a seafood bar with oysters, lobsters, shrimp, and more. Although mom and dad made sensible, balanced food choices, each of the four O'Donnells went wild with the dessert station. In the center of it all was a chocolate fountain that Erin found simply fascinating. They gorged themselves on cakes and pies, ice cream and chocolates. When the frenzy finally subsided, they all looked at each other and broke out in laughter, with crumbs flying everywhere.

It was probably just as well that they enjoyed their Easter Sunday together as a happy family, attending Mass, trying to forget their worries, breaking bread, and reconnecting with each other. God made sure of that. What He apparently didn't want to trouble Pat about was something going on at the same time not more than ten miles from Fort Belvoir. Outside a small, white townhome in the Old Town section of Alexandria, Virginia the killer sat in his pickup truck. He stared at the old, white-painted brick townhome with black shutters, sandwiched in near suffocation between two other units made of the same kind of brick. The row of homes was ancient, literally built in the late 1700s when our founding fathers, men like George Washington, Thomas Jefferson, and John Adams roamed the area, quite possibly having looked at this very same place on a few occasions following a night of drinking at Gadsby's Tavern. The bricks were wavy, and a few of the homes even appeared to buckle from the pressure the others on either side placed on them. Although these structures were old and worn, they were almost priceless parcels of property. This was the "high rent district," with million dollar townhomes sought after by the yuppie nouveaux riche of the Washington elite class.

But the psycho could care less. He had other reasons for being there. Evil, sick, disgusting reasons. On his lap was a torn page from a northern Virginia telephone book. He circled the last name, Swank, noting how there were only three Swanks in the entire area...and two of them were similar. There was a Robert D. Swank and a Robert D. Swank, Jr. It was the former's townhome outside of which he sat, assessing correctly, that it was the home of the Air Force major general he envisioned a few days earlier at the meeting Dr. Davis attended.

His plan was simple. He would invade the home, force entry, and kill the general's wife first. Then, under threat of a violent ending, he would demand Swank lead him to his psychic nemesis, and once so led, he would kill Swank before killing his enemy. He sat for over an hour. Observing. Surveilling. He wanted to confirm his vision of Swank's face, the big bully he had seen--if not admired slightly--because of his lack of political correctness…something the killer himself loathed. He watched and waited patiently until the front door opened. Standing in the doorway was the visage he had seen from his psychic state. He now had the target confirmation he needed. Swank held a cell phone in his hand and seemed to be looking outside his door for someone. The killer strained to listen in.

"Hey, Son, your mom and I are looking forward to seeing you and Bobby. Wait, I see you now!

Swank waved to someone down the street as he flipped his cell phone off and placed it in his pants pocket. The killer trained his eyes in the same direction, and then, like a gift perfectly wrapped up and placed under the Christmas tree, he saw the two figures approach. One was a tall man, about thirty-five years of age, balding slightly like his dad, but the spitting image of the general himself, if not a bit thinner. And clutching his hand was a young boy, perhaps eleven years old, little Bobby…the general's grandson.

My, my, my. I may have to rethink my plans, he thought sickly.

Robert Senior and Robert Junior hugged each other in the doorway, and for a brief second, General Swank, the growling pit-bull of a man, smiled. He swooped Robert D. Swank III up in his big strong arms and mussed up the scrawny lad's dark brown bushy hair.

"Hi, Grandpa!" Bobby chirped.

"I missed you guys so much!" the general beamed, this time grinning even more.

Appearing suddenly next to him in the doorway was his wife, a somewhat tall and slender blond woman, perhaps in her early fifties. The madman was once a Navy Ensign whose brief career ended when he insulted an Admiral's wife one night following a drunken binge. He harbored a great deal of animosity toward flag officers…and their wives, so his current pursuit intrigued him all the more. He thought Mrs. Swank was surprisingly fit and looked like a typical general's wife...the kind who wore tennis outfits and practically lived at the Officers' Club, sipping mimosas and eating watercress sandwiches with the other wives, wearing their husbands rank and falsely fawning over each other while looking down their noses on anyone of junior rank.

"Oh, Dahling, it is so good to see you," she exclaimed in a forced snobbish voice, turning her cheek to accept a kiss from her son, not wanting him to hug too tightly and mess up her hair.

"Hi, Mother," he smiled handing her a small Easter basket containing a bottle of single malt scotch and assorted colored eggs. "Bobby dyed these just for you."

"Oh, they look, um, well wonderful, Bobby," she offered, but her tone suggested she really found them dreadful. Her eyes were focused more on the scotch. "Let's go inside and enjoy our Easter supper together. We had everything catered today!" she said gleefully, prodding them all back inside, firmly shutting the door behind her.

From across the street the assassin sat and tuned his mind in to the townhome like hitting the scan button on a radio. He was a powerful psychic, with many years spent learning to understand and control his abilities. He channeled up and down the paranormal frequency band in his brain, quickly passing by the whispers, comments, giggles, and cries from nearby apartments and townhomes until he found the right place to stop. When he heard Sandra Swank's snooty voice beckoning the family to the table, he locked down the on the signal and began to generate a visual image to accompany it.

Within seconds it was as if he had teleported himself into their dining room, seated at the elegant long table, and watched as the family bowed heads in prayer led by the general's son. Standing behind General Swank was someone he had not detected originally, a young woman in her early twenties, wearing a long-sleeved, blue Air Force uniform with two stripes on her arms. With head bowed the pale-faced blond waited patiently for the next order.

"These people have a servant?" he said softly to himself.

"Kathy, Dahling, serve us the appetizer," Mrs. Swank commanded, looking impatiently at the airman.

"Yes, Ma'am," she replied carefully setting down fine china plates each containing salmon and whitefish cakes, drizzled with white horseradish cucumber sauce.

Little Bobby grimaced a grossed out look to his dad, who tried to suppress his own snicker. The appetizer was followed up with small bowls of San Francisco crab meatball chowder. Bobby's eyes lit up seeing it because he loved soup. He quickly grabbed his spoon and was about to dig in and devour it, when Mrs. Swank chastised him.

"Bobby, a gentleman waits for everyone at the table to be served before first eating himself!"

He erupted into a fit of laughter. "Grandma, I can't eat myself!" This brought chuckles from all the Robert Swanks in the room, all three, but the missus was not amused.

"Er hum," she said clearing her throat. "So, Robert, tell me what is the latest with you and that tawdry tramp ex-wife of yours. How is the custody battle going?"

"Mom, please don't call her that," Robert junior asked, putting his arm around little Bobby's shoulder. "It's still hung up in the Louisville court system. I'm just lucky I get to spend time with Bobby a couple times a month. But sometimes that's a struggle because Janet likes to conveniently forget when it's my time with him, and takes off on weekends a lot."

"Hmph! Probably out at some bar somewhere," she crowed taking a long gulp of the scotch her son brought.

The beast outside took it all in, savoring every tidbit of scandalous detail about the Swanks and their family troubles. His mind raced along as if he were a jogger on a dirt path, enjoying all the sights and sounds of his surroundings. But then he suddenly stopped. He reached a point in his new awareness where something clicked in his mind. A new revelation. A new plan. Suddenly he recalled the CRYSTAL ROUNUP rules from the black globe memento in Dr. Davis' office. They instantly made sense to him, and they offered him an opportunity and a new direction to proceed. In particular, he loved the one that prohibited work on family member abductions.

I'm going to Louisville, he thought. *I'm going to pay the little whore a visit.*

~ 15 ~

"Boss, any word yet on Woody? I've prayed for him all weekend," he asked, standing in the CCVC hallway while he watched the cleaning crew remove the last bundle of trash bags filled with blood-damp rags, erasing every hint of the crime scene where Dr. Davis had been shot.

"No. Listen, I know this won't go over well with you, but the Attorney General does not want any CRYSTAL ROUNDUP operatives going near Bethesda, he thinks--"

"WHAT!" Why?" Pat nearly shouted in anger.

"We don't know why this guy tried to kill Woody. My guess is he wanted him to reveal who you are. Do you have any idea if he gave you up?"

"NO! He didn't. I mean, he never would. Boss, look, I have thought hard about this, and I get no impressions at all that Woody gave anything up. My sense has been that this guy thought Woody was the psychic in all this."

"Well, the AG was real clear. We need to stay away just in case this nutcase is still looking for you. Once this is over, I promise you we'll go visit him."

Jake had been standing there listening to the two men talk,

his back to Dr. Davis's office. It appeared to Pat he was repulsed by the messy scene and was afraid to even peek inside. He held the morning stack of new Amber Alerts in his hands, and was about to speak when the colonel cut him off, motioning for the two to follow him into Pat's office.

"Gentlemen, before we talk about the new alerts, I want you to know what we learned from Suzanne. She described the guy she let in as a tall, middle-aged white man, burly, but not the blue collar type. He pretended to be some kind of federal agent, and when he flashed his credentials, she noticed scars on the back of his hand, like you described for us. Naturally she's very distraught over all this, and I've given her the week off to collect herself."

"Did we get anything from local surveillance cameras?" Pat asked.

"Not a thing. The few that cover the area around the CCVC didn't pick him up anywhere near the building. We're publishing a wanted poster based on Suzanne's sketch, but it's not much to go on at this point."

Jake set the batch of reports down on Pat's desk. "John, what do we make of the fact the killer maybe printed off Dr. Davis's clinical notes?"

The colonel shrugged his shoulders, then shook his head. "We're afraid that if he took a classified report out of here with program info it could cause severe damage to the SAP. I don't know if you saw the news over the weekend, but the media did pick up on the disparity in how two of the kids were rescued last week."

He shot Pat a nervous glance that didn't need much interpretation. Pat knew the colonel still stung over his gaffe in handling some of the reports last week.

"Does the CCVC have a good media plan for this one?" Pat asked.

"Yes and no. The PA guy downstairs is not briefed into the program. Jim Connors is working with him to come up with some plausible explanation for the mix up, but I'm afraid it's probably not going to go away any time soon."

Pat didn't like the answer because he knew he had screwed up and let his mentor down. He spun his chair around and looked out the window at the stop and go traffic on Wilson Boulevard for a few moments. The program was threatened, and Woody was clinging to life. He felt it was all his fault. To top it off, being unable to visit Woody at the Bethesda Naval Hospital was the cruelest cut of all. While he understood it on an intellectual level, it made no sense to him in his gut…no sense at all at an emotional level that at the moment was consuming him.

"Okay, let's just focus for now on finding some kids. That will help take my mind off Woody for now, I guess," Pat shrugged.

"We need to work on your ability to control things," Jake started to say, hesitating, even stammering his words.

Pat gave him a curious glare, unsure where he was going with this. Once more he had a bit of apprehension over what Jake had in mind, considering how the hypnosis idea went horribly wrong last week.

"What I mean is, we need to figure out how to adjust the power settings on your psychic gift, if that makes any sense. Last week it was like your abilities were running at full throttle. You nearly burned yourself out between the dreams and the sessions in here. Control is key, and with it I hope we can help you find a crevice in that brick wall the killer puts up to keep you out."

Pat stood up without saying a word and walked over to the sofa and plopped down, closing his eyes. He thought about the gentle admonition the Virgin Mary gave him in church Easter Sunday, to love everyone even those with whom he had disputes.

This is going to be tough! he thought. "Okay Jake, let's look at the Amber Alerts. I'm open to any suggestions at this point."

Dr. Jacobsen grabbed the stack from his desk, but handed him just the top report instead of the entire stack which Pat typically liked to review in one shot. "Just this one. Let's try one at a time today and see where it takes us. I have a feeling you have been overloading your mind and letting the cases overlap."

He rolled his eyes as he took the report from him. *Yeah, I know Mary, no squabbling,* he thought.

The little girl was but five years old, one of the youngest he had ever tried to rescue. At just three feet tall, the little imp was reported missing during a city-sponsored Easter egg hunt in Montgomery, Alabama. In the mass of children, more than five hundred it was estimated, she seemingly vanished without a trace the day before. He studied her picture and read the details over and over with the hope that something would come to him. With his eyes shut tight, he clutched the report on his chest, both arms across it as if to protect the pages as much as he wanted to protect the brunette doll whose picture graced the front of the document.

He suddenly had a sensation he hadn't felt in many months,

one that signaled his descent into a psychic state. A rapid, plunging feeling coursed through his body making him believe for a moment that he was being sucked through a giant water pipe. And in a half second more, he was tossed out into a wide open park amidst hundreds of screaming and frantic children rushing to outdo each other and find the most eggs.

He stood up as an invisible spirit in the park, struck by the heavy, dense mugginess of Montgomery even in the springtime. He started to sweat immediately. The humid air had a certain quality to it he had never experienced before. It had a sound, like big stacks of newspapers falling and smacking concrete. He smiled to himself, realizing at that precise moment his synesthesia was kicking itself back on. That special sensory-blending condition of his had been seemingly dormant for the past several days. He was hardly aware of its absence until this moment.

Standing next to him in the instant vision was the brown-haired soul he hoped to rescue. Her parents were with her…mom holding her hand as she tugged hard to be let free to pounce on every egg in sight. She held a pink basket that was laden with shiny, plastic green grass, but with only two poorly-dyed eggs to grace it.

He could feel her frustration. She wanted desperately to break free from her mom for just a moment to grab as many eggs as she could, but mom's grip was tight. "Please, Momma, please let me do this! I won't git lowst, prommus!" she pleaded with her.

"Come on, Honey, let Sally go for just a few minutes. We can watch her. It's the only way she's gonna git any eggs!" the girl's father pleaded, siding with his daughter.

Pat watched as her mom reluctantly let go. Sally's eyes beamed bright and wide, and she bolted! Like an eager puppy managing to break free from its leash, the girl shot out so fast her parents couldn't keep up with her as she ran into the thicket of children clamoring for egg prizes. They screamed her name, but she never looked back. She was so focused on securing for herself a basket full of the colorful holiday treats, that the last thing on her mind was her parents' instructions.

In an instant, he found himself standing with her clear on the other side of the park. She continued to skip along, looking for eggs well beyond the yellow tape boundary established by the egg hunt organizers. Suddenly, she realized she had gone too far, and was lost. She started sobbing and calling out for her mother and father, but they were still back in the madness of the egg hunt, searching for her in their immediate area.

"You lost, Honey?" came a raspy voice from a bench nearby.

Pat hadn't seen the man before, although he had been there all the while. The homeless man, haphazardly dressed in torn rags of clothing, was lying down on the bench no more than ten feet away. He literally blended in with his surroundings as if he wore clever urban camouflage. The hobo sat up and motioned for her to come over to him. He was a scrawny old man, with unkempt gray and black hair, mostly missing teeth, and a foul odor from not having bathed in weeks, if not months.

She reluctantly approached him, and when he spotted the basket of eggs, now numbering over ten, his tired yellowed eyes lit up. "I can help you find your momma if you give me some eggs," he offered.

Pat's senses were working hard on this one, unsure just yet what the old bum's intentions were.

"Come on, Sweetheart, we can look for them right over here," he said taking her hand and leading her to the south entrance, barely twenty feet from the bench.

Pat walked along with them and watched as the man seemed to be looking for someone to help him, but no one paid attention. It troubled him to see that no one noticed, much less cared, that the old tramp and the sweet, clean sprite he was with were clearly mismatched. It should have sent up flags, but it didn't. He seemed to be getting frustrated trying to help the girl, and it was starting to get dark.

"Come on, you can stay with me tonight, but tomorrow I have to take you to the police if we can't find your mom and dad."

He led her down a couple of side streets to a filthy alleyway in the heart of downtown Montgomery. There was a pile of cardboard boxes and scraps of plywood with sharp splintery edges arranged in a box shape at the back end of the alley. "Your palace, my princess!" he smiled, bowed slightly, and opened one end of the box to let her step inside.

In it was everything the man owned: a few old pairs of trousers, a couple of torn coats, and some cans of soup. The girl sat on the pile of clothes, her skinny legs sinking down into the fabric.

"I'll sleep outside the front door, by the moat," he winked. "To protect my princess tonight!"

When he said these words, she giggled and handed him the entire basket of eggs. He took two and gave the rest back. Small tears began rolling down his face, leaving a trail of clean creamy skin as the salty moisture washed away old accumulated dirt.

"Thank you," she whispered.

"God bless you," he said to himself softly as he wrestled with finding a good position to sleep on the hard asphalt.

Pat walked back out of the vision as casually as he had strolled the alley way with the pair moments before. As he had done so many times in the past, he related his impressions out loud. The colonel was on the phone finishing up his call with Jim Connors who promised to set in motion the events needed to find the little princess.

"She's going to be fine. There's a tenderness about the old homeless guy I never imagined I'd see," Pat offered.

"Shall we find some more kids?" Jake suggested with a big grin.

He nodded as he took the next report from him, catching out of the corner of his eye a smiling Colonel Helmsley. When Pat looked more directly at him, the colonel gave him a thumbs up. It was as if his boss sensed the renewed bond between him and Jake.

"Okay, let's rock and roll!" Pat grinned.

For the rest of that day the men worked through the remaining three Amber Alerts from the past seventy-two hours, taking each case on its own and patiently plucking from the ether all the clues Pat could scramble up. When they knocked them out, they proceeded to work on a half dozen more older cases from the weeks preceding the resurrection of the CRYSTAL ROUNDUP program. By the end of the day, all ten children had been rescued safely and were home with their families once again. The trio was excited to have solved so many cases in such a determined, systematic way. Pat was not the least bit exhausted or stressed. It felt right to him, and he noticed with each new case, his sense of power and control grew. What the men neglected to consider was the obvious--that solving so many cases in one day only threw more logs on the fire of media interest. What had kindled the week before was about to erupt into a conflagration of unwanted attention. One other thing was missed during the excitement as well. In his zeal to solve new missing children cases, Pat paid no attention at all to the serial killer who was still on the loose. When work ended for the men that day, the maniac was halfway to Louisville, Kentucky, having revised his devious plan for getting closer to his psychic enemy. It was a detour to be sure, but a necessary one in the killer's mind. He was patient. He knew the ultimate prize, the psychic cop, could wait.

~ 16 ~

It was unseasonably warm in northern Virginia the following morning. An unusual, early day thunderstorm locked in both the moisture and the heat, with temperatures already in the mid 80s by 0700, with an unforgiving forecast of upper 90s for the daytime high. The weather itself probably should have served as an omen of some kind for Pat, but he didn't regard it as such, at least not on a conscious level. His work the day before gave him such hope and confidence, that he slept soundly that night. Looking at his reflection in the bathroom mirror, he noted his baggy, swollen eyes were starting to look more normal again.

He went from room to room of his modest colonial home, kissing first his wife, then his two cherubs, goodbye. He paused momentarily in his den after strapping his official duty handgun to his waist, followed by two additional black steel magazines of 9 mm copper ball ammunition in pouches on his left hip. But it was as if on some subtle plane of awareness he believed the forty-five rounds of ammunition he had at the ready were not enough. He opened the small den safe once more, and reached way into the rear for his back-up handgun, a

Kel-Tec P32 semi-automatic. It was in a tiny canvas holster that he strapped to his right ankle under his pant leg, secure and out of plain sight. The diminutive gun measured less than three inches across the barrel and looked very much like a child's toy, but it was anything but a plaything. The lightweight, miniature pistol carried eight deadly rounds of hollow point ammunition. Most significantly, Pat was not authorized to use it for official business, though many OSI agents did anyway. He knew that carrying it alone could get him fired, but he reasoned things these days were anything but normal. He felt justified.

When he approached the CCVC, traffic was horribly snarled on Wilson Boulevard. He inched along until he came to the building and realized why. Lining the boulevard in front of the Center were several news teams with their large vans and trucks arrayed in a neat row. All had either telescoping antennae or satellite feed dishes extended to provide live linkage with their home stations. He walked past the crowd of reporters and their crews, many of them televising live shots with the CCVC building in the background, doing on-the-air interviews with anchors. No one seemed to mind at all the steady, moderate rainfall that doused them as they spoke; most were wearing raincoats or were covered by umbrellas held by assistants off camera view. He noticed off to one side a dark wooden podium bearing the CCVC logo was set-up under a blue tarp with about two dozen microphones bearing news station icons mounted on the top. A spaghetti bundle of black wires and cables flowed from the side and off in all directions, crudely taped to the sidewalks before terminating inside each of the vans.

No one seemed to notice Pat as he walked along, into the

lobby, and up to his third floor vault. When he stepped into his office, he was startled to see the Attorney General sitting on his office sofa, the one he used to generate his paranormal visions. The fifty-two-year-old, silver-haired Harvard Law School alumnus seemed amazingly casual and relaxed. There was not even a single visible wrinkle in his Giorgio Armani tailored suit, even though he sat cross-legged while flipping through a magazine.

"Hey Pat, great to see you!" Colonel Helmsley boomed upon his entrance. "I think you already know the AG, Ryan Coppock."

He walked up to Coppock and extended a hand.

General Coppock stood to greet Pat, towering slightly over the six foot one inch Special Agent. "Agent O'Donnell, it's great to see you again!"

"You too, Sir."

His shake was firm and vigorous, but not nearly as painful a squeeze as he had given Pat the first time they met eighteen months before. This time the AG's handshake felt *political*, like he was now in a campaign-mode of some kind. Pat quickly put it all together in his mind, realizing the Attorney General had come out to address the media swarm outside the front of the building.

"Have a seat, Buddy; we need to talk about how I'm going to handle the press today. It seems your work is so exceptional, it's caught the attention of a suspicious and conspiracy-minded media!"

"Sorry if I caused you any trouble, Sir," Pat said meekly, taking up a seat on a side chair. Colonel Helmsley walked over with a document bearing, in large red letters, the word, DRAFT, on the top and bottom.

"Here, take a look at this, the proposed press release. General Coppock will take the podium downstairs in about an hour and cover what's in this. Jim Connors worked with the unwitting Public Affairs folks to ensure no CRYSTAL ROUNDUP info was compromised."

He looked at the one page document and read silently to himself:

"The Department of Justice is intensely proud of the work that goes on every day at the Child Crime Victim Center. Since its partnership with DoJ a decade ago, more than 60,000 children have been recovered through the clearinghouse efforts of the men and women who work here and at our sub-centers throughout the United States. But one important fact must always be kept in mind. The Center is just that, a clearinghouse. It is not a rescue center itself. The real work of finding and rescuing missing or exploited children occurs at the grassroots level where citizen and law enforcement meet. While the professionals here at the Center serve to help connect the many law enforcement agencies together to solve tough cases, and while it has a robust television and radio network to inform the public, it is not in the operational business of finding children. It is clear to me that in the past week and a half these grassroots efforts have resulted in a dramatic surge in cooperation between the public and local law enforcement. I want to thank all the alert citizens throughout the nation who witnessed things that were out of the ordinary, or who spotted children reported missing via the Amber Alert System, and who ultimately decided to contact emergency services personnel. Why we have seen a sudden increase in reported cases these past ten days or so is difficult to assess right now. I want to believe it has more to do with good people doing good things and looking out for their fellow Americans. Ladies and gentlemen, I want to see more of this! What has happened recently is a good thing! I encourage all Americans to take an active role in their communities and immediately report anyone or anything they find suspicious. Thank you very much for coming out today. I will be happy to take your questions now."

"Well, Sir, it looks like you have carefully deflected ownership of the rescue efforts away from the CCVC, while avoiding the sticky issue of explaining the mix-up in cases from last week," Pat said handing the press release back to Helmsley.

"Precisely!" Coppock snapped with a grin. "And when the question about the mixed-up cases comes up--which I'm sure it will--I plan to shrug my shoulders and tell the press we simply don't know. Because the calls came in to local law enforcement from concerned citizens, these questions are best handled at the local level. I'll keep deflecting to protect CRYSTAL ROUNDUP. And you!" he winked.

The colonel had rolled the press release into a tube and was tapping it on his knee as he sat. "You realize too, Pat that we're parsing words a bit in this. While the Center has overseen the recovery of thousands of kids, most have been parental abductions, runaways, or kids who simply got lost. The recovery rate for stranger abductions, which the bulk of what you accomplished recently represents, is less than ten percent across the board. If anyone re-crunches the numbers, and omits everything but stranger abductions, it will be apparent the surge is genuine and extraordinary."

Pat took it all in as he sat there, mindful of the competing forces at work right now. On the one hand he had his central calling, his one Supreme Truism in life, as he called it, to find abducted children, while on the other hand it was apparent he was getting so good at it, that there was now subtle political pressure to slow down.

Just then Jake briskly walked in with two empty hands pointed at the ceiling, pumping them upward in the air. He had a big smile on his face and was chanting like a school kid, shaking his head back and forth, his long black hair swinging wildly. "It's gonna be my birthday, in just a week, yeah my birthday. Gonna be twenty-one on my birthday, yeah my birthday, gonna get drunk as a sailor on my birthday!"

"Ah hum, Jake, this is the Attorney General, Mr. Ryan Coppock. We were roommates at the Air Force Academy many years back," Colonel Helmsley said making the introduction after clearing his throat.

Jake turned white as a sheet. "I'm sorry, Mr. Coppock. I'm Dr. Jacobsen, assistant to Dr. Davis."

Coppock gave Helmsley a smirk and shook his head. "Well, um, happy birthday…I guess, Son. I have actually heard a lot about you. Are you getting ready to run Pat through some reports to find children?"

Jake nodded. "We only had two from last night."

The AG's eyes lit up. "You know, I've never seen Agent O'Donnell in action. Mind if I stay for this session?"

Pat cringed inside, feeling like he was about to become a circus freak show attraction. But he also didn't want to offend the AG. "Sure, Sir, but just one problem. You're in my seat."

Coppock let out a hearty laugh and stood up to switch seats with Pat. For the next forty-five minutes he watched in amazement as Pat transcended into the realm where his visions took control and brought him to the scenes of two abductions. In painstaking detail he described everything he witnessed both with his psychic mind and with his synesthesia, as well. But this time, with his eyes uncharacteristically closed, Pat did not see that Colonel Helmsley was not on the phone with Jim Connors relaying in real-time the events he witnessed. Based upon prior orders from Coppock, Helmsley was told to slow the pace of rescues for the time being, to give the spike in rescues a chance to synchronize with the press release. Coppock wanted to take some pressure off the Special Access Program. He hoped the media interest would wane, so that business as usual could continue for the program.

~ 17 ~

The former-Naval-officer-turned-killer became an investment broker when his military career abruptly ended. He was good at it, too. His genius for spotting fast rising stocks was almost legendary on Wall Street. He churned hundreds of thousands of dollars each week in the early 1980s, never once buying high, and never once selling low. It was during those days that he unlocked the real secret of his success, his psychic ability to peer into the future just far enough to know which investments were winners and which were losers. But he became greedy. He stole from trusting investors who were eager to make a fast buck, and in the late 1980s when the market tanked, it all caught up with him.

He spent two years in federal prison for his white collar fraud offenses. It was while he was in the can that he decided to get a tough appearance, for survival. He adorned himself in tattoos, most of them on his arms and chest, and he shaved his head bald. The real advantage he had while in the federal clubhouse was his big, muscular size. The tattoos served to add to that bad-ass aura which kept him safe while there. That was, at least, until he decided to tangle with the prison's informal leader, the Latino gang banger with a large following. That bit of disrespect earned him the scars on his hands.

These days he was independently wealthy. He managed to squirrel away enough of his legitimate earnings in offshore accounts to evade the tax man. When he wasn't killing, he spent his time in casinos where he multiplied his nest egg significantly…his special gift enabling him to make the right bets at the right times. But his lust for making money, although on hold while in jail, was secondary to his real desire…to kill young boys. Locked deep down inside the sociopath's complex mind was a sickness so severe that it could baffle even the brightest minds in the field of psychopathology. That is, if anyone ever cared to look. He didn't hate his mother. He came from a good family with no history of abuse. He never killed small animals as a child. He lacked the typical hindsight indicators that armchair therapists and media pundits point to with amazing clarity after a killing has occurred. His desire to kill was inexplicable. Even he had no idea why he did it, other than the fact that it felt good. It felt right to him.

But unlike his penchant for making money, which got so out of control because of his consuming greed, he was in command of the killings. He faithfully kept to his steady goal to murder one boy per year. It was just enough to scratch his twisted itch, but not enough to keep law enforcement hot on his trail. As a result, he never blipped on anyone's radar as a serial killer.

His only frustration with prison was that it forced him to take two years off from his killing spree. Now that he knew he was being pursued, he felt the urge to make up for lost time. His recent killings of two boys in the space of one week was one way to do it, but it also put him at risk of being discovered. But then, he enjoyed the added rush from taking such a chance.

The killer had driven slowly about the countryside before stopping on a rural road to read a map. In contrast to the stormy wet weather of northern Virginia this day, Louisville, Kentucky was basking in warm sunshine that lit up its pastures and fields and farms, sending jolts of dark green rays throughout the city and its suburbs. Horses grazed contentedly on grasses and hay as if there was nothing in the world to care or worry about, no sense of fear about the human who sat in the truck near their fence.

On the seat next to him he had the rolled-up TOP SECRET report from Woody's computer, along with a piece of white paper on which he had scribbled an address he plucked from a local telephone book for *Swank, J.* But it wasn't Janet Swank's house he was searching for at that moment. He needed something more to prepare for his new, sick plan. He needed a base of operations. A safe house. Plus a new vehicle.

He had done his homework. Traveling across the mighty Ohio River into Indiana, he headed for a suburban area known as Silver Hills, just south of New Albany. From the air it looked like a miniature version of the Rocky Mountains out west. The rolling hills that formed the community seemed to be a throwback to the agricultural era that once made the region flourish. Nestled among the crests and valleys were small family farms separated from each other by miles. Neighbors didn't really know each other so well these days, making it ideal for the killer to find sanctuary. This, combined with an unfriendly terrain that visually obscured everything beyond a half mile in any given direction, meant he had excellent cover and concealment as well.

He cruised along Indiana State Road 111, gauging the perimeter that ran along the Ohio River. Although he tried to see deep down into the community to his west from that point of view, he saw nothing but slopes and trees that swallowed his gaze, revealing nothing beyond the outermost edges of the undeveloped neighborhood. He turned onto Budd Road. It trekked back through some side roads, to even smaller roads still. He spent a good three hours learning the area well, until he spotted two homes set far back and away from everything, and from each other, that he assessed had the greatest potential for meeting his disgusting needs.

He sat parked at the end of one road watching the first home for several hours. It was an older, small red-brick ranch style house with slab-gray shutters that did not seem to match well. He waited until he spotted a man come out the front door carrying a large tool box. The young, mid-twenties man set the box down in front of a vintage 1969 cherry-red Mustang convertible and popped the hood. *Too young, probably others home, too connected to others in the area,* he thought as he fired up his engine and headed to the second home on his list, two miles to the west of this one.

He slowly slinked his truck to the side of the road on which the home sat in such a position he felt the occupants could not see him, but close enough for him to watch and wait. This time he didn't have to wait too long. An old gentleman, perhaps in his late eighties, ambled out of the front door, his elderly wife not far behind him. They carried some garden tools and began working together to plant fresh wildflowers in small, stylish boxes in front of their modest, wood structure farm home. A large SUV was parked in the driveway, from which they walked back and forth pulling small potted flowers and plants from a cardboard box through the open rear hatch. The killer smiled to himself, deciding this was the best place to set up shop, but there was one problem. He had to evict the current residents first. He decided to wait until nightfall to carry out his operation.

His dinner was hurried yet satisfying. Stepping into the men's room of a New Albany Applebee's restaurant, he carried a garment bag containing a business suit. He quickly changed clothes, the conservative dress giving him the appearance of a federal agent. When he stepped outside to the cool, evening air he saw the sun was just going down. Nightfall would soon follow, and by the time he reached Silver Hills again, it would be pitch black.

He sat in his truck in the restaurant parking lot, carefully getting his handgun ready. With a full magazine of ammunition in the stock, and silencer tightly screwed in place, he headed out for his target. When he arrived, not only was the sky as black as coal, but low clouds prevented even the smallest dollop of moonlight to come through and light up the hills. He approached the old couple's home and pulled into the driveway using just his parking lights to guide him along the slightly serpentine gravel road. He parked about ten yards from the front porch, cut the lights and the engine, and listened for a moment. There was not a sound to be heard for miles except for busy crickets off in the thicket of woods and trees.

He rang the doorbell twice before either the man or his wife responded. He was about to ring it a third time when he heard some footsteps from the other side. The old woman pulled a sheer curtain aside from a clear glass sidelight to get a peek at the caller. The killer raised his badge and gave her his signature, deceptively-charming smile. The silver-haired woman, head and hands shaking from Parkinson's, squinted through a pair of gold-rimmed bifocals. When she opened the door, the psycho put her at ease instantly with his naturally magnetic personality. He told her why he was there—a ruse, of course, but a plausible enough reason to acquire her trust in order to gain access. He needed that. Otherwise, he would have to do his dirty work on the front porch, a messy prospect he wanted to avoid.

"Honey, it's a detective at the door. He wants to talk with us about a suspicious vehicle someone reported seeing in the hills last week."

"Well, tell 'em to come on in!" the old man called back, his voice raspy and brittle.

The killer stepped inside, pulled the door closed behind him, and watched for a second as the old man hobbled toward them from the kitchen where he had been having dinner. He looked pudgy in his white undershirt, red suspenders, and blue jeans. The killer noticed his right leg appeared crooked, and it slowed him down en route to the front door. The wrinkled old woman turned her back on the madman for a moment to face her husband. The killer wasted no time at all. He quickly drew his hand gun, and grinned at the old man, whose face became instantly horror-stricken.

"What's the matter, Dear?" his wife asked.

A soft, almost silent round tore through the psycho's barrel, just over the woman's right shoulder, and screamed dead center into her husband's heart, dropping him instantly. When she began to react…tried to scream and run toward her husband, another quiet round ripped from his gun and into her back. She fell two feet away from her mate, loudly hitting the carpeted floor. But she wasn't dead. She reached for her husband with her right hand, inching her crooked fingers along the carpet in painful spasms.

The killer fished through the old man's pockets for keys but found none. He located the woman's purse on a kitchen counter where he found a set. He jingled the keys as he walked past the old woman. She was making slow moaning, gurgling sounds. Like a trained assassin, he pointed the gun at the back of her head and delivered one final round to her skull, ending abruptly the noise she was making.

"Sheesh! I thought you'd never stop making such a racket, Granny!"

He went back outside and moved the couple's SUV off to the right of the road so he could pull his truck into the garage and hide it. He went back inside and picked up the old man. The killer was strong, and he had no difficulty cradling the stocky old man's body in his arms. He carried him through the kitchen and out a back door to the rear yard of the country style farm home. Under the blanket of a pitch black night, broken only occasionally by a moonbeam or two busting through the low clouds, he brought the man's body to a shed at the far end of the property line. He pulled the door open with his right foot and clumsily plopped the man's corpse, chest up, inside. The body landed with a clunk, head and shoulders propped up by a large bag of lawn fertilizer.

The killer returned to the home to retrieve and carry out the wife's body. She was a lightweight in contrast, and when he reached the shed, he coldly tossed her, like a big burlap bag of potatoes, on top of her husband before swinging the door shut, never once looking back.

In some strange way, when she landed on her husband's chest, his right arm swung over and down across her. It was as if the laws of physics were intentionally kind in arranging this. He appeared to be clutching her lovingly, even in death. But perhaps it wasn't just the force of gravity at work. Perhaps God had seen to it that this old couple, married for over sixty years, would be welcomed into heaven as the loving man and wife they were when their souls left earth.

~ 18 ~

"What do you mean you didn't pass along my intel to the Operations Center? These kids are in real danger, Sir! Every minute we wait is almost a guarantee they'll be killed!" Pat shrieked at Colonel Helmsley the morning after his session with the Attorney General. He paced about his office nervously as he thought about the absurdity of curtailing his efforts to find children.

"I know how you feel, but the AG was unambiguous. We need to slow things down to avoid overexposing the program," the colonel replied, but from the look on his face, Pat could tell he was conflicted. He knew Helmsley was a good man with a good heart, and this decision was tearing him up inside.

"Sir? You really need to readdress this with Coppock. Remember how CRYSTAL ROUNDUP got off track the last time? It was precisely because she feared exposing the program that Vicky and her two henchmen murdered people just to protect it. That same kind of tortured logic is leading us down the wrong path again. What's more important, saving kids, or protecting the program?"

The colonel stared down at the floor as he sat in one of Pat's side chairs. Dr. Jacobsen was in the opposite chair, taking it all in. Pat could tell Jake was confused because he was not a part of the Special Access Program world when the original disaster struck. He knew little about the extraordinary, bizarre thinking that went into Vicky's decisions to kill people just to shield the existence of a government program.

The colonel started to nod. "Okay. Damn, you're right, Pat. I'll call Jim Connors now and get the rescues started. I need to talk with Coppock this afternoon on the media issue anyway."

Pat let out a loud sigh of relief. The colonel went over to Pat's desk and made the call, giving Connors the particulars from the psychic state the day before.

"Any news on Woody or finding this killer?" Pat asked when the colonel hung up.

"Woody has not improved at all, so keep praying. My FBI team is very engaged on this, running down dozens of leads, but nothing so far. Have you been able to come up with anything?"

"No, Sir. I'm sorry, but I can't seem to pick up anything."

The colonel lifted up a folder from his desk. "We got three more Ambers overnight. Let's work on these for now."

"How did the press conference go yesterday?" Jake asked, interrupting before Pat could take the stack and read them.

"Well, the media seemed to grab the storyline like we had hoped. At least for now. But since we're ramping back up again, I'm not sure how much longer they'll keep buying it," Helmsley stated, shaking his head in doubt.

"Perhaps we should do a little bit of deception or disinformation," Jake offered rather bluntly. "Surely the government engages in that. Just look at JFK, Roswell, and all."

Pat started to laugh out loud. "Damn, I thought it was too good to be true! Just when I saw a glimmer of hope that you were melding into our team, you go and spout out all that loony conspiracy theory garbage!"

He looked at Helmsley and expected to see the same kind of reaction, but the colonel appeared stoic at the moment, lost in serious thought. Pat knew that in his last job on active duty as Director of Security and Investigative Programs for the United States Air Force, the colonel was the nexus for all security programs at the infamous Area 51 in Nevada. It was the existence-officially-denied air base where the Air Force tested newly-emerging technologies. Colonel Helmsley was the official denier of the pop-culture belief that the government had recovered a crashed flying saucer in Roswell, New Mexico in 1947, and that alien technology was being reverse-engineered at Area 51.

"Sir, you aren't giving this nutty stuff serious consideration, are you?"

"Well. Sorta. Look, maybe we can gin up a cover or cutout operation for the program. I don't know yet what that could be, but I can have my old staff back at the Pentagon come in and consult. We can involve the interagency focal point officers. I think we need to give the media something that indicates we have a robust effort ongoing, but one that misdirects their attention away from you."

Pat started to nod, understanding exactly where Helmsley was headed. He smiled at Jake who had a mixed look of deep confusion and mild elation--the latter clearly over being the one who sparked the idea.

"So we own up to having a hand at finding children, but we

make it appear the effort came from another direction, from a unique source or method?" Jake asked slowly, measuring his words carefully.

Colonel Helmsley grinned. "Perhaps a carefully planted 'leak' to the Washington Observer will 'force' us to 'partially' admit the existence of a program of some kind, without acknowledging the truth."

Pat saw Jake was suddenly getting uncomfortable, actually more like incensed.

"So you people do this all the time, don't you? I knew it! I knew our government lied to the public!" he stammered.

"Jake, we have no obligation, moral, legal, or otherwise to inform the public about intelligence sources and methods. We spend millions, sometimes billions, of dollars developing technologies and operations that we risk losing if revealed," the colonel told him matter-of-factly.

"Yeah. Not to mention sensitive operations involving human agents--LIKE ME-- who could be killed if exposed!" Pat sneered, becoming more bellicose.

"Well, I don't like it. It's unethical," Jake snapped back.

"GUYS! KNOCK IT OFF!" the colonel shouted.

Pat shrugged his shoulders, smoldering from Jake's comments, resurrecting again his original doubts about Jake's loyalties to the program. "Sorry, Sir." He looked away embarrassed.

Colonel Helmsley opened a briefcase he had on Pat's desk. "It's time we discussed some of the new technology we designed for the CRYSTAL ROUNDUP program. Remember the magic minivan we used that changed colors and had all that satellite technology on board?"

Pat nodded his head. He strained to see what the colonel was now holding in his hand. It looked like a personal digital assistant, a small thin box no larger than a three by five index card. It had a shiny plastic screen that lit brightly when the colonel hit a button.

"Get ready for the future gentlemen. This gadget has a real-time satellite link with the NRO's constellation of GPS, imaging, and infrared satellites around the globe, all two hundred and thirty-seven of them. That's classified TOP SECRET, Jake."

The screen glowed bright white at first, followed by a large red banner that read SPARK//AVALANCHE//RHOMBUS, the National Reconnaissance Office's codewords for the satellite technology. He handed it to Pat.

"It will take a little practice to master the touch screen features, but with this you can look at any point on the globe down to one eighth inch resolution. And by the way, we added an enhanced feature. Six of our satellites use a mild burst of gamma ray radiation to develop three dimensional x-ray images of what's inside buildings and structures. You can peer through rooftops with it," he smiled.

"Dear God! I hope I never lose this thing, it would compromise so much if it got in the wrong hands!" Pat exclaimed holding the cool, slim device in both hands.

"We're ready just in case. Memorize these numbers," the colonel said handing him a business card bearing a colorful floral design and a business logo that read, "Flowers by Francine."

Pat was puzzled.

"If you lose it, dial the business number immediately and enter the fax number right below it. That's the password for the device. It will send out a beacon signal worldwide which will find the unit and fry it instantly. It works even if the device is switched off. There won't be much left but a clump of plastic."

Jake suddenly appeared intrigued by it all. "I only thought this stuff existed in the movies," he said in amazement.

"See why we have to keep some secrets, Jake?" the colonel asked rhetorically. "We didn't want to introduce this technology right away because you were doing so well on your own, Pat. But I'm hoping that it will help you find the serial killer. Maybe if you pick up a tiny clue, despite the force field he seems to have erected, you can use this device to fill in some blanks."

"Is it also a cell phone?" Pat asked.

"Yup. It has a built in Fortezza card. Secure up to TOP SECRET, Special Access Program material. Everything you need."

The sound and smell of bacon grease and frying eggs filled the old man and woman's rural home in Silver Hills. The killer hummed to himself while a local radio station blurted out classical music in the background. The frying pan's sizzling and crackling noises seemed out of sync with the high brow sounds of Wolfgang Amadeus Mozart's Piano Concerto Number 24. Even more disgusting was how the madman so casually prepared breakfast when barely fifteen feet away in the couple's small living room, the bloodstained carpet hadn't yet dried. Nor had he made any effort to clean up the mess.

He sat at the kitchen table with his platter of food piled high, slowly eating and enjoying his meal, occasionally waving his hands with fork and knife in the air as if conducting the symphony that played through the old transistor radio's crackly monotone speaker. He tried hard in the past few days to pick up clues about the other psychic--the man at the opposite end of his life right now…the cop who was trying equally hard to find him. But like Pat, when he searched for clues, the killer also came up empty. Neither man seemed to be able to break through the barriers preventing them from seeing each other.

It's just as well, the sociopath mused. *Today is the day I get my bait. And soon, I will trap my prey.*

When he finished his meal, he carefully placed each plate, pan, and utensil in the dishwasher and turned it on. From any outsider's perspective it would appear he had moved in and intended to stay awhile. Before departing in the couple's SUV, he examined the home in detail, going room by room, looking for and damaging all manner of ability to communicate with the outside world. He cut phone and cable lines to ensure their internet service, if they even had any, was disconnected. He found two cell phones and crushed them, along with a dusty old cobweb-covered ham radio set in the garage.

The ride over the Ohio River into Louisville, Kentucky was pleasant. The SUV's expensive XM satellite radio system belted out soothing numbers from a commercial-free classical music station. But in contrast to the ancient radio in the couple's kitchen, the SUV's stereo system was pristine and clear with deep bass tones he thoroughly enjoyed. With the address to Janet Swank's home memorized, the business suit-wearing killer easily navigated his way there.

Her neighborhood was quiet. By this time in the morning,

most of the community was away from home, the majority of its citizens off to work in the downtown Louisville area. He drove around the neighborhood several times, making mental notes of all the streets and roads, peering through backyards from side streets, examining vantage points, looking for neighbors with open windows. He wanted to make sure he had several contingency plans in place, with multiple and redundant ingress and egress routes, in the event Janet eluded him, managed to escape out a back door, or cried out for help and was heard by a neighbor.

He parked his vehicle directly behind her home on a back road that ran parallel to hers, providing essentially the same exit route that leaving from the front would afford. There was no fence separating her yard from the home behind hers, making for a short walk. Everything about the place was dreary. The home was tiny and somewhat dilapidated, with torn window screens, chipped white paint laying bare the wood that formed its siding, and piles of junk in the yard and back porch. A few toys littered the yard made mostly of clumps of broken sod and dried crusty earth.

Janet was a dancer in a local gentlemen's club, this much the killer was certain about based upon the conversation he intercepted Easter Sunday outside the general's home. She worked nights and slept days, leaving little Bobby to fend for himself while she rested. *No wonder his father was in a fight for custody,* he thought. He had done his homework and knew the neighborhood school buses would not arrive for another thirty minutes. The situation was ideal for a daytime abduction. Virtually no chance of witnesses, and with almost certainty she and the boy were home alone right now.

"Hello, Son, I'm with the police, is your mom at home?" he asked when Bobby opened the rickety front door.

"Um, my mom is sleeping. Can you come back later?"

"Well, I can't really. I must speak with her now. It's very important," he insisted, taking a step inside the home and pushing the door shut behind him.

While it was clear Bobby didn't like the boldness of the intrusion, the young boy didn't protest, either. "Okay, just a minute, let me get her," Bobby responded as he bolted up the noisy stairs to the upper level.

He could hear grousing going on between mother and son as he waited in the living room, subtly scanning the home's drab interior. He captured a variety of clues from the physical and psychic world in an effort to analyze Janet's lifestyle. She had a penchant for wild men whose names she never cared to learn, and for Jack Daniels…lots of it. He knew that despite paying generous alimony and child support, Robert D. Swank II's money wasn't spent well. Janet clearly had little interest in pleasant amenities like decent furniture and clothes for her son. He strolled around the room before taking up a position at the foot of the stairs, out of view of anyone who should step down them at this moment. The thought suddenly occurred to him she might have a boyfriend sleeping over, a twist in his plan he hadn't anticipated. He didn't sense one, but he couldn't be sure.

"There's nobody here, Bobby!" he heard her grumble, voice strained and tired from a night of heavy boozing, smoking, and flirting. Her footsteps were getting louder as she came down the uncarpeted wooden stairs.

When she reached the bottom, he grabbed her with his right hand and pulled her close to his chest from behind, his gun pointed at her head in his left hand, the cold steel silencer pressed tightly against her temple. "Don't make a sound! Bobby, you too. Get over here. Do exactly what I say or I will kill you both right here, right now!"

She shook violently against him, nodding her head in compliance. Bobby suddenly made a motion as if he planned to flee, but his mom stopped him. "No, Bobby, don't! Listen to this man!" she pleaded in a harsh whisper.

"Good thinking, Mom! Here's what we're gonna do. We're all going upstairs where you will pack suitcases for you and Bobby. Get some decent clothes on and we will walk to my car."

"What do you want? Look, I have a little money, and I have, well you know something else I can suggest, if that's..." she started to say before he stopped her. Her sexual favor offer might have tempted some men, but she obviously misjudged this particular one.

"Shut up, you tramp!" he snarled, jabbing the gun tighter against her head. "Let's go upstairs slowly!"

They proceeded first to Bobby's room, where his mother threw a few things in a small bag, but the killer insisted she pack almost all his clothes, everything she could fit in the biggest suitcase she had. Then they went to her room, a pigsty of a place with underwear and lingerie strewn about. He demanded she change clothes in front of them, though he made Bobby turn his head. Once her suitcase of clothes was packed, he told her to get a piece of paper from her nightstand and pen a note to be left on the kitchen table:

Bob,

I can't let you get custody of Bobby. My boyfriend and I are taking him away where you can't find us.

Janet

"Okay, now we're going out the back door. You walk ahead of me, holding hands and smiling. Do NOT try anything stupid. I've killed many, many people. Two more is child's play!"

They played their roles well, and no one ever noticed them as they slipped away in the stolen SUV. Janet sat in the passenger seat, occasionally glancing at the killer's gun which he kept tightly clutched.

"What do you want with us? Where are you taking us?"

"Shut up!" he screamed. "Not another word or you both die, Bobby first. You want to watch that, Janet?"

She began to wail. He smacked her hard across her face with the back of his right hand. He gave Bobby a menacing stare in the rearview mirror when he did. The two of them settled down long enough for the psycho to get them across the river and into the Silver Hills neighborhood without detection.

Once they arrived at the old couple's home, he hustled them inside quickly and pushed them at gunpoint to the upstairs level. He bound their hands and feet, and covered their eyes and mouths, and placed them in separate bedrooms with as much light blocked as possible to disorient them. He ordered them to keep quiet, and told them he planned to spend time in each room without them knowing he was there, and he would instantly kill them if they made a sound. Before leaving them alone, he inserted foam earplugs in their ears to keep them in silence and unsure if he was nearby. He wanted to generate as much fear and isolation as he could.

From that point, his plan was to sit back and wait. For the next several days, he put them on a regular schedule where he allowed bathroom and meal breaks, but only one at a time. Neither mom nor son saw each other the entire time there, and never once did the killer give them any evidence that the other was still alive. His plan of isolation and disorientation was so effective, each was hopelessly broken and dispirited within a few days.

~ 19 ~

With no warning at all, the electronic monitors in Dr. Davis's Bethesda hospital room screamed out an alarm. His heart had stopped, the monitor displayed a flat line graph, and his blood pressure dropped precipitously. Grace Davis had fallen asleep moments before the equipment that monitored her husband's health went haywire. She was in an ugly green vinyl side chair with her arm raised high onto Woody's bed, lovingly clutching his hand in hers. When the machine erupted with its warning, the short-cropped, gray-haired woman woke instantly in a panic. She clutched his hand even tighter while screaming for help.

"Someone, please come and help my husband!"

The hospital staff was way ahead of her. Within seconds, two nurses and a doctor from the floor rushed into the room with a crash cart. They had heard the alarm at the nurses' station and sprung into immediate action. Tears streamed from Grace's face when the nurses gently prodded her away so the doctor could do his work. The light-skinned African American woman stepped back and held her hands together and prayed.

The doctor was a tall, thin, Navy Commander. He ordered

one nurse to tear open Woody's pajama top while he warmed up a portable defibrillator, adjusting the joules setting expertly.

"Clear!" he screamed before almost instantly applying the paddles to Woody's chest.

The electrical jolt made a loud thump sound and forced Woody's chest to rise up and then drop as if he were somehow stuck to the paddles for a moment. The doctor looked at the monitor which remained flat line. Grace Davis, panic-stricken, began to sob harder.

The doctor readjusted the joules setting and readied the machine for a second jolt.

"CLEAR!"

BAM! Woody's entire upper torso came off the bed at least ten inches before crashing down hard. As his body came down, one of the nurses excitedly spoke, "We're getting a pulse now, and his BP is rising."

The doctor looked at the monitor and saw that his pulse had returned to normal, his blood pressure was low but acceptable, and his respirations were perfect. He wiped his brow and turned to look at Mrs. Davis.

"He's gonna be okay, Ma'am."

She thrust her arms around him, gave him a strong hug, and then surprised him with a gentle kiss on his cheek. Mrs. Davis returned to her green vinyl chair and clutched Woody's hand once again, but this time she didn't immediately fall asleep. She talked to him nonstop, hoping that, despite his coma, what she said would penetrate his strange state of consciousness and register somewhere in his brain. She wanted to give him a reason to hang on, to live, to come out of the coma, to regain consciousness, and to be the same man she married almost thirty-five years earlier. She chatted to him for five hours until her eyelids became droopy and heavy. She was fast asleep, still clenching her husband's hand in a never-let-go hold of hope. No sooner had her eyes shut, when Woody's fingertips—on the hand that she held so gracefully--gently, barely imperceptibly, twitched.

Although Pat, Colonel Helmsley, and Dr. Jacobsen were prohibited from visiting Woody because the Attorney General feared compromising their cover, or worse, drawing the killer's attention to them, they were at least there in spirit.

Pat sat in his office with his hands folded, head down in thought and prayer for more than forty-five minutes, silently reconnecting with his faith and with the Blessed Virgin. Frequently, when he was in deep prayer like this, he received subtle, elusive impressions. He never ascribed them to his psychic abilities, not even in the year and a half since discovering his gift. Rather, he understood them in a spiritual context. He even likened them to a form of prayer in reverse…direct feedback from God. They were messages sent from heaven without words--disconnected in time and space…merely thoughts secretly inserted into his mind. This time the impressions were extraordinarily elusive. There was some deep meaning to them that he failed to grasp, let alone understand in cogent thought. His thoughts wandered again.

He took stock of what he had done in the week since Dr. Davis was shot. While he did a splendid job finding and rescuing many children--no one could argue this was an ignoble endeavor--he failed to make any progress in finding the serial killer who remained at large. Perhaps it was because the psycho was a hard target of sorts, one who actively blocked Pat's efforts to learn more about him. Perhaps it was because Pat enjoyed finding lost children, and there were so many cases to solve. Whatever the reason, despite his ongoing struggle to home in on the psychotic psychic's stealthy signal, nothing he tried seemed to bear any fruit. He was growing increasingly frustrated at his failed attempts, and he knew he needed a new strategy. *Maybe that's what you are trying to tell me, God…I need to look at this differently.* He walked over to Colonel Helmsley's office where he and Jake sat reading reports.

"Guys, I want to try to work harder on the serial killer case today. I'll put some energy into the regular batch of Amber Alerts, but I need to get back to finding this guy soonest."

Colonel Helmsley nodded. "I agree. Here's the latest case update from the Bureau. It's not much, but maybe it will trigger some new insights for you."

Pat read through the thin document, barely three pages long, one of which was Suzanne's artist-created rendition of the killer. But not even seeing his sketched face helped him much at the moment. Then, out of the blue reaches of Heaven, a new thought occurred to him, something that had slipped below the depth of his conscious mind the past seven days. It suddenly appeared in his brain like a harsh slap in the face. Those subtle clues God was pushing into his skull began to take shape and become clearer.

He stood up abruptly and walked out of the colonel's office, leaving his boss and Jake sitting there dumbfounded. He jogged down the hall and into Woody's office. Although the crime scene had been cleaned up, the memory of the room was still gruesomely clear to him.

He sat down in the desk chair and tried hard to see through Woody's eyes. He wanted to connect back in time to the day of the attack and see if he could hitch a ride onto his dear friend's memories for just a scent of events. *The killer may be able to block me from seeing him, but Woody won't!* he thought, smiling to himself and wondering why he hadn't thought about this before now. He grew excited with the new concept of using Woody's impressions as a conduit to events--making himself a cutout in it all. If he could hack into Woody's memory, the killer might not even detect him!

He closed his eyes and held his head in his hands, with his elbows resting on the light brown desk blotter. First, there were quick feelings of being startled. Then anger. And then, a sense of violation. They all filled his mind like a syrupy mix, oozing in and around his brain cells until the transformation to Woody's thoughts became complete. He looked down at his hands on top of the desk, and saw his skin color had changed. The fair skinned, Irish-American Patrick O'Donnell was mentally inside the memory of the African-American Dr. Davis, and his hands were now old, brown, and wrinkled. He looked up and saw the killer standing there, his semi-automatic Sig Sauer with silencer in his hand, demanding to know how Woody knew about him. It was now abundantly clear to Pat that the killer thought Dr. Davis was the psychic, and that Woody never gave him up, though he really never needed proof. He never doubted that for even a moment.

He saw his right hand reach for the telephone, and he felt the searing pain in his left shoulder when he grabbed the receiver off the hook and hit the number nine button. He had never been shot in real life, but for the first time, through Dr. Davis, he experienced the sharp, burning pain and felt his left arm go numb. He witnessed his right hand try once again to hit a number button, only to be greeted by the soft blow-dart sound of yet another round from the killer's gun. It tore through his right arm with incredible force and unbearable pain. He saw his hands shake, blood all over them and his shirt, as he made one last attempt to complete the 911 call. He stared right in the killer's cold green eyes and saw the sneer on his sick face as the final round was delivered…a perfect trajectory with barely any attempt at aiming. The killer sent the bullet silently through the barrel to Woody's head.

Something took paralyzing control of Pat at this moment in the memory. He could almost see the bullet roaring toward his head in slow motion, helplessly watching it inch closer and closer. But suddenly, he felt the strange force of another body slam into him from the left side, almost knocking him from the chair. It was as if he had been standing on a busy street, and an invisible Good Samaritan rushed to tackle him away from the path of a speeding bus. The force dislodged him from Dr. Davis's memory, but not from the scene. He now found himself standing in the doorway looking at Woody, but back inside his own mind once again. He knew deep down that if he waited a moment longer—and if the mysterious interloper had not shoved him out of the way--the bullet that entered Dr. Davis's skull would have ended the memory and prevented him from seeing what happened next. Worst case, it would have killed him. He also found it odd that the killer did not seem to be aware of his presence in the room once outside of Woody's memory. It proved to be a freebie at the moment, an opportunity perhaps because he had been a stowaway in Woody's mind and the killer simply didn't realize he was there.

Pat stood behind the killer now and watched as the man casually walked about the room and picked up his spent cartridges, placing them in his pants pocket. The man walked over to Woody's desk and read the clinical notes on the computer screen. The realization he had that he shot the wrong man was apparent to him in the vision, and what infuriated Pat the most was his cavalier attitude about the mistake. One thing was for sure…the madman thought he had killed Woody, assuming the bullet to his head had done the trick. That mistake saved Woody's life. If the killer had any inkling that Woody was still alive, he would have finished the job. Pat was certain of this.

The printer behind the desk hummed and churned out the five page report. He watched the man roll it up and turn toward the door, seemingly making eye contact with him. Pat realized instantly that the killer knew he was present, but the degree to which he could see Pat's face was unclear. He jumped from the psychic state as if he were throwing himself from the side of a fast moving train, making a getaway before he could be confronted. The last sensation he received was a trace of a thought coming from the sociopath. Something about Fox News.

"Christ! That was powerful!" he moaned looking down at his pale pink hands.

Colonel Helmsley and Jake had been standing in the doorway without saying a word the entire fifteen minutes or so that he was in his obvious state of psychic exploration.

"I can tell you he knows Woody's not the psychic, and he may have plans to send his report to the news media."

"Nice work, Pat," Jake offered. "Any idea where he is now?"

Pat shook his head. His thoughts were interrupted by the sudden ringing of his cell phone. He pulled it out but didn't recognize the caller's number. "Hello? Yes, this is Pat O'Donnell. Okay, sure." He looked at the others as he covered the mouthpiece with his hand. "It's Sean's school. He needs to talk with me. Mind if I have some privacy?" The colonel and Jake nodded in understanding and left him alone, closing the door on the way out.

"Hiya, Dad!" came the enthusiastic voice of his eleven-year-old boy.

"Sean, everything okay? What's going on?" Pat had never received a call from his son at school before, and immediately sensed he had an important update on the search for the killer.

"I'm fine, Daddy. I know you were just thinking about that bad guy, and I want you to know I kinda had a daydream here at school. I pushed you out of the way when he tried to shoot you through that other man's mind."

Pat felt the blood leave his entire body. His legs felt so wobbly he thought he might collapse as the impact of his son's psychic intervention hit home. He paused for a moment to recompose himself. "Thank you, Buddy. Thank you so much," he whispered into the receiver.

"It's okay. Sometimes kids gotta help out their parents!" he giggled, obviously feeling exceptionally proud of his actions. "But there's more, Dad."

While Pat was ever mindful of the lack of communications

security over the line they were using to talk, he also knew Sean's visions were the only real clear link to the psycho who actively blocked him. It seemed, at least for the time being, the killer was not aware of his son's parallel efforts to see him.

"Go on."

"Well, he's kinda far away right now. I'm not sure where, but there's lots of horses nearby. And he is still planning to find you. He's real mad that you keep trying to find him."

"Did you stay real quiet and not let him know you were there?"

"Yes, Daddy. I didn't make a sound, and he didn't see me."

"Okay. Keep working on this when you can, but don't try too hard. We can't afford to let him know you exist. Be good, love you, Buddy!"

Pat left Woody's office and found the other two waiting for him in his office.

"Everything okay at home, Pat?" the colonel asked.

"Uh, um yeah, yes, Sir. Everything's okay. Sean just needed permission to attend a school outing next week. He forgot to turn in the slip that was due today." Pat handled his hastily-made white lie like a wide receiver with greasy hands. He fumbled about it unconvincingly, one of those character traits he had--a total, utter, complete inability to tell effective lies.

"Okay, well let us know if you need anything," the colonel said with a cautious eye, signaling he hadn't bought the lie. "Listen, the interagency group wants to meet next week. They just called and said they have some solid HUMINT on both bin Laden and Saddam Hussein's whereabouts. They want to see if you can fill in the gaps. Oh, and they also have some ideas to support the deception plan which the AG agreed to consider. I spoke with him while you and Sean were on the phone."

He glanced at Dr. Jacobsen who appeared clueless.

"HUMINT is Human Intelligence, Jake. Agents and informants in the field kinda stuff. Our community has a lot of acronyms you'll need to learn," he said with a wink.

"We'll meet at the FBI conference room again at eight in the morning next Monday. It promises to be a full day for us there."

"Okay, Boss, will do. After lunch, I'd like to hit the stack of Ambers again. I think I made some pretty good progress on the killer today, and I plan to give it a lot of thought this weekend. But for now, I feel compelled to keep finding these lost souls."

Back in the Silver Hills subdivision of south Indiana, the killer sat in the old couple's living room, munching on a cold ham and cheese sandwich on toasted wheat bread, garnished with Dijon mustard and a pickle slice. Upstairs in the master bedroom, Janet Swank was sleeping, tied to the bed in the same clothes she wore since her abduction three days earlier. Her son, Robert D. Swank III, was shackled similarly in a guest bedroom at the opposite end of the upper level of the farm home. They were both so hopelessly disoriented in the dark and soundproof confines of their makeshift dungeons, that the thought of even trying to escape had long ago vanished from their minds.

Janet's employer, the Kentucky Gentleman's Club, had not bothered to try and track her down. Like so many women they had seen come and go over the years, they assumed she up and left with no warning, drifting to a new town and a new job. Little Bobby's school tried calling Janet the past three days to see where the boy was since he had not been to classes. Voice messages on the home answering machine went unreturned. As did voice mail on her cell phone. Finally, in one last attempt to determine what was going on, the school called his father in Virginia, knowing he had visitation rights and would likely know where he was.

Of course, Robert D. Swank II had no idea there was even a problem. Upon receiving the disturbing call from school, he placed several frantic calls to Janet's phones, even one to the club where she worked. He realized he had few options at this point other than to make the drive once again to Louisville. His greatest fear, and the scenario he fully expected to find played out, was that Janet ran off with their son to avoid the custody battle which she was likely to lose given her lifestyle and less-than-adequate parenting skills. He had been duped masterfully into taking the action, the fruitless journey. He was merely a single domino in a series of events the insane killer maestro had quickly orchestrated to snare his ultimate prize.

~ 20 ~

He always found the hugs and kisses he received from his children and wife some of the richest blessings God had given him. He felt that even if he were to lose his psychic gift, or stop experiencing synesthesia, he would never look back so long as he had his family forever. This Friday evening, upon returning home, Sara greeted him at the door wearing a short tan skirt and light green blouse with bundles of red hair bouncing off her shoulders. She had reapplied her makeup just before he arrived and had put on a white pearl necklace with matching pearl earrings. A few puffs of her favorite perfume scented her neck. She was absolutely radiant. When Pat saw her, his heart flooded with the same feelings he had when they first met in college in Pennsylvania some fifteen years earlier. She gave him a very sexy smile and pulled him in for a tight hug. He dropped his briefcase in the foyer, already beginning to breathe fast before their lips even met. At this moment he had an intense urge to tear off every stitch of her clothing and make love to her standing up right there with the door open.

"Easy there, my leprechaun. There will be time enough for this after dinner," she teased pulling him off her. "My, it has been a long time!"

"Damn, Sorcha! You know I want to take you right here," he said almost breathlessly.

"Come on, stud, I have a nice dinner planned. You look like you could use a treat...or two," she said with a sparkling wink as she led him by the hand into the kitchen.

His children were waiting there as if on cue for a surprise party. "Daddy! Daddy!" they screamed, rushing him, thrusting their arms around his neck as he knelt to greet, hug, and kiss them at least ten times each.

He realized now how consumed he had become in his work that he was not spending as much time with his family as he had in the past. The CCVC work was intense, and he typically didn't get home until late in the evening. He would later learn that Sara had called Colonel Helmsley, insisting that Pat get kicked out of the office early that day so she could surprise him with a special meal.

"Hmmm. What smells so good?" he asked trying to decipher the myriad of scent hints reaching his brain. His synesthesia was in turbo mode, and it worked feverishly to interpret the multiple, overlapping senses the smells created for him. He had the sensation of warm mud in his hands that made popping and gurgling sounds. He looked into the pot on top of the stove.

"Dublin Coddle!" he exclaimed, seeing the simmering concoction of potatoes, sausages, and bacon, bubbling inside.

"And barmbrack bread in the oven, along with some boiled cabbage. And for dessert, it's gooseberry crumble!" Sara added, putting an arm around his waist. She leaned in for a whisper. "Well, that will be your first dessert, handsome."

His heart thumped again as he took in a deep breath, wanting nothing more than to gobble the food down and run to the bedroom for that second sweet treat Sara just promised.

"Here you go, Daddy," Sean said handing him a warm bottle of Guinness stout.

"You guys are amazing! I love you all so much!"

They sat down to eat dinner with Erin leading them in grace. Pat didn't want to burden them with the news of Woody's heart attack that he learned about just before coming home. While Erin prayed, he said his own, special prayer for his friend, asking God to protect him and ensure his heart didn't give out again. The doctors thought his prognosis was worsening, and that another episode of cardiac arrest would probably kill him. For now, he wanted to put this trouble out of his mind and reconnect with his family.

The meal was splendid, and in combination with a couple pints of ale, the hormonally-charged Irishman could take neither his mind nor his eyes off his bride.

"Sean, can you and Erin clean up the table? Mom and I have some important family business to talk about, so we need some privacy," he asked as plainly as he could.

At eleven years of age, Sean was certainly old enough to know what kind of business they might have in mind, and combined with his psychic powers, Pat could only hope he didn't decipher it.

"Oh sure, Daddy," Sean replied innocently.

Once inside the bedroom, door closed and locked, Pat practically devoured Sara. He began kissing her neck wildly, taking occasional nibbles as she struggled to unbutton her blouse. He didn't want to wait much longer and reached up and nearly tore it off. She fell backwards onto the bed, landing softly on the downy bedcover with Pat on top. Although he straddled her gently, there was no mistaking his determination. He was not about to let her slip out from under him.

He hastily unhooked her front fastening bra, clumsily almost, like a teenager exploring the backseat of the family car with his first girlfriend. Her firm and conical breasts were slightly moist from perspiration, and they heaved up and down rapidly as her own arousal swelled. He yanked her skirt off roughly, followed by pantyhose, then thong. On his knees now, he stood up partially and looked down at her naked body. He smiled while pulling his tie and shirt off. Sara pulled him down and ran her hands across his smooth, muscular chest, kissing his mouth hotly before clutching his back with two strong, long-nailed hands. It was abundantly clear to Pat that his wife had no intention of letting him slip away, either.

He broke her hold for a moment to quickly undo his belt buckle and zipper, which when undone, opened rapidly under the weight of his 9 mm Beretta. He slipped off the bed for a second, looking back at Sara with a sexy smile, sliding his pants and his ankle-holstered backup gun under the bed. He did not want her to see that he had been wearing it. Back on top of her, the only items Sara still had on were her pearl necklace and earrings. And a heated smile.

Pat made love to her like it was their first time and their last time. He was in total control, executing with precision a sequence of kisses, nibbles, licks, caresses, and thrusts designed to drive Sara wild. It worked. He drove her to the edge once, twice, three times before allowing her the release she craved.

When he was unable to hold back any longer, there was a

flash in his mind, like a bright arc of white-blue light as he achieved a veritable violent release. The timing could not have been more perfect as she let go along with him, dragging her nails down deeply in his back, clawing him like a wild animal, and gently sinking her teeth into his neck. Pat didn't even realize it at the moment, but she had torn his flesh, and the two of them had slid so far to the right as one, they were nearly off the bed.

In gentle waves their mutual oxytocin rush subsided, but it didn't completely go away. They both breathed heavily…deep, heaving, gasping, oxygen-searching breaths, as if they had finished a marathon race together. He lay on top of her, kissing her sweat-soaked face softly, slowly becoming aware of the searing pain on his back from her nails, and the bite she placed on his neck. Their pretzel mass of arms and legs began to unravel. Pat rolled off to his right, while Sara readjusted herself back to near center on the bed.

"Oh, my God! Oh, my God," she panted.

He turned to kiss her lips again. "Ay lassie, ders nuttin better than wild Irish lovemaking!" he teased in a brogue, brushing her damp hair from her face. "But I thinks da misses got a wee bit rough!" he cried turning his back toward her.

She gasped seeing the long nail marks down both sides of his back. "Oh, Baby, I'm so sorry. I didn't even realize I had…" she started to say, but stopped halfway as she traced a hand over his wounds. They weren't as bad as they seemed initially, with a just small amount of oozing blood to accompany the red scratches.

"And what's this?" he asked pointing to his neck that was made sore from her love bite. In the dim glow of the night light he watched her stare with big guilty eyes at the outline of a bite mark that promised him a hickey in the morning. "I haven't had one of these since I was fifteen!"

"Let's shower together, Sweetie," she purred in his ear. She giggled, took him by the hand, and dragged him to the bathroom.

For the past two weeks, Pat had put in place a kind of subconscious barrier of his own, blocking with his paranormal powers the ability of the killer to penetrate his mind or his environment. But during their lovemaking, he let his guard down. Perhaps it was the intensity with which he and Sara made love, or perhaps that bright flash of light that accompanied his orgasm somehow created a chasm. Whatever the cause, the effect was to allow a momentary lapse in his psychic security.

The killer sat back in a large leather recliner in the old man and woman's farm house in Silver Hills, sipping an ice cold beer while watching television. When the fragments of an unsolicited vision seeped into his mind, he hit the mute button on the television remote control. He received a flooding erotic sensation, hints of extreme passion and lovemaking in which he found some deviant delight. The psychic voyeur strained to see and hear the experience more clearly, but was unable to gain much more than an occasional moan or groan of pleasure.

The killer enjoyed his fuzzy show and the subtle sensations he was receiving. But what really got him off was when that chink in the armor appeared. That bright flash of light in Pat's mind had created a microscopic schism, a mental keyhole that enabled the sicko to peer in and spy upon him and Sara. The killer leapt upon it. In a split second he received two important impressions: *Pat* and *Sara.* It wasn't much, but it was a start. He filed the tidbit of data away in his brain as the gap in Pat's defenses subconsciously and automatically sealed itself up again, preventing a further look. As fast as it opened, the gap was quickly closed tight.

He was just about to turn the volume back up on the television, when he caught a glimpse of something else by way of his psychic peripheral vision. Huddled outside *Pat* and *Sara's* bedroom door was a little boy, about eleven or twelve years old. He was secretly listening in on his mom and dad, his inquisitiveness about such adult matters drawing him there quietly, trying to learn whatever secrets he could about the mystery of sex.

Although Sean was eavesdropping on his parents, he was also aware of the killer's attempts at much the same. His curiosity came with a price. He let his guard down like his dad. And when he did, the killer saw him. Sean looked upward suddenly, right into the eyes of the maniac. A gush of fear overcame him as he closed his eyes tightly, hoping to disconnect the link between him and the killer at that moment. It worked. He forced the sicko offline, but not before revealing himself. The killer smiled, opening his eyes in the recliner, riveted back now from his vision.

"You little punk! You and your dad share the gift. Oh it's going to be such fun killing you both," he cackled, casually swigging down the rest of his beer.

~ 21 ~

Monday morning came before he knew it. He had spent almost every waking weekend moment immersed in his family life, trying not to let his work intrude into his home. There was only one time during the weekend when he sat in his den checking emails that he thought about the scheduled interagency meeting. He tried to locate both Usama bin Laden and Saddam Hussein, but he found them to be elusive. But then again, his was merely a half-hearted attempt. Pat was still so focused on finding children--and the serial killer hunting him--that he paid little attention to the two men most wanted by the United States in its Global War on Terror and Operation Iraqi Freedom. He stared in the mirror after tying his tie. The bruise on his neck was small but visible, and unfortunately for him, it was high up near his jawbone, making it impractical to wear a turtleneck to cover it. Even if he had one.

There was also one other important matter that was not on Pat's mind this weekend. It was the place where his job and his family intersected, a crossroads of grave danger he hoped he would never have to traverse. He was unaware that Sean inadvertently exposed himself to the killer. And Sean never told Pat about the encounter because he worried that doing so would reveal him as a snoop, trying to listen in on his parent's romp, although in reality he heard little more than muffled moans. Unlike his father who had zero capability to tell a lie, Sean had a great poker face. He never let on to his parents that something worried him, and they never sensed it either.

Pat strolled into the FBI conference room a few minutes before the interagency meeting began. Although he was the star of the show, and at past meetings had been treated as a celebrity, this time the mood was somber, no doubt because of Woody's assault and comatose state. Colonel Helmsley waited for a few more key members to arrive before he began the session.

"Morning, Pat. Say, what happened to you? Vacuum cleaner hose attack you?" he teased seeing the hickey adorning his neck.

"Funny, Boss, say where's General Swank? Normally he's here on time."

"Dunno, haven't seen him, but if he's not here soon, we'll have to--" he began to say, but stopped when Swank abruptly strolled in, his shoulders uncharacteristically hunched down slightly.

Pat watched as Swank kept an eye on him, but it was an awkward stare this time, one that suggested he wanted to talk with him. It wasn't the intimidating, fire-breathing dragon of a glare to which he had been accustomed. The general looked terrible. His drawn face looked hastily shaven, and his uniform wasn't as crisp as normal.

"Ladies and gentlemen, it looks like we're all here," the colonel began as he shut the door firmly. "I'd like to begin with a moment of silence for our dear friend Dr. Davis who is still in a coma. He desperately needs our prayers."

When Colonel Helmsley bowed his head, Pat made the sign of the cross and hung his head as well. Everyone in the room did much the same except for Dr. Jacobsen, but Pat was starting to get used to his quirkiness. When the moment ended, the colonel outlined the agenda for the meeting. The first order of business was the need to develop a denial, deception, and disinformation campaign to cover CRYSTAL ROUNDUP and provide a rationale to the media to explain the sudden surge in successful rescues. He introduced the man who replaced him in his former active duty assignment as Director of Security and Investigative Program Oversight, within the Office of the Secretary of the Air Force, the "AAZ" as it was known.

Colonel Chris Jordan was a lanky southerner with a deep drawl. He spoke slowly and with determination, as if to ensure each word came out perfectly despite his thick accent. Standing in a red Polo shirt and tan cargo pants, he sported a farmer's tan that Pat imagined was permanently one of his features, probably something he grew up earning as a young man working on the family farm. Despite his simplistic charm, the blue-eyed gray haired gentleman commanded a mission so secret, few inside the government were privy to it. He oversaw a multi-billion dollar budget that was in the black, the details of which not even the Congress--the branch of government Constitutionally-chartered to appropriate the budget--was allowed to know about.

"Ladies and gentlemen, as ya'll know we need to devise a strategy to head off the current media interest in CR. It has become even more urgent now with the likelihood that the serial killer has a copy of some of our documents."

The subject itself was so serious the entire group was silent as everyone kept their attention focused on Jordan. Everyone that is, except for General Swank. Pat was nervously conscious of the general's attention on him, making him fidget in his seat. He did his best to listen to Jordan, but his preoccupation with Swank caused him to look in his direction every few moments or so. The general never took his eyes off him.

"We have a proposal to consider. We would like to generate a false technology assessment that describes a satellite capability to image the entire country every few seconds. Every square inch of each of these fifty Yoo-nited States, kinda like a huge security surveillance camera system for the naayshun," Jordan said matter-of-factly.

Pat could not believe what he was hearing, thinking the technology was so farfetched that it would be perceived by the media as the hoax it really was. "Wait a minute. You mean you plan to leak a document that suggests we have been imaging every square inch of the USA, so we simply go back and look at the recordings of the last known time and place a kid was spotted to see what happened to him?"

"Precisely. Remember PROJECT ECHELON, the National Security Agency's global communications eavesdropping system that caused a stir in the media a few years back? Lawdy, that ruma had the press seeing June bugs faw months!" Colonel Jordan laughed.

Pat nodded his head, recalling the alleged system for intercepting virtually all telephone calls, emails, and instant messages sent around the globe. Supposedly the United States, Great Britain, Canada, New Zealand, and Australia were cooperating to collect and analyze billions of communications around the globe daily in an effort to locate terrorists and head off future attacks.

"The press didn't wanna believe us when we towd 'em it didn't exeest! We plan to add some elements to the reeport to tie it to ECHELON and seal the deal on both," Colonel Jordan said with a tone of total conviction.

He still wasn't convinced. "So we say we have this satellite capability and all, but what happens if someone in either NSA or NRO leaks the truth that we don't?"

The National Reconnaissance Office focal point officer had been silent the entire time, but he jumped in at this moment. The old, slightly hunched over civilian, with streaks of gray and jet black hair, unfolded his hands and gave Pat a long, thoughtful look.

"Patrick, we really do have this capability. But we don't use it this way yet because computer data storage has not advanced at the same rate as our ability to eavesdrop. Once we solve the ability to assemble and store trillions of terabytes of data per second, we will implement the program. The President has approved."

"Jesus! You mean to say--" Pat began but Colonel Helmsley stopped him.

"Pat, we think this is a good thing to get out there for a couple of reasons. First it provides the cover we want. Of course we'll deny it's real, making it even more believable to a conspiracy-minded press. It also serves as a deterrent for all kinds of crime. Imagine for a moment how people will behave if everything they do outside of a building is photographed, archived, and made retrievable for later investigation!"

He didn't like what he was hearing. It all sounded too Orwellian for his liking. He was about to protest when the FBI liaison spoke.

"The Bureau has been helping in this regard. We're developing a data mining system called CARNIVORE in which we plan to dump all manner of communication intercept information we need for law enforcement purposes. That's the vanilla reason. On the black side, we're beta-testing some computer and software capabilities the National Security Agency created. If CARNIVORE works well on a small scale, it will join ECHELON as a place to store what ECHELON produces."

It almost seemed to Pat that everyone in the room knew about this idea before the meeting, except for him and Dr. Jacobsen who sat silently with a look of confusion and disgust. There was no doubt in Pat's mind that the Berkeley-boy hated the sinister sound of things.

"So how do we go about leaking a document to the media?" Pat asked, looking at Colonel Helmsley.

"We have a CIA agent working for the Washington Observer as a journalist. He will *receive* the leaked document and take it to his editors. Of course, the paper will require him to fact check the story before they run with it. He will do behind the scenes interviews with some of the people in this room who will confirm off the record such a program exists."

Finally, Jake had had enough. "You people make me so sick!" he shouted before storming out of the conference room in a huff.

While his departure drew some chuckles from the rest who remained, his clear displeasure caused Pat to revisit his concerns about Jake's loyalty to the program. *I sure hope he doesn't do anything foolish like tip off the media to the deception.*

The group spent the next hour talking about the nuts and bolts of the deception effort before taking a break. When Pat headed out of the room and made a beeline for the bathroom, General Swank grabbed his arm in the hallway.

"Pat, we need to talk, can we get together for lunch?"

The general's question rattled him. For starters, he never called him Pat before. It was always "Major O'Donnell!" with a definite stern, almost angry delivery. And, the general never suggested they go to lunch together. But Pat did not need to be a psychic to know something was bothering the man right now, and he obviously needed to talk to him.

"Um, okay, sure, Sir. I think we're probably going to finish early anyway since I don't have a lot to offer on the hunt for UBL and all." He did his best to drill into the general's mind to see what was troubling him, but nothing was to be found.

"Great! There's a nice deli a block from here."

Once the break was over, the group reassembled in the conference room for discussion of the second major topic of the day...the two simultaneous wars being waged at that moment, and the hunt for the most-wanted men in the world: Usama bin Laden and Saddam Hussein.

"Folks, I really tried to pick up some clues this weekend, but not much is coming through. As you all know, we had a pretty good lock on UBL a while back, but the best I'm able to discern is that he is constantly on the move. Ever since we almost obliterated him in the cave in 2001, he has not stayed in the same spot more than one or two days at a time." He looked around the room and saw the disappointment.

"What about Saddam Hussein?" the State Department focal point officer asked. "He's become a political pain in the ass for the President."

Pat closed his eyes for a moment when the question was asked. He had a sudden, almost spasmodic sensation that an impression was about to come through. "Where is Saddam from originally?" he asked.

The State Department official told him he was born in Al-Awja, near the culturally-important city of Tikrit. "Why do you ask?"

Pat closed his eyes again. "He's near Tikrit. He's being sheltered by friends and relatives in the area. It won't be long. Tell the HUMINT teams to source taxi drivers and family members, because they will know. We're gonna find him in December of this year." Then a smile traced across his face. "He's going to be in a hole in the ground. I don't know why or how I know it, I just do."

The room was stunned. Everyone sat with jaws open, seeing for the first time, most of them at least, the CRYSTAL ROUNDUP Operations Officer, the OPSO, in action. Everyone was attentive to what Pat had to say except for General Swank who sat with a worried look on his face, constantly checking his watch. Pat gave him a nervous look. Whatever was on the general's mind was huge. It was obviously even bigger than Global War on Terror or Operation Iraqi Freedom at the moment. Pat was beginning to become alarmed. He almost did not want to find out what it could be.

~ 22 ~

The general did not say much as they walked together to the deli on 10th Street in Northwest Washington, DC. Ever conscious of protocol, Pat walked to the left, allowing the general the position of honor on the right. He was beginning to sense this was a broken man, completely disconsolate over something huge. Mindful that it may be a matter of national security, he also certainly was not going to ask in the open. They walked along silently, almost as if strangers, though it was apparent they were together. The general seemed to just stare at the pavement below, only occasionally looking ahead to avoid bumping into passersby. Ordinarily, a two star general in his service dress uniform would garner a glance or two by the hundreds of office workers, lobbyists, political staffers, and even tourists who riddled the downtown streets during lunch hour. But today, the aura he exuded was subdued and sad, so much so, that he seemed to blend in to his surroundings like the street tramp from Montgomery.

The restaurant was a quintessential New York style delicatessen, decorated with hundreds of pictures and other memorabilia from the Big Apple. Pennants from the Yankees and Mets, autographed portraits of Mayor Koch and Governor Pataki, subway posters, ball caps, Coney Island maps…everything seemed to be thrown on walls and nailed or glued down chaotically. But that randomness added to the atmosphere the deli tried to create. The employees were hurried, harried, and abrupt, with no sense of decorum, not even for their patrons.

"Hey, what can I get for yous?" the Italian-looking, mustached-man behind the counter shouted when they walked in, his Bronx accent thick, almost a touch overdone. He wore a green bib apron over a white undershirt that had badly stained sleeves. "Hey, a man in blue! Danks for your service, Sarge!" he said to the general.

"I'm not a sergeant, I'm a major general," Swank replied, gritting his teeth, trying to maintain his cool.

"Yeah, yeah. Whatever, Chief. Waddya wanna eat, huh?"

"I'll have a hot pastrami on rye. Pat, it's my treat, what about you?"

He saw the abuse the general just went through and was not about to stir up anything more. "I'll have the same."

They sat in a booth as far back in the tiny shop as they could go, nowhere near the plate glass windows that were street side, and far enough away to have some privacy. It was dark back there, with just a small amount of light coming from a couple of bare bulb lights hanging from the greasy ceiling by long black cords. The general sat across from him and stared down at the table for a few minutes in total silence. Pat studied him the entire time, getting more worried about what he was about to bring up. The general wiped some crumbs from the table with his bare hand as he suddenly began to speak, ever so slowly.

"My grandson has been abducted. I need your help."

"What? Sir, are you serious? When did it happen? Any idea who has him?"

"My ex-daughter-in-law. She's been fighting for sole custody with my son for nearly a year. She took off with him last week, left a note at her house in Kentucky."

Pat instantly understood now why the general seemed so melancholy all morning. But he wasn't prepared for what came next.

"I want you to help us find Bobby. Hell, I never imagined I'd ever say this, but I have come to be a believer in you, Pat. I know I was your biggest skeptic and critic before, but ..." he said, his voice trailing off. He stared at him as if searching for an indication Pat would assist.

"Sir, I can't really help. I mean, I'd love to and all, but the CRYSTAL ROUNDUP program has rules I must follow, like--"

"I know all that, Pat...no family abductions, Oversight Committee approval and all, but I'm not asking for you to work this officially. This has to be under the table."

For as many years as Pat loathed the general, at this moment he felt genuinely sorry for him. Here was a man--a two star general in the Air Force--practically begging Pat to help him on a very personal matter. He looked around the restaurant, mindful of the need to be discreet in their conversation.

The general pulled a white paper napkin from its chrome cube holder on the table and blew his nose. Pat could tell he was sobbing slightly, trying his best to maintain some respectability, but in this situation he was no longer a major general. He was a grandfather who loved his grandson dearly, and desperately needed Pat's help.

"Look, Sir, I'll see what I can do, but you can't tell anyone at all that I'm helping you on this. I think Colonel Helmsley would neuter me if he knew. And if I come up with any information to help, you need to alert the proper law enforcement folks. I can't go operational to aid in rescuing him, deal?"

The general nodded in acceptance and reached across to grip Pat's arm. He gave him a tight squeeze and whispered, "Thank you!"

This new, human side of the general was something to which Pat had a hard time adjusting. Part of him wanted to believe this was a real change--perhaps a permanent one. But at a deeper, more visceral level, Pat was afraid the man eventually would revert back to being the anger-seething bully he always knew.

A petite young woman came out of the kitchen at that moment. She was olive-skinned, like the man behind the counter, and was a spitting image of him, minus the moustache, but no doubt his daughter. "Here yous goes boys, lemme know if I can getcha anyding else."

While they both admired her inner-city charm, there was something eternally grating about her and her father behind the counter. Pat and the general smiled at each other, secretly sharing the bond.

The plates were piled high with a generous portion of potato chips surrounding giant pastrami sandwiches sliced in half, with about a full pound of meat per plate, practically spilling out from all sides. It was hot and steaming, and it smelled wonderful. While Pat added a touch of Dijon mustard to the undersides of the rye bread, General Swank filled him in on every detail about his grandson and his parents, hoping to provide Pat the clues he needed to psychically link up with the mom and son who were on the lam with the mom's boyfriend.

He listened intently, making a few notes on a piece of paper napkin, occasionally wiping crumbs from his mouth as he and the general talked for another hour while devouring their lunches. Pat began to see General Swank in an entirely different light during their meal. He *was* human after all. He was not the monster Pat had come to know and fear.

The general reached for his wallet, pulled out two pictures, and gave them to him. One was of little Bobby from just a few months back, and the other was a wedding photograph of his son and Janet.

"She's beautiful."

"She was a beautiful woman the day that picture was taken, but we never had a clue she would turn into a pole-dancer. A girl from the wrong side of the tracks," as my wife would say.

"General, I'll do my very best, but I can't promise anything. My energy lately has been so directed at CR ops involving stranger abductions, that I'm not sure I'll be able to get any signals on this one."

"I understand, Pat. Is there anything coming to you about this, like right now?" he asked somewhat gingerly. "God, it would be wonderful if you could just point me to where they are staying."

Pat hated the idea of trying to work his magic in a public place. Although he was confident he could control things, he had had plenty of strange psychic states where things did not go so well. Like the near-death hypnotic vision. Or the dream fight with the killer. But he knew he needed to at least send the general a warm signal that he was sincere.

"Let me try something."

He closed his eyes, keeping his right eye open slightly to watch for people who might walk to the back of the restaurant where they sat. But he really did not try too hard, the awkwardness of the situation made it difficult for him to concentrate. Nothing at all came to him. After about five minutes of this psychic-lite effort, he opened his eyes wide and gave the general a disappointed look. "I'm sorry. I'm just not able to get anything right now."

"I will be praying for you and Bobby as you work on this," he said once more giving Pat's forearm a tight pump.

While the two men finished off their gluttonous platters of artery-choking pastrami, the killer sat in the Silver Hills home he had commandeered, smiling with eyes closed in the old man's well-worn brown leather recliner. He had a mental connection with General Swank ever since he witnessed him speak at the first interagency meeting. He knew the general was his conduit to the psychic cop who was pursuing him...and at this precise moment he received flashes of thought, weakly transmitted at best, but slight impressions nonetheless. The psycho knew his plan was working. The general's son found the note, alerted him, and now the search was on for Bobby and mom. And as he predicted--actually as he had planned for--the general went to the one person he knew could help, the man at the center of this secret program…the killer's real prize.

But Pat's subconscious barrier was up and running at full

strength. Although the killer picked up fragments of the scene, he was unable to see what the general saw, and unable to hear what the general heard, but he was able to understand bits of what he thought. The name *Pat* kept ringing in his head. *Pat!* he thought. *Pat* with a small son of his own whom he had seen crouched down outside mommy and daddy's bedroom door trying to spy on their sex. He mentally tucked the note away for future reference. It brought the men one step closer to each other.

The sweet sounds of a Brandenburg concerto by Johann Sebastian Bach poured from the couple's stereo in the living room all throughout his reverie. He had been tracing his hands back and forth conducting the air to the orchestra in his mind. When the piece ended, his link was severed, and his eyes opened widely. A sick smile appeared on his face.

"I'll make that call soon, very soon," he snickered to himself as the next Bach number began playing.

~ 23 ~

Pat found himself leaning over an old wooden fence that was slightly higher than his waist, his elbows planted firmly in place. It was made of bare wood stock, long since turned gray, a split rail design with a rough, jagged, and splintery surface. He was entranced by the thoroughbred horses that ran swiftly, proudly, and freely in the pasture as he watched. There were about a dozen of them, mostly solid dark brown, and two or three with some white streaks on the sides that looked like lightning bolts. They were enormous creatures that at once were both big and powerful, while soft and graceful all the same. The pasture of tall grass was wide open and seemed to go on for miles in all directions. While he had no idea where he was, at his special level of dream awareness he knew he was probably down in Kentucky where General Swank told him earlier that day his grandson lived. The grasses were deep green, no doubt some blend of the famous bluegrass from this region. The hay-like scent of wild grass reached his brain, along with the freshness of a southern spring that told him this event was near real-time.

He was so interested in watching the horses that he almost

forgot why his multifaceted brain likely brought him to this place. He looked about him for something to stand out, as was often his experience, but for the time being there was nothing to his vision except the horses, the pasture, and the fence. He concentrated as hard as he could on the dream, but what he needed to search for was something that had been in front of him for a week or so. There was something Sean told him after they both had separate nightmares about the serial killer that was literally the tree he missed in spite of the forest. It was right in front of his nose…and then it hit him. Hard.

Well, he's kinda far away right now. I'm not sure where, but there's lots of horses nearby. And he is still planning to find you. He's real mad that you keep trying to find him.

Suddenly, Sean's innocent and vague clue about horses took on the mantle of an evil premonition. Those haunting words seeped into his sleeping mind and tore him from his dream with a strong jolt. He may as well have fallen off a cliff in his dream because the sensation was just as strong and designed by his subconscious mind to wake him up. Instantly.

But even if his brain had not so willingly connected the dots to shake him from his spell, an external force at that precise moment was equally determined to do the trick. A loud banging on his front door, accompanied by the frantic, constant ringing of his doorbell drew both Pat and Sara from bed. It was just before midnight. Sara hastily pulled a bathrobe around her as she walked behind him to the stairway. Pat had his Beretta in hand, having kept it at the ready inside his nightstand.

"Who can that be, Pat?" she asked, clearly shaken up by the intrusion.

"I'm not sure, but grab a cell phone and get ready to call

nine-one-one if I give you the signal."

Pat went down the stairs slowly, aiming his gun at the front door. It was dark outside, and he couldn't see who was standing there through the long vertical sidelight windows on either side of the door framing. He flipped the outside light on, and was shocked when he saw the familiar face of General Swank, wet from a gentle nighttime shower. He looked back at Sara. "It's okay, Sorcha. It's work stuff. You can go back to bed."

Although it was clear from the expression on her face that she didn't want to go just yet, that she wanted to make sure Pat wasn't speaking out of duress, she reluctantly trotted off, back upstairs to bed. He opened the door and ushered the general inside. He was soaked from head to toe in pajamas and bedroom slippers. His feet made sloshing sounds as he stepped onto the hardwood floor of the foyer.

"Sir, what's going on?"

The general was shaking, ringing his wet hands in despair. "Bad news. I got a call from some guy who says he has Bobby and his mom."

Pat's worst fears were starting to come true. The combination of Sean's warning about the killer and horses, his new dream about horses, and now General Swank's call were adding up to a more sinister outcome than he could have anticipated.

"Come on in and let's talk in my den."

Pat led the way to his home office on the main floor, opening the glass-paneled French doors and flipping on a dim light on the cherry wood desk. The general sat in a side chair next to the desk while Pat landed in his high back black leather chair, setting his gun down next to his computer keyboard.

"Tell me about the call, Sir."

"This guy calls my house about an hour ago, says he has them hostage. He let me speak with Bobby for like a second, so I know it's real. He says he'll kill Bobby if I don't tell him who you are! Pat, this guy says he knows about CRYSTAL ROUNDUP! He called you the OPSO!"

What he needed to tell the general would not be easy. He stared at him for a few moments, trying to come up with the right words. Deep inside he knew he had to make the right decision and alert his team. He was way over his head again. He got up and opened his electronic safe and pulled out his STU key and inserted it into the special telephone on his desk.

"What are you doing, Pat?"

"Sir, this is going to be tough. The guy that has Bobby is the serial killer we've been hunting for a few weeks now. I know you got a briefing on the matter, the guy who shot Dr. Davis."

Pat picked up the receiver and started to hit a few buttons, but General Swank pushed the cradle button down harshly.

"Who are you calling?"

"I need to alert Colonel Helmsley. This guy is on our radar, so your grandson's abduction is in our mission set right now."

"NO!" the general boomed, startling him.

"What do you mean? I have to alert the team. This is huge. I mean, it's all happening because of the program, not in spite of it!"

Pat picked the receiver up again, but the general smacked it down one more time.

"NO! Pat, I, I, I can't let you. This guy said you need to keep the CR people away from this. He said if I don't bring you to him, he'll slit Bobby's throat!"

"Jesus! You know I can't go operational, it's against the new rules."

"And he knows that, too. He said you must act alone, that you can't tell anyone else in the program, or Bobby and your own son will be killed!"

Pat's eyes widened. The sudden revelation that the killer knew about Sean was something he didn't see coming. Despite his warnings to his boy about lying low, he wondered if Sean had slipped up and let the killer peer in and see him on the sidelines, gathering clues for his father.

"Oh, my God, I don't know what to do now. Did he say where he and Bobby are?"

"No, but he said he'll call me back in a few days."

"He called your landline at home, right?"

"Yeah, why?"

"Hang on, Sir."

Pat got up again and put the STU key back in the safe, then fished out the TOP SECRET personal digital assistant device Colonel Helmsley gave him. He fired it up and entered his password.

"What's your home phone number?"

He entered each digit as the general relayed it. He hadn't experimented much with the device since receiving it, so he clumsily meandered through the functions and prompts until he found the National Security Agency feature for running traces of telephone calls. Three clicks on the touch screen later, and he had a hit on the only call received at the Swank's Old Town Alexandria townhome within the last three hours.

"Here we go. A call came in from a cellular phone. I don't

recognize the area code. Let me see if I can do a reverse-number search."

Pat plugged away at the touch screen and button functions until he commanded the National Security Agency's enormous telephone records database to process the number.

"Anything?"

Pat shook his head. "No, it came from one of those disposable cell phones. Let me see if I can get the satellites to triangulate the location where the call was made."

He fiddled around a bit more until he had controlled a constellation of low earth orbit satellites to register the call's transmission history back to the NSA's powerful analytical computer system. The enormity of the operation was lost on the two men as they stared at the tiny PDA screen. Three huge communications satellites, each much larger than a school bus, synchronized together before beginning the beaconing process on the cellular phone's call, tracing it back to microwave towers throughout the United States. Each satellite collected transmission data from its unique stationary position above the Earth, then fed it back to the NSA where high speed computers processed the data into precise geographic coordinates. Within seconds, and at a cost to taxpayers of nearly a half million dollars, the results were ready and displayed on the screen.

"It indicates the call came from Silver Hills, in Indiana," Pat said, taking a notepad out of his desk drawer and jotting down the coordinates. He also established a bookmark in the PDA's history log so he could easily come back to the location. "Let's see if we can image the location with infrared," Pat suggested as the general strained to see the tiny device he held in his hands.

The screen display changed from its simple map overlay to a

dark black color. It seemed to flicker a few times as if adjusting itself to the lack of light in the area the overhead satellites were scanning. Slowly, the black blob began to turn gray, and then into a grainy mix of black, gray, and white. The outline of a small farmhouse appeared, displaying itself like a picture snapped through a night vision scope.

"Pat, I can't tell anything from that picture. Too fuzzy and small!"

O'Donnell pulled a long black cable from his desk and attached one end to the PDA and the other to his desktop computer. Using simple Microsoft software that came with the computer, he established a link between the devices, and suddenly on his large flat screen monitor, the same image appeared with a higher degree of resolution.

"You do realize, Pat, that your computer is now contaminated at the TOP SECRET level?" the general asked.

"Sir, at this point in time, I don't care. Finding Bobby and stopping this nutjob are what really matter!"

"I like your style, Pat," the general said, smiling for the first time this evening. He gave him a comforting pat on his back.

"There's one more thing, Sir. Let me see if I can do this properly," he said, his voice trailing off while he manipulated the handheld's controls. "There, in a moment we should be scanning the structure using gamma ray bursts. With any luck, we can look inside the house and see who's there."

Although the general was well-versed in the technology he was using, he had not seen the device in action and was as fascinated by its application as Pat was.

"Oh, my, God!" General Swank cried out seeing the image of the upstairs bedrooms appear, as if the roof of the home were peeled away, permitting them to peek inside.

It was not a perfect image, and not entirely clear, but it was enough of a gradient to allow Pat and the general to see Bobby and his mom in separate bedrooms, tied up on the beds.

Pat looked at him silently. The general had reached his hand out and caressed the screen, across his grandson's image. Tears welled in his eyes. "We're going to rescue you, Son. It's gonna be okay, Bobby." He turned to look at Pat. "So what's next?"

He shook his head, contemplating what he was about to suggest. He knew it would violate every tenet within the CRYSTAL ROUNDUP program, and probably get him fired, or even court-martialed, but he knew he had to do it. This was no ordinary case, he reasoned. As if ordinary were ever a standard in the paranormal world in which he was now firmly embedded. He also knew he had to respect the general's wishes because this particular nemesis meant business. It really wasn't so much about General Swank and Bobby anyway. Pat was sure of this now. He was the object. He was the reason Bobby was kidnapped. And he had to fix the problem. No one else could do it.

"I leave for Silver Hills in the morning, first thing."

"I'm going with you!"

"Sir, I can't let you. I'm the guy he wants. If I don't act alone, he'll kill Bobby!"

"All the same Pat, I have to be there when you find Bobby!"

He looked at the general and knew he was not about to back down. "Can you handle a gun?"

The general nodded with a smile. "Got my own Colt forty-five at home. I'll swing by here tomorrow at seven sharp, packed, racked and loaded!"

"Okay, Sir, and I mean no disrespect, but follow my lead on this one, okay?"

"You got it, Pat. You got it! You're the boss!"

Pat snickered inside. Never in his life could he have imagined hearing those words come from General Swank's lips. Never.

~ 24 ~

As soon as the general left the O'Donnell home, once more getting pelted by the rain as he walked to his car parked in front of their colonial home, Pat went to his bedroom and took Sara by the hand to Sean's room.

"We need to talk with Sean. I know this is going to sound confusing and all, but I think he is in danger."

He could tell Sara was not amused at all. Although she stayed in the bedroom while General Swank was in the house, she was savvy enough about Pat's business to know that once again he was getting in over his head, like he did a year and a half ago when he began his psychic journey. The journey that nearly got her killed. And while she now knew about his and Sean's abilities, she also understood the gravity of these psychic powers and the potential threatening forces they could unleash in others. She scowled at him as they entered Sean's room and woke him from his deep sleep.

"Hey, Buddy, wake up. Sean?" Pat asked as he gently shook the boy's scrawny shoulders.

The soft glow of a seashell-shaped nightlight plugged into an outlet near his bed provided just enough light for them to see his angelic face.

"Hiya, Daddy, what's wrong?" he whispered while his eyes fluttered, unsure if they should stay opened or close again.

"Sean, we need to talk. This is real important, and I won't be mad at you, but I need to know the truth!" Pat was stern, but he lovingly assured his son he could be completely honest.

Sean looked down and away from his father as he sat up in his bed. It was as if he already knew what this was about, his fear and shame very apparent. Pat reached out and took his hand and grasped it tightly and warmly.

"Yes, Daddy. What do you want to know?"

"Did you let the bad guy see you in your dreams? Does he know about you?"

Pat saw tears welling in his eyes, quickly becoming bloodshot and swollen. He rubbed them with his two small fists, sniffling away the moisture that began to consume his face and puffy sinuses.

Sean nodded tentatively. "Uh huh, but I'm real sorry, Daddy! I am. I shouldn't have been spying on you and Mommy. I'm sorry!"

His whimpers were now a full-scale emotional assault, complete with salty tears flowing like rivers down each cheek. His face was bright red, and he shook trying to get his words out over the heavy heaving spasms he began to experience.

Pat pulled him close to him as he sat on the edge of the bed. "It's okay, Sean. It's okay," he said consoling him as best he could. "Tell us everything."

Sean proceeded to confess his sins, albeit with great hesitation and trepidation. When he disclosed how he had spied on their lovemaking, their "sex stuff," as he called it, Pat shot Sara a glance with a mild smile. She seemed more embarrassed than anything, although Pat found his son's curiosity slightly intriguing. The boy never once made eye contact with his parents.

"Daddy, you let your own wall down for a minute. And the bad guy was able to look inside our house. And he saw me with my ear to your door."

Pat gave Sara a momentary, worried look. "Did he see your face?"

Sean nodded and began to cry again. "But I tried real hard to push him out of my mind, and it worked! I closed my eyes and concentrated real hard, and when I opened them, I knew I broke his vision!" he stammered, fighting back another spasmodic wave of tears.

"That was good work. I'm proud of you for knocking him offline like that. But remember, you can always tell me or Mommy--I mean, you *must* always tell us everything you experience about this guy, okay?"

He sobbed out a yes.

Pat caressed his light brown hair and leaned in to kiss his forehead. "Get some sleep. We love you."

When Sara finished tucking him in, she and Pat left the room.

"What the hell is going on, Pat?!" Sara growled when they retreated to their bedroom.

He knew that look was not one to take lightly. Her Irish genetic makeup had kicked in, and he knew if he tried to talk his way out of things, she might just physically assault him.

"It's that killer I told you about a few weeks back. Sean's in danger. We're all in danger!" He pulled her close and embraced her tightly for a moment before whispering in her ear. "Sorcha, I need you to take our kids in the morning and go up and stay with my mom in Pennsylvania." It was almost as if he feared the killer could see and hear everything in their room at the moment.

"What? Is it really that serious? I mean they have school and all."

He loosened up his hug and ran his arms down to her wrists. It was a subconscious gesture, but by doing so he drove home his point. With his strong hands on her knife-wound scarred wrists, he looked right in her eyes and nodded. "Yes, Baby. This is the real thing. We have a chance this time to get out in front of this threat, to prevent another--"

Sara interrupted him by putting a finger to his lips. "Shhhh. I know, Honey. I understand. It will be good seeing Mom again," she whispered before leaning in to kiss his lips. "But what are you going to do?"

"I have to go find this guy and take him out. He won't stop until he kills us or I kill him. I don't see any middle ground on this one, Sorcha."

She jerked back away from him, her mouth open in shock. "No, Pat, it's too dangerous! You can't do this alone. Leave it to the local police to find him!" She grabbed his pajama top with both hands and began shaking him.

"It's complicated. He has General Swank's grandson as a hostage. If I involve other authorities, he'll kill the kid first. This guy is a psychotic genius, and he means business."

She pressed her head against his chest and listened to his heart beat. He could sense she was starting to resign herself to the situation. "You be careful. I'll go pack some bags, and we'll be on the road early. I'll call the school from the car."

"One more thing. Call Colonel Helmsley in the morning and tell him we all had to bug out to Pennsylvania on a family emergency. Let's say some old uncle died or something. Tell him I'll be in touch in a few days."

Sara was startled by his request. "Why Pat? You mean he doesn't know about this?"

"Listen, like I said it's complicated. He'd have a cow if he knew I was going after this guy alone. Please, just trust me on this!"

She shook her head and walked off.

He racked out for a few more hours, but it seemed like mere minutes. Before he had rested enough for it to even matter, he was awake again, wondering if what he had just gone through had all been a cruel dream…a hoax of some kind planted in his mind by the sick psychotic for his own personal amusement. But it was very much real, and although he wished he could simply shake it out of his head, he knew better.

The groggy-eyed OSI Special Agent grabbed a steamy hot shower, put on a pair of tactical cargo pants, clipped his shiny gold badge to his wide belt, and strapped on his leather holster and extra ammunition magazines. From his nightstand he retrieved his official OSI handgun, the 9 mm Beretta, inserted a magazine, and sent the steel slide screaming forward to load its first round. He pulled out his Kel-Tec backup handgun, the unauthorized easy-conceal semi-automatic pistol, and strapped it, loaded, to his ankle. He put on his dark blue windbreaker jacket--his official OSI raid jacket with pull down patches bearing an embroidered OSI badge on the front, and the words FEDERAL AGENT in bright gold letters on the back. They were, for now, tucked neatly out of sight, but were ready to be displayed at a moment's notice.

Sara was still sleeping just before he departed, so he gave her a soft, quiet kiss on the cheek and caressed her bright red hair. Tiptoeing stealthily, he proceeded to his children's rooms and kissed them goodbye without rousing them. He made the sign of the cross before leaving Erin's room and said a hasty prayer, asking for God's grace and divine protection for him and his family.

General Swank was waiting at his front door, rather impatiently, when Pat opened it at precisely 0700. He was dressed uncharacteristically in blue jeans and a red, white, and green plaid outdoorsy shirt, looking more like a lumberjack than a two-star general. A denim jacket concealed his Colt .45 pistol which he flashed to Pat briefly as a sign of assurance that he was ready for anything this day. Most of all, Pat knew he was ready to rescue Bobby at any cost.

"Sir, please try to tuck your gun out of sight a bit more. I'm the only one with a badge, and the last thing we need is some local PD or sheriff to hook you up on the way."

The tall and imposing general nodded hesitantly as he pushed the gun and holster back more on his hip, his blue jacket now covering it completely. "You ready for this, Pat?"

"Yes, Sir. I hope we can take turns driving. It will help us get there without a lot of stopping and ensure I'm not too drained when we arrive."

"You got it. Listen, let's take my Suburban. I think we could use all the power we can get today."

Pat agreed and hopped in the passenger side, allowing the general to drive the first leg of the long journey to Louisville.

Although the big, powerful SUV handled well on the highway, enabling them to travel fast without lumbering up steep hills, it also sucked gasoline by the boatload. They made several refueling stops along the way, occasionally combining them with fast food and restroom breaks. Before long, the back floorboards contained all manner of empty bags, drink cups, gas receipts, and newspapers as the men journeyed swiftly, but just slow enough to keep them under the radar of state police vehicles along the way.

About halfway through the trip, Pat's cell phone rang. He looked at the caller ID display. "It's Colonel Helmsley," he whispered to General Swank as if he feared the colonel somehow could hear him before he actually answered. "Hello, Boss. Yes, uh huh. Thanks for the condolences, and for your understanding about missing work." He gave the general a nervous smirk, not too terribly proud of his lies. "Well, I'm not sure. My mom is taking it pretty well, so I hope we can be back in the area in a couple of days. Okay. I'll call you then. Cheers." He flipped the phone off and put it back in his raid jacket pocket.

"I take it John bought the deception?" the general asked slyly.

"Yeah, not one of my best moments, Sir. Let me drive for a bit, okay?"

They switched off driving at that point, for the second time that day, when they were about three hundred miles east of Louisville, on the outskirts of Charleston, West Virginia. It was there that they encountered considerable traffic delays because of construction on Interstate 64. Their original estimated arrival in Silver Hills of 1700, became an actual arrival of 2000 due to road work and two serious accidents along the way. Delays and detours betrayed them.

It was pitch black when they rolled into town. They snaked through the low lying hills of the rural community until they were a half mile from the old couple's home. Pat parked the SUV on top of a small hill overlooking the farm home and killed the lights. He lowered his window to listen to the night. The grassy scent of the pasture from his dreams reached his brain. Although they were nowhere near a horse farm, the evening's breezes carried the aroma from some great distance. The nighttime was eerily silent, and low, swirling, dense fog made it difficult to see more than a few yards ahead. Deathly quiet. Ominously black. The two men looked down and saw nothing below. No lights were on in the home. It was a black mass surrounded by black misty air. From that glob of darkness something else seeped forward into Pat's brain. It was a paranormal clue, a teaser he hoped he was wrong about. There was a sense of death about the place that struck Pat hard in the lower abdomen...two deaths to be precise.

Oh, my God. Please no. Please don't let Bobby and Janet be dead, he cried inside.

He was not about to break this kind of news to General Swank. The last thing he needed right now was an unbridled two-star general storming inside the farm home, potentially into an ambush, putting both their lives at risk. No matter how ugly things got, he had to maintain control. His law enforcement training and experience were what he needed to rely upon. Not his emotion. And certainly not the general's emotion.

~ 25 ~

Fearing they would be seen and exposed if they drove to the home, Pat decided it was best to hike the half mile or so down the hill, using the main roads to guide them in the darkness. They may as well have been blind. They walked slowly, using their shoes as virtual red-tipped canes, tapping a few feet ahead at a time, cautiously ensuring they did not go too close to an edge and fall down a steep incline into the rock and brush below. Pat held his Beretta in his right hand, the general a few paces behind with his Colt. Each man was ready for anything…an ambush by the killer, even a wild animal. Pat's adrenaline was rushing now, and although he had his fair share of dangerous missions catching fugitives and terrorists, he was never without sight like this night.

I wish I had a pair of NVGs! he thought, mentally kicking himself for forgetting to bring night vision goggles to let him see in the dark--and shoot with precision if need be.

Every slight sound they heard, no matter the source, was frightening and magnified exponentially. Even the general, a veteran of several tactical intelligence combat missions in Vietnam, trembled as he anticipated being pounced upon or simply shot at in the blackness of the cool spring air.

Their eyes began to adjust to the dim light ever so gradually. When they were within fifty yards of the home, Pat looked back at the general and could make out his face. The general nodded, letting Pat know he also could see him well enough now. They picked up their pace, the excitement of being within minutes of rescuing little Bobby was beginning to well within General Swank. Pat could sense it. The general started to walk faster, now slightly ahead of Pat. He grabbed the general by the arm and pulled him back harshly. "Sir, follow my lead!" he whispered sternly, reminding the two-star that he was the boss of this operation. The general nodded, somewhat meekly.

The home was just a few feet away, and Pat instinctively hunkered down, walking semi-squatted to lower his profile and reduce himself in size as a target. It was hard to do over such a distance, harder still for the tall, muscular general who had two weak knees following multiple surgeries for combat injuries he sustained in Southeast Asia. Pat's rugged, tactical hiking boots disturbed the gravel bed in the driveway, making slightly muffled crunching sounds, like someone munching on a bowl of dry cereal. He did his best to stifle the noise, but in the stillness around them, it was loud. It forced him to slow his pace when all he wanted to do at this moment was rush the house and barge in.

Stepping up on the first wooden stair leading to the wrap-around country-style porch gave off a *CREAK!* He took a deep breath. Another step. Another loud *CREAK!* He looked back at the general and whispered, "We're gonna have to bust in loud and in charge. I'll jump to the right, you go to the left, and let's clear one room at a time."

The general nodded his understanding. Pat stood at the top step and listened for any sound he might be able to pick up. He tuned his mind in to the home and came up with that fuzzy image of death again. And one living breathing person. He was certain now the killer had murdered Bobby and Janet, and was lying in wait, ready to strike and kill them both.

With one fluid motion Pat charged the front door, smashing against it with his right shoulder like a defensive tackle. The old, dry-rotted door and frame gave way easily, splinters and shards of wood spraying everywhere as the door crashed inward, pulling Pat with it. He fell to the floor and instantly rolled himself off to the right and upright. Slapping the side wall next to the doorframe quickly, he hit two light switches sending beams of bright, almost blinding light into the room.

He screamed, "POLICE! Don't move! Don't move!"

General Swank was right behind him, Colt pistol pointed out straight ahead, screaming along with Pat, uttering the same warning. The room was silent and still, except for the occasional fluttering of dust particles from the door-breaking episode moments ago. Stepping over the pile of debris, Pat cleared the right half of the room while the general did the same on the left. Off to one side was a large bloodstain on the carpet from the old woman. It was now brown and dry. But Pat could only guess it was from either Bobby or Janet, and the hopelessness of it all began to sink in. He watched as General Swank spotted the stain. His eyes widened in grave fear, clearly thinking the same as Pat at that moment.

Room-by-room they swept through the lower level of the home rapidly, determined hands deftly holding their pistols. Pat motioned for the general to get behind him and bear left as they climbed the stairs. There was only one area of the house where the killer could be, and it was upstairs in the bedrooms where Pat was certain the general was about to find his dead grandson.

He climbed quickly, hitting a light switch along the way, flooding the hallway with bright light, hoping to send the killer on the move so they could see and hear him. Like the downstairs, the upper half of the farm home was deathly silent. They first burst into a back bedroom where they had seen Bobby's outline from the reconnaissance satellite the night before. The door swung open quickly when Pat kicked it, and once the light was on, they found the bed--indeed the entire room--empty. In some respects Pat was grateful it was empty. At least they didn't find Bobby's body. He was certain the boy was dead, but he still wanted to hold out hope.

They proceeded slowly down the hall to the next bedroom, the one that was vacant on the x-ray image the satellite's gamma rays generously provided. But it, too, was empty. Pat's heart raced as they approached the final room, the master bedroom, the one they saw Janet lying in. He was convinced that not only would they find the two bodies there, but the psycho would be waiting for them, armed and ready to shoot and kill them. He thought about the bizarre cat and mouse game that was being played out and wondered who was chasing whom. If all this was an elaborate set-up, he fully expected a heavy gun battle, with everything at stake on the table at this moment.

He listened outside the door, his head against the framing for added protection, and heard muffled sounds, more like slight movement. He began to sweat profusely, anticipating the firefight, praying that if there was even the slightest chance either Bobby or Janet were still alive they would not get caught in the most certain cross-fire. He looked back at the general and held his left hand up, three fingers extended. General Swank understood the signal. Pat slowly counted down, lowering one finger at a time, mouthing out the words while looking at the door.

THREE—TWO—ONE! When his left hand made a fist upon reaching number one, Pat kicked the door with all his might, knocking it off its hinges and sending it into the room, hitting the bed.

They both screamed loudly, "POLICE! Freeze!"

The only light in the room came from the ceiling fixture in the hallway, and in the semi-darkness, they could make out the figure of Janet lying on the bed, still, lifeless. Pat pushed open the closet door and found it empty. The last possible hiding place, the adjoining master bath, had a closed door.

"He has to be in there," Pat whispered to General Swank, raising his Beretta to eye level. Something seemed to take a hold of him at that moment. Assured now that his nemesis was hiding in the bathroom, and recalling the words he spoke to Sara earlier that he had to kill this man, that there was no compromise, he aimed his gun at the center of the door. Closing his left eye, taking a second or two to adjust his grip and stance, he gently squeezed the trigger.

The double action semi-automatic pistol clicked once to pull the hammer back, then a second time to slam the hammer down, driving the firing pin into the copper ball round in the chamber. A deafening boom filled the room as the bullet screamed out of the barrel and through the center of the door. Within half a second, another gentle squeeze of the trigger sent a second round ripping through the door. General Swank gave him a startled, disturbed look.

"Major O'Donnell! What the hell are you doing? Bobby could be in there!" he screamed, keeping aim with his Colt .45 on the door.

But Pat knew Bobby was already dead, just like Janet on the bed. He glanced at her motionless body. There was only one living soul in the house, and it was the killer, and all Pat cared about at that moment was killing him. He ignored the general . He lunged forward and kicked the bathroom door open. When he flipped on a light, he was not prepared for what he saw. His mouth hung open in shock.

The room was empty, except for chunks of broken door and ceramic tiles, the unkind bullets having wreaked havoc on the interior. Scribbled on the mirror in what appeared to be semi-pasty blood were the words, *Too late pig!*

Just then slow, soft moans from the bedroom drew the men back to where Janet lay. Pat holstered his warm weapon and rushed to the bed, rolling her over onto her back, yanking the blindfold off, then the ear plugs, then the tape over her mouth.

"Janet. Janet?" Pat cried trying to get her to respond and open her eyes. He could see she was groggy and thought she was probably drugged. He had assumed she was dead all along, and could not have been happier to see she was still alive.

She began screaming. Pat and the general grabbed her and held her down until she could realize who they were. It was clear she thought he was the killer and her time had come as he had promised her so many times.

"Janet, it's me, Grand Pop. You're alright. This guy is gone, but he has Bobby! Do you know where they went?"

"Bobby! Bobby!" she began to scream, calling for her son whom she had not seen in many days. She was not sure he was even still alive.

"It's okay, Janet. We're gonna get you out of here. We'll take you back to Virginia with us. Tell me everything you know about this guy," the general said.

Janet was shaking so uncontrollably, Pat knew it was pointless to probe her right there on the spot. He and the general picked her up and helped walk her downstairs. When she saw the bloodstain on the carpet she began to scream and cry.

"What is it?" the general stammered.

"He killed the old man and woman, and showed me the bodies in the shed out back. He said he was going to do that to me and Bobby if we made any noise!"

"Sir, keep her here while I go check out the shed. I'll go get the SUV and come down for you both!"

He grabbed a flashlight from a kitchen counter and turned on the back yard flood lights, making his way to the shed. He carried the flashlight in his left hand while his handgun was firmly in his right. As he got closer, he could hear a peculiar soft humming sound. It grew louder with each step. He flicked on the flashlight and aimed it at the door. When he pulled it open, the swarm that greeted him was huge. Thousands of busy flies danced and dove over and on top of the corpses, their bodies bloated from decomposition, the stench rancid and heavy. He nearly heaved when the wave hit him. The wife was stacked on top of her husband, and both faces were turned toward the door, almost posed it seemed to Pat. Their eyes were milky and swollen, and in the glow of the sliver-handled flashlight, he saw dozens of maggots wiggling around, in and out of their eyes around the sockets they were slowly munching open. He turned away to cough and to try to control the natural reaction he had to regurgitate.

He pushed the door shut again, realizing now what his mild psychic impression about the house meant. These were the two dead bodies he sensed, and Janet was the one living soul in the house he assumed all along was the killer. It was a much better turn of events than he originally expected. He now held out renewed hope that they would find and rescue Bobby.

The psycho arrived in northern Virginia as the scene in Silver Hills unfolded. In some strange and twisted irony, when Pat and General Swank were plugging along westbound, in the bumper-to-bumper traffic on the jammed up Interstate 64, about halfway through their journey, the killer was travelling east. On a slow stretch of the highway, where construction crews shifted lanes to two way traffic, one lane each, their vehicles passed each other without either of them realizing it. Both powerful psychics had built their brick walls of defense so strong, that each blocked the other from seeing him.

The serial killer pulled into a cheap motel on Route 1 just north of Fort Belvoir, in a seedy section of Alexandria that was riddled with liquor stores and pawn shops, and where the sound of gunshots was as common as firecrackers on the Fourth of July. He tossed forty dollars on the counter and told the clerk to give him a room around the back so he had less noise. In the cover of darkness, he parked his vehicle out of sight of the highway, then walked to the back and opened the SUV's hatch door. He looked about the desolate parking lot for signs of life before pulling Bobby, bundled up in a blanket, from the back and carrying him through the cool night air to the room.

"Here we go, little fella," he whispered. "Home sweet home."

He dropped Bobby to the floor near the bed, the little boy's head smacking the filthy carpet hard. He cried slightly under his wrapping. The psycho opened enough of the blanket to reveal his face, smiling upon seeing the tears streaming down his cheeks. He kicked Bobby's side--surprisingly gently--just enough to get his attention.

"Shut up! I need to get some sleep!"

With that admonition, the killer fell back on the bed and was fast asleep.

~ 26 ~

The SUV's tires spun rapidly with little effort on the gravel road in front of the old farm home. They kicked up chunks of stone, dust, and dirt when Pat hit the accelerator hard, causing the rear of the vehicle to fishtail along the winding driveway back to the main road. The old couple's home shrank in his rearview mirror, lit only by the eerie red glow of his taillights. The fog had lifted considerably, making for a cleaner, clearer getaway. He pulled his TOP SECRET personal data assistant from his jacket pocket. With one hand on the wheel, the other worked the PDA's keypad to bring up a special function he discovered over the weekend when he experimented with its features. After a few keystrokes, the LCD screen displayed a menu titled, *DECOY PHONE.* He entered the telephone number for the old couple's home, and then was presented with an option, *USE VOICE ALTERATION?* He hit the *YES* button. He looked back at General Swank and Janet, sitting in the bench seat behind him, and was immediately struck by the tenderness the general seemed to provide her at this moment. He held the sobbing young woman close to him, one big strong arm wrapped around her shoulder, her head resting on his chest.

"I'm going to call nine-one-one and report the deaths, but don't worry, no one will know it's me. Please keep silent while I make the call."

The general nodded, patting Janet's arm, gently comforting her.

He drove frantically through the low hills, quickly making his way to one of the major highways on the outskirts of the rural community. The glow of city lights began to emerge as he sped his way toward them. He made the final few keystrokes he needed to complete the call to the emergency services personnel. After two rings, the operator picked up. On her screen it showed the call originating from the old couple's home, complete with address and grid coordinates to make it easy for first responders to find it. When Pat spoke in his normal, deep male tone, the operator heard an old woman's voice come through at her end.

"I want to report a murder. You need to send police right away. The man and woman are in the shed out back."

Pat hung up without waiting to hear what the operator said next. A few minutes later, he pulled onto Interstate 64 in time to witness a convoy of emergency vehicles screaming their way over to State Highway 111, leading them into the farm community.

Janet's sobs had begun to subside when they were a few miles east of the area and safely away from the house of horrors where she and Bobby had been held. Pat sneaked an occasional glance at her and General Swank in the rearview mirror, especially when they would pass brightly lit highway signs that threw bursts of visible light into the SUV, giving him a clearer look. He was astonished at how General Swank, the man he had started seeing only recently in this new light, was really a gentle giant. For all his boorish, blustering, and bullying behavior, and despite the likelihood that he probably disliked Janet over how she treated his son, the general cast it all aside at this moment. Right now, in the middle bench seat of the SUV, General Swank was a perfect father-in-law, a loving, tender, caring, compassionate man. Although it was virtually anathema to him, Pat harbored a secret feeling. A budding new emotion. He might actually be starting to like the old man…something he never saw coming barely a week before.

"You dun good back there, Sir," Pat offered with a half smile in the rearview mirror.

The general beamed at him. "Not so bad yourself, Major! I must admit, though, you shook me up shooting into the bathroom like that."

"Sorry, Sir, but I knew Bobby wasn't in there. I just thought the killer was in there alone." He lied, of course, because he actually thought Bobby's body was inside. He had to say something to comfort the general. But deep down he realized he had acted irrationally. He knew he had to be careful to prevent his emotion--indeed his assumptions—from overtaking reason and prudence. He recalled Woody's admonition when he screwed up the information from his uber-crazy, eight-visions-in-one dream. He needed to slow down on the guesswork, and focus firmly on facts.

He looked at Janet's reflection. "Can you talk now? Are you able to tell us anything at all about this guy?"

She nodded between sniffles, wiping her eyes and nose with her fifth Kleenex tissue. She related to the men the entire episode that had begun one week earlier, everything from the abduction from her home, to how the madman kept mom and son separated and isolated. The blindfolds. The hearing protection. The scheduled bathroom and meal breaks. While she maintained her composure quite well, it was all lost when she began to talk about Bobby and his currently unknown whereabouts.

"I don't know where Bobby is! I don't know if he's even alive!" she wailed, grabbing a handful of new tissues from a box on the seat next to her.

Both Pat and the general knew they could not reveal any details about how they came to rescue her, no information at all about Pat's psychic abilities. He gave her a long look in the rearview mirror before speaking.

He sighed, then grinned. "Janet, Bobby is alive. He's fine. This guy needs Bobby alive for reasons we can't tell you, but rest assured, he's fine."

She began to sob harder, a mix of anguished, grief-stricken cries over not being with her son, and happy, comforting cries because of his assurances. For the next few hours, they journeyed in silence while Pat mentally tallied everything he knew about the killer in his head. Although it was late, he decided to give a call to Sara to see how they were doing in Pennsylvania.

"Baby, I wanted to check in with you. Everything okay?"

"We're all good here, Pat. And your mom says hello and to stay safe," she whispered so as not to wake anyone else in her mother-in-law's old home in the town of Kingston.

"I just wanted you to know that things went well on this mission, but we didn't find this guy yet. I need you to stay put and out of sight up there. It isn't over yet."

"Okay. I love you, Honey. And your little ones know something is up, especially Sean. Don't worry, he told me to tell you he hasn't had any new dreams."

"That's good. Maybe this guy is blocking things real well, now that he knows Sean can see him, too."

He looked back to make sure the general and Janet had not heard what he had just whispered. Both were fast asleep, Janet cradled in his arms and out like a light.

He hung up and flipped the radio on to help keep him awake. Choosing a classic rock station, Pat worked the buttons until he had pumped the music to just the front speakers, keeping it as quiet as possible behind him so the pair could sleep. The heavy rock sounds and pulsating rhythms did the trick. Although he was exhausted, he managed to stay alert and focused, as he continued driving for another two hours.

But the peaceful mood was broken when General Swank's cell phone suddenly rang, loudly, waking him and Janet from their power naps. She sat up when the general removed his arm from her shoulder to fish his phone from a jacket pocket. Pat muted the radio instantly.

"Hello," he said with a worried look that Pat saw in the mirror. He cupped the phone's microphone and whispered, "It's him!"

Pat fumbled with the PDA and began entering a series of commands designed to trap the originating call's number and location. In so doing, he was also able to listen in to the conversation, having turned his special PDA into an extension phone of sorts. He held it tightly to his ear.

"Look, you sonofabitch, if you hurt my grandson I will personally kill you!"

It was at that point Janet realized what was going on. She began to scream, trying to yank the phone from the general's hands. He pushed her away as he listened to the killer.

"Oh, that sounds like Mommy!" he sneered. "I take it you and your psychic wonder boy found my message, then." He chuckled with the realization that the general was with Janet somewhere on the way back from having rescued her.

"Where are you? Let me speak to Bobby!" the general demanded.

"Nah, I don't think so. I'll be in touch. We have so much more we need to discuss. Before this is over, you will give up the psychic and I will kill him and his little boy. You need to decide which life is worth more, Bobby's or theirs." He hung up abruptly.

"Shit! He's gone! Were you able to locate him?" he asked Pat with an angry growl.

"Yes, Sir. Sure did. It's the same cell phone he used to call your house. But this time, he's calling from Route 1, near Belvoir. I need to back-search the GPS coordinates to see what's located there, if it's a house or restaurant, or what."

Janet had a confused look. "What the hell is going on? Just who is this guy, Pops? How can you track calls like that?"

The general once again placed an arm over her shoulder to comfort her. "Shhh, Janet. Pat's a federal agent, and what you just overheard is very sensitive. You can never tell anyone about it, okay?"

She nodded her head reluctantly. "Okay, but will you be able to save Bobby tonight?" she asked.

"I hope so, Janet," Pat said pulling into a rest area so he could complete the search. He worked the keypad, generating a satellite image of the precise location of the call's origination. "Looks like it was from the Sunset Motel. A real dive from this picture. Wait, let me zoom in a bit more."

Janet tried to lean forward to look at the display for herself, but General Swank gave her a tug. "No, Honey, you can't look at that stuff. It's TOP SECRET."

"Okay, the call came from room one-twelve. Let me see if anyone is in it." Within seconds his display captured the X-ray image of the room, and the outline of the killer on the bed, and Bobby on the floor on a blanket, clearly bound at the wrists and feet. Bobby moved as Pat watched.

"Bobby's fine. He just wiggled a bit!"

Pat turned around to give them both a huge smile. Janet, while overjoyed at the great news, was still awestruck by how he was able to receive this confirmation. "Who the hell are you?" She almost sounded frightened with her question.

He did not respond. Pat was busy setting in motion what he hoped would be the termination of this mission--the rescue of Bobby and the capture, or even better—the killing, of the psychopath. He peered into the rooms adjoining the one where Bobby lay. Finding a man and woman in room 113, in bed, frantically making love, he decided it was the prime locus for the next call he needed to place. He obtained the room's phone number from deep within the National Security Agency's archives. And like he did when he called 911earlier, making it appear to come from the old couple's home, he dialed emergency services in northern Virginia. The software once again disguised his voice.

"Hey man, I think someone's getting' killed in the next room! Some kid was screaming, then I heard a man scream he was gonna kill him, a lot of noise like he was beatin' the shit out of this kid. Now it's quiet, man. Room one-twelve. Hurry!"

The operator never got a chance to ask the street-smart thug-sounding man who he was. He identified the calling number as coming from the room next to 112 at the Sunset Motel, a place he was all too familiar with from numerous emergency calls for fighting, shooting, drug dealing, and prostitution. The 911 operator dispatched Fairfax County Police to the scene.

"I'm beat, General, can you drive a bit?" Pat asked as he hung up. "I'm pretty sure we'll see some action at the hotel soon."

"Yes, why don't you keep a visual on it while I drive so we can confirm the rescue."

Pat thought that was a great idea. He slid over to the passenger seat and buckled up. As the general drove off, he once again worked the controls on the PDA to bring up a satellite image of the motel. It took a few minutes, but when the display came into focus, he could see three police cars at the back of the structure. A fourth came to a screeching stop near the others as six uniformed officers approached the door to room 112 with guns drawn. Janet had leaned forward in her seat now that no one was next to her to constrain her. Pat didn't fuss. He knew it violated all security protocols, but he felt her status as Bobby's mom trumped all that for the moment. Her jaw dropped when she saw the scene on the tiny screen, like a small television broadcast from a hovering helicopter.

The officers crept up to the motel room door with guns drawn, three on each the left and right sides of the doorway. They did not bother to knock or announce themselves it seemed. One of the officers kicked on the door, but it took three good kicks to bust through to the other side. The six officers flooded in. There was no sound to the scene as Pat and Janet watched it play out, which only enhanced the suspense. He pressed a few more keys and generated an X-ray image so they could peer inside and see the rescue first hand.

And that's when the disappointment came. Pat's head dropped when he saw that the only people in the room were the six officers. The killer and Bobby were gone. Apparently the psycho's instincts were keen, and he must have realized the general had a way of tracking and locating him, so he decided it was best to move. He left the cell phone he used to call the general powered on, sitting on the bed, and was two miles away down the highway when the police arrived.

"I'm sorry, Sir. We were just too late."

Janet sat back in her seat, rubbed her tired eyes, and began to cry hysterically for the rest of the ride back to Virginia.

~ 27 ~

The sun was coming up when the trio arrived in Old Town Alexandria. General Swank had called his wife from the road an hour before, and she was less-than-pleased to learn her "skanky tramp ex-daughter-in-law" would be staying with them indefinitely. Pat heard enough of the one side of the conversation to understand it, his psychic abilities filling in the rest for him. What bothered him, and what he could sense troubled the general the most, was that Mrs. Swank seemed more upset with Janet staying at their home than she was with the news Bobby had not been rescued. The general slowed his Suburban as he approached the old colonial townhome with its semi-sagging fascia, put his emergency flashers on, and came to a stop.

He looked back at Janet in the mirror and gave her a smile. "Welcome home, Honey."

"Thanks, Dad."

Pat reached back and took her hand and gave it a squeeze before opening his door. He saw a bond between her and the general that seemed to grow stronger during their ordeal over the past twelve hours. He stepped out and stretched, arching his back and taking in a deep breath of the cool, fresh spring air. When he did, his badge glittered bright rays of gold sunlight, and his holstered gun was exposed briefly when his jacket opened wide.

Sitting in another stolen SUV, watching them arrive from a block away, was the killer. He outfoxed them again, and this time he took the offensive. He was drawn immediately to Pat, knowing instantly he was the psychic cop who had been chasing him. And if there was any doubt at all, it disappeared the moment he saw the badge and gun. He studied Pat's face and build, his stature and apparel. He pried mentally at his brain, seeking a crack or a gap into which he could insert himself somehow, to analyze, to assess, and to understand this adversary. All he needed was an opportunity...and then, like a parasite, he would latch himself onto his host, and suckle and drain him--drink up every drop of thought and knowledge with the ultimate object being to knock down his defenses. To control. To weaken and to make Pat vulnerable to any form of manipulation or torture he could develop in his devious mind.

And he found it. Pat was exhausted from the ordeal and was subconsciously diverting huge sums of energy, mental and physical, to his body as he took Janet's arm and helped her up the small steps to the front door while the general went to park the vehicle in a nearby lot he rented. This reapportionment of power meant that he devoted much less of it to the psychic brick wall he had built, and by doing so, left a small crack in its foundation. The killer envisioned it like a door that was slightly ajar, so he pushed it open slowly, trying not to make a sound.

He tiptoed into Pat's mind and looked around, impressed at its complexity and expanse. Like an old, Cold War Soviet KGB agent, the killer snooped about until he found the ideal spot to plant a bug. It might just as well have been the cliché microphone under the table routine. It didn't matter. With the virtual device now in place, tucked away in Pat's brain, the killer could read his thoughts, understand his emotions, learn his past, anticipate his future, and most importantly, bring him to his knees whenever he wanted.

One thing about Pat that impressed him the most was his synesthesia. He had no idea what he was experiencing at the time, and didn't even know what to call it, but when he first heard color, and saw sound, and tasted texture, the psycho was amazed. It was a power he found delicious in a sick sense. He even had a momentary thought that he might just spare Pat's life a little longer so he could continue to experience this pleasure.

He watched as Pat walked up and rang the doorbell. Deep within Pat's mind his synesthesia gave him the sensation of bright orange light and a taste of chalk, but he hardly dwelled upon it. Although he was accustomed to this blending of senses that he rarely paid active attention to it, the killer took notice. The orange light and chalky taste were incredible to him, so much so, that he literally clapped his hands softly, as he sat in his SUV and watched. Bobby made a sudden muffled noise under the blanket in the back.

"Keep quiet you, little bastard!" he snarled.

Mrs. Swank appeared at the door in a silky, pastel- yellow bathrobe, a cynical smirk on her snobbish face. She was holding a tall glass of red juice with a celery stalk sticking out of the top.

"Hello ma'am, I'm Major O'Donnell, and I think you know Janet," Pat said awkwardly. The impression he had of Mrs. Swank, as an elitist and arrogant general's wife, were confirmed the moment he saw her.

"Yes, I know, come in," she said in a bothered voice. "I have a pitcher of Bloody Mary's on the counter, so help yourselves."

"Oh, none for me, thank you. Janet, can I get you one?" Pat offered.

On any other day in her life Janet would have jumped on the chance for a stiff morning drink, but today her mind was focused on something much more important--finding her son.

"No thanks," she replied.

Mrs. Swank had wandered off, leaving Pat and Janet standing in the foyer, to make their way into the townhome on their own. It was her cold, smug way of showing her disapproval of her new houseguest. They walked into the small living room and took seats on two elegant, stuffed side chairs and waited for the general to return.

General Swank walked in and saw them alone. Pat could see his jaw tighten, clearly incensed over his wife's rudeness. "Janet, why don't we get you up to our guest bedroom. Take your time getting yourself refreshed and rested, and I'll make sure my aide, Kathy, brings you some of Sandra's clothing to wear until we can go out and get you some new things."

Janet stood and tugged at Pat's arm. "Thank you for rescuing me. But, find my baby, please!" she begged, just before giving him a goodbye hug.

"I'm all over it, Janet. Get some rest, and welcome home."

Once she was upstairs and out of hearing range, the general turned and asked him, "What's next, Boss?"

"Maybe I should call Colonel Helmsley--"

"NO! This guy will kill Bobby if you involve him."

"No, Sir. What I meant was I want to call and see if he has any news on the FBI investigation into Dr. Davis's shooting. Maybe the Bureau will have some new clues I can use to generate new impressions."

"Yes. Gotcha. Let's do that."

"How about we head over to my house. Look, Sir. Just drop me off. My head is starting to hurt like a truck drove through it. I want to take a little time laying down on my sofa and thinking about this, in my own unique way."

He could tell the general didn't like the idea because he had been so insistent on being there when Bobby was rescued. He gave Pat a tight-jawed, squinty-eyed stare. "Hmmmph. Well, if you think it will help you come up with new evidence, I guess it's worth a try. But call me if you get anything!"

Pat nodded. "I will call if I can, but understand this could get on a fast track very quickly."

The two men left and walked to the general's vehicle. Pat was so exhausted, that his eyes became droopy as soon as he plopped down in the passenger seat. Within a few seconds of pulling away from the curb, he was fast asleep, and incapable of knowing about the SUV, with the serial murderer at the wheel, keeping a loose surveillance on them as they made their way out to Burke.

When they were about five minutes from his home, Pat's cell phone went off, jarring him awake. He looked at the caller ID display. "It's Colonel Helmsley," he said to General Swank.

"Morning, Sir."

"Hey Pat, how are things up in PA? You holding up okay?"

"We're all fine. Like I said, he wasn't a close uncle, but I wanted to be here for my mom."

"Well, let me know if you need anything and take your time there. Listen, let's go secure. There's something you need to know about."

Pat fumbled with the buttons until he had a secure link. "Sir? Got you TS at this end," he said with a pesky feedback echo over the static-filled line once the TOP SECRET banner appeared.

"Same here. I wanted you to know the AG approved the deception plan and the CIA agent at the Observer planted the story with his editor yesterday. It headlined this morning, and is being picked up by the wire services right now. Hold on tight--it's bound to be a blockbuster by the end of the day."

"Roger that, Sir, I'll check the local news up here and see if they have it yet. I sure hope this works!"

"Me too!"

"Say, anything new from the FBI on the killer?"

"Not really much of anything, unfortunately. They are working it hard, but this guy's like a ghost."

"How about Woody?"

There was a pause. "No change there either, Pal. Good news is he's still holding on. Keep praying."

"I will. Out here."

Pat hung up, glancing at General Swank while he played with the radio controls to tune in a local Washington, DC talk news station. "Nothing new from the FBI, Sir. My only hope at this point is to try to link in with the psycho when I get home. The colonel also told me the deception plan is in the news. Here we go."

He found an all-news AM radio station. The commentator was mid-sentence in the story when Pat stopped the station scan:

"... at the Pentagon. No word yet from the National Security Agency, but a spokesman for the Secretary of Defense said he could not comment on a subject as sensitive as satellite technology, so I guess we won't be getting a confirmation or a denial as of yet. Recapping today's story for folks who may be joining us now, a highly placed source has told the Washington Observer that the NSA and National Reconnaissance Office have built and fielded a network of spy satellites that have been mapping and recording every square inch of geography in the United States. This massive archive is behind the recent surge in child abduction cases that have been solved in record time. Apparently the government can go back to a crime scene and look at captured images leading up to the crime itself, giving investigators the clues they need to solve them. George Orwell must be rolling in his grave. We have to take a commercial...."

Pat flipped the radio off. "I sure hope that helps deflect attention away from me. If the public were to find out I'm a psychic and about the existence of the CRYSTAL ROUNDUP program, we'd be blown out of the water!"

The killer listened to it all with a huge smile. The surreptitious, psychic listening device he had secreted in Pat's brain enabled him to listen in on his and Helmsley's TOP SECRET conversation, defeating the best encryption system taxpayer money had bought. He particularly enjoyed the news story, thinking the entire deception plan, while ingenious, was too much like science fiction to be taken seriously. He was confident that when he provided the news media with the real truth behind the CCVC's sudden success, it would expose Pat as a psychic. *Posthumously, of course,* he sneered inside his sick mind.

He reached down and patted the large manila envelope on the passenger seat that was addressed to Fox News in New York City. Inside were Dr. Davis's TOP SECRET clinical notes, containing a running history of his work with the "OPSO" in the CRYSTAL ROUNDUP program. Anyone reading the report would clearly understand what it was all about, despite not mentioning Pat's name. The linkage between the Department of Defense and the Department of Justice, the nexus to the Child Crime Victim's Center in Arlington, and the clear, central mission of the program--to find abducted children, would all be exposed and made ripe for investigative journalists to tear apart.

"Well whaddya say, Bobby? Wanna come with me to the post office? As if you had any choice!" he chuckled just as he watched the general slow his vehicle to a stop in front of the O'Donnell home. "You know Bobby, I have half a mind to stick a note in this package with Pat's name and address, but that would be too easy. I'll let the media chew on it a bit, make them work a little at trying to figure out who the OPSO is, er, was."

The psycho watched through Pat's eyes as he dragged his feet into his house, fell back on his bed, and held his head tightly. Then, it was like a giant water sluice had been opened. The harder Pat tried to psychically connect to the killer, the faster the information from his brain gushed out and into the killer's mind. The mental tap was hemorrhaging out his thoughts, his memories, his entire life to the serial killing maniac. Everything there was to know about Patrick Sean O'Donnell was now in the psycho's mind.

The killer drove off and found a local post office in a nearby shopping center. He gave the clerk cash and a bright smile, left the overnight delivery package in the care of the United States Postal Service, and sped off to look for another sleazy motel to rest for the night.

"Tomorrow's another day, Bobby. But what a big day it will be! Tomorrow, you, this cop, and his son…are all gonna die."

~ 28 ~

He had no idea he had fallen asleep. When he eventually woke at 2100 that evening, he was angry with himself for having wasted so much valuable time. His fruitless effort at trying to lock onto the psycho's psychic signal only added to his exhaustion, knocking him out cold for the last twelve hours…twelve hours during which anything could have happened to Bobby.

Pat shuffled into the kitchen, still in his tactical clothing with one gun on his hip and the other on his ankle. He grabbed a bag of greasy Lay's potato chips from a counter and started to devour handfuls of the salty, oily chips. Mid-way through the fat snack orgy, out of the corner of his eye, he noticed a blinking light on the answering machine on the counter. When he hit the message button he broke out into a big smile hearing Sara's voice.

Hi, Baby. I tried calling your cell phone but couldn't reach you. Please call me if you get this. Sean says he needs to speak with you right away.

He became excited with this development, knowing that Sean's insistent message was most likely going to be the only morsel of information about the bad guy he would get that night. He pulled his cell phone from his cargo pants front pocket and called Sara.

She answered in a whisper. "Hey, Pat, is everything okay? Everyone is sleeping here, I don't want to wake them."

"I'm hanging in there, just worried about you guys. Do you know what Sean wanted to tell me?"

"He only said it was about this bad guy. Something real important."

"I hate to wake him, but I have to talk with him."

"Okay, be right back."

In the space of two minutes, while he waited for his son to pick up the phone, Pat finished off the potato chips. He crudely wiped his mouth and slimy fingers with a paper napkin just in time to hear his son's high-pitched voice.

"Hiya, Daddy, it's Sean," he said cutely, as if he needed an introduction.

"Hey, Pal. It's good to hear your voice. What's been going on?"

"Dad, this is serious. This guy is inside your head. I don't know how he did it, but he got in there, and he can read all your thoughts. He followed you to the house today, but he didn't kill you because he wants, he wants," Sean's voice trailed off into sobs as he spoke, unable to get his final words out.

"He wants what? Sean, what does he want?"

His boy took a deep breath to control his weeping. "He wants to kill me first, and make you watch!" With those words he broke out into a loud wail, dropping the cell phone and grabbing his mother for comfort.

Sara picked the phone up. "What's happening? What do we do?"

"Honey, listen. If Sean's right, and if this guy can read my mind somehow, then you, the kids, and mom are in danger. Get everyone out of the house now, get on the road!"

"What? Pat, what? Why? Where do we go?" Sara stammered in confusion.

"Look, go anywhere. Hell, go someplace far away--I don't want to know where you are because if I do, then he does. Be random. Change locations every day. Change directions abruptly, make U-turns frequently. Look for tails! Call the police if you spot anything suspicious!"

"Christ, Pat! I will, but call me every day to make sure you're okay."

"No!" he said abruptly. "I'm sorry, Sorcha. Look, we can't be in communication until this is all over. Any contact between us will expose you guys to him. And please tell Sean to turn everything off...no sending or receiving. He'll know what I mean."

"Okay, but please be extra careful. I'll go round everyone up here. I love you, Sweetie!" she said in a this-may-be-the-last-time-we-speak tone. He knew her worry…could almost synesthetically taste it as he hung up.

He contemplated the significance of Sean's insight--indeed his warning about the freak's ability to read his mind. A disturbing sense of wide-open vulnerability began to settle in, like when he eventually learned that FBI agent Vicky Desantis had his entire home bugged a year and a half ago when he first worked in the CRYSTAL ROUNDUP family. But this time, instead of his spoken words and visible actions, it was his thoughts that lay bare. Like nightmares he had had as a young boy about going to school in his pajamas, Pat felt incredibly exposed, mentally nude, with no ability to cover up or close the blinds.

For the first time since he began his psychic journey, he had an appreciation of what it was like to be on the other end of a mind reading experience--the readee, as it were, instead of the reader he had come to be. And he didn't like it. Nor did he know what to do to stop it.

As much as I hate having to call my socialist friend, I think I need to talk with Dr. Jacobsen, he thought as he leaned over a counter, elbows on the hard marble surface, cell phone in his hands. The phone rang three times after he hit Jake's number on speed dial.

"Hello? Pat, is that you?"

He heard Jake's voice over a lot of background noise. There was loud music, laughter, chanting, and screaming reminiscent of a frat party out of control wherever Jake was.

"Jake. We need to talk. It's very important!"

"What? I can barely hear you, hang on."

He next heard Jake's muffled voice as he covered the cell phone with one hand, obviously trying to hush the wild party crowd.

"Can you hear me now?" Pat asked.

"Yeah, sorry about that. My birthday is a couple days away and some of my friends from Berkeley are here early to help me celebrate. Wish you were still in town, maybe you could have come over!"

Pat rolled his eyes trying to picture what that must be like. A few dozen of Jasper Jacobsen's nerdy hippie classmates wearing peace signs in a marijuana smoke-filled room like a Cheech and Chong movie, chanting "Give peace a chance!"

"Listen, we need to talk. Something very serious is going on and I need your help. On the QT--I don't want Colonel Helmsley to know about this just yet in case it isn't anything at all. Look, I never left town. It's complicated. Can you come over to my place?"

"Crap. Well not really, Pat. I'm a bit fried right now, been drinking a lot here. Can you come on over here?"

He shook his head silently then took in a deep breath. "Okay, Jake. I'll come over right away," Pat said hanging up.

It was almost 2230 when he arrived at Dr. Jacobsen's apartment that was within walking distance of the CCVC. He approached the door and heard the steady sound of a party, increasing in volume with every step. He rang the doorbell four times, then finally banged on it harshly before he heard the din start to soften from the other side. When it opened, he was face-to-face with a gorgeous, blond-haired girl no more than nineteen years old. Dressed in a tight, short denim skirt and a rather stylish silk, white blouse, she took one look at him, glanced at the gold badge on his belt, then shouted to the room over her shoulder. "Looks like the cops are here to break up the party!" She turned to once again make eye contact with Pat…very alluring and sexy eye contact. "Well officer, would you please come in?"

Pat stepped inside and looked around at the six others in the room, one of whom was Dr. Jacobsen holding a beer bong. Despite his expectation of a 1960s style love fest, a la Woodstock, the group of teens and twenty-somethings was relatively conservative in appearance. There was no hint of smoke in the air at all. No drugs to be seen. Jake put the beer drinking device down with a grin.

"Hey everybody, this is my colleague, Special Agent Patrick

O'Donnell!" He said the last four words in a deep, authoritative tone, drawing chuckles from his friends. They all said hello in unison, except for the blond girl who greeted him at the door.

"Well, with you it makes eight for the party! I'm the odd girl out, so you can be my date tonight." She slid her arm under his and held his hand, then placed a soft kiss on his cheek.

"Uh, hello everyone, sorry to interrupt the party, but I just need a few minutes of Jake's time," he said breaking the awkward grip of her hand. She gave him a playful pout as she let go.

"Come on, Pat, grab a beer and let's go talk in my bedroom," Jake urged.

"I'm fine thanks, let's just chat," he said walking ahead of Jake, leading the way to the bedroom.

"What's up, man, you look frazzled! I thought you were in Pennsylvania for a funeral."

"Listen, I have reason to suspect this guy--the killer--has somehow managed to tunnel into my brain, like a wiretap. He's able to read my thoughts, maybe even hear and see all that I do like a hidden camera!"

He took a seat on the edge of Jake's bed. Dr. Jacobsen stood and stared in confusion as Pat related his concerns. Despite his expertise in this arena, he appeared to be at a loss at the moment for advice. He had never encountered a situation like this--in fact, had never even imagined such a scenario when he studied psychic phenomena at Berkeley...two high-powered psychics locked in a mental battle with the price of life and blood on the line.

"Let me do some research. I'll call--"

"Jake, this is the real-world! I don't have time for research!"

Pat practically shouted as he stood up, placing his hands in his pants pockets. When he did his gun was visible, causing Jake to jolt back.

"Why did you bring a weapon here? This is a gun-free house!"

Pat rolled his eyes. "I need you to focus, Jake. Forget the left coast and help me out. We're not in a lab. My life--and potentially yours and everyone connected to CRYSTAL ROUNDUP is on the line!"

"Alright. Alright! Let me think."

Jake paced about his room nervously as Pat sat down again and looked around.

"I have an idea. It might or might not work."

Pat could sense uneasiness in Jake's tone of voice. "What is it?"

"Well, I know you had a bad experience with truth serum back when Vicky Desantis ran the program. But a small, controlled dose might be enough for me to relax you to the point I can help you locate and wipe out the lock he seems to have on you."

Pat stood up and walked around the room in small circles as he thought. He hated the idea. It wasn't just the bad experience he had with the use of soporific drugs in the last series of operations, it was also the fact that when Jake hypnotized him in his office a few weeks back, it nearly killed him. If he went under at a time when the bad guy was watching, combined with his mental wiretap, Pat feared he would surely die.

"What kind of controls would you have?" Pat asked.

"Total. Like I said, a mild dose is all I propose." And as if he could read Pat's mind at that moment, he added, "I think we're probably safe right now. This guy's probably asleep."

"Okay," he nodded. "But I don't want to be under any more than ten minutes."

"Easy. Let me get my stash, er, I mean my medical bag. Don't worry, I'm licensed to do this," he added, giving the nervous Agent O'Donnell a reassuring smile.

Jake returned a few minutes later with some alcohol pads and a syringe. He tapped out the last few air bubbles, and sent a small spray of clear liquid a few inches out of the tip. Pat rolled up his sleeve and waited for the injection.

At Jake's instruction, he counted in reverse from one hundred, but didn't get much past ninety-seven when his eyes became droopy. He fell backwards to the bed. He was semi-conscious, although his body felt heavy and weak.

"Can you hear me, Pat?"

"Yessssss," he replied slowly, drawing the word out with a hiss.

"Examine your mind. Think about *how* you think, how you process information. And look for something that shouldn't be there. Something out of place."

Pat concentrated as best he could, the sodium pentothal making it easier for him to think about this one single, central topic. Unfettered by distractions, the drug enabled him to practically take a look inside his own brain, as if it were removed from his skull and sitting in his lap. The serum seemed to enhance his synesthesia as well. In one mental flash, he smelled a black tarry scent, like freshly-spread, sticky asphalt on a highway. It was surrounded by red, oozing blood that carried a sharp sound, a tinkling chime sound, like the tapping of a wine glass with a fork. He felt like he was wading through a dense, warm swamp, thick as pea soup, making it difficult to move his legs.

This strange orchestra of sights and sounds represented a journey he was on—a journey inside his own mind. Deep in the swampy ooze of brain matter and blood was an object that did not belong. It was a dark black glass orb, and the tinkling, tapping sound he heard was his own mental machete making its way toward it, occasionally striking its surface. Until finally he reached it. Although just a symbol of the mental listening device the killer planted in his mind, it was the only way his brain could make sense of it.

He reached down into his own brain matter with both hands, feeling the slimy, warm blood and brain tissue slowly flow around his hands. It felt like thick, warm, wet Jell-O. He felt the object…a cold, hard-surfaced, round crystal of a device, the size of a baseball. When he pulled on it, the suction-like vacuum it created made it seem stuck. He pulled harder and harder with all his might. It finally began to give way, making a wet smacking sound at first, followed by a sloshing, slurping, *POP* noise as it came free. Pat nearly fell backwards on his read end in his symbolic journey. His brain cells and blood rushed to fill the void. Suddenly, he felt like a giant malignant tumor had been removed from his head.

He carried it out of the swamp. He stood on the edge of the muck, his feet soaked in brainy grime, but no longer encumbered. He looked across a vast expanse of nothingness to the tiny outline of a brick wall off in the distance. With all his might, the former high school baseball pitcher lined up, and then flung the ball as hard as he could toward the brick wall. It travelled straight and fast, and if it had been a baseball, he was sure this pitch would have clocked in at over 100 miles per hour. Smiling, Pat watched the device rocket and whistle toward the wall. When it struck the barrier dead center, the thick, coarse brick and mortar construction seemed to explode. Sharp chunks of rock and cement erupted from the surface, flying like a dust storm in all directions. After a few moments, the scene settled, and the damage came into clear focus. The device had punched a neat hole in the wall, about four inches in diameter, and then continued on through to the other side. Pat knew he had accomplished two very important things. He removed the spy equipment the psycho installed in his mind, returning it to its rightful owner in the process. And, he finally broke through the psychic's heretofore impenetrable brick wall force field. He weakened the killer's mental defenses.

"Pat, can you hear me?" Jake shook him frantically, apparently trying for the last seven or eight minutes to wake him.

"I'm okay," he said sitting up and rubbing his eyes. "I think it worked, Jake. Better still, I think I may have clocked this guy in the head with his own device! Damn, I'm tired."

Jake had no time to comment. Pat had fallen back on the bed and was fast asleep in seconds.

~ 29 ~

When the sunlight flitted into Jake's bedroom, striking Pat's face, he squinted and slowly tried to open his eyes. He was groggy still from the mild dose of truth serum Jake gave him the night before, and in his muzzy state of being, he had an awkward sense of not knowing where he was. Thinking Sara was cradled next to him, his arm around her shoulder, he pulled the woman in close and kissed her hair. But her distinctly different scent drove itself like a screaming freight train into his mind, shattering the fuzzy dreamy feeling he initially had. He jerked his arm back, waking her up. The blue-eyed, blond beauty who had greeted him at the door the night before was now snuggled next to him in just her bra and panties. Pat looked down at his own clothing, fearing the worst, but grateful to see he still had everything on that he fell asleep in, to include his raid jacket, gun, pants, and tactical work boots.

"Christ! What are you doing here? Please tell me nothing happened last night!" he demanded as he pulled himself away from her and sat up on the edge of the bed.

She giggled. "Morning, gorgeous. Don't worry. You were a gentleman, but it's not like I didn't try." She blew him a playful kiss.

"How old are you?"

"Eighteen. But I like older guys, especially sexy ones like you."

"Gee, thanks!" he said sarcastically, not actually taking the "older guy" comment as a compliment. "What time is it?" he mumbled checking his watch.

"Early, like eleven o'clock."

"Damn, I've got to go. Look, I'm sure you're a sweet kid, but I'm happily married," he said waving his gold wedding band at her. "Be good, okay?"

"Bye bye, Honey," she said with a small yawn and a big smile. She curled up in a ball and went back to sleep as Pat slipped quietly out the bedroom door.

In the living room was a pile of bodies. Fast asleep. The other six partiers, to include Jake, were sandwiched in and around each other like a drunken game of Twister gone horribly bad. Empty beer, vodka, whiskey, and wine bottles littered the place. It reeked of stale beer, cold pizza, and sour Chinese take-out. He tiptoed carefully through the mess, deftly and deliberately setting each footstep down in whatever small amount of open floor space he could find. An occasional snore would spurt out from one of the sleepers, startling him momentarily. Once he cleared the room, he slid out the front door and into the bright sunlight and fresh cool air. He took in a deep breath and realized just how nasty Jake's apartment smelled in hindsight.

Pat was at a loss over what to do. He drove off in no particular direction to collect his thoughts. He concentrated on his mind and the experience he had the night before of ridding his brain of the virtual bug the killer had implanted there. While he could not be certain the mental brain surgery he conducted was successful or not, he had a high degree of confidence. Still, to be extra cautious, he decided not to contact Sara and the kids until the whole ordeal was over. He was as sure now as he was when he began hunting for the psycho that it would only end when he killed him. But how to find him now was proving to be a vexing problem.

The killer woke and immediately clutched his head in anguish. It ached fiercely, throbbing as if pounded by a hammer while he slept. Inside his motel room in the slums of Anacostia, he sat up and cried out when the wail of a police car siren screamed past his door to a crime scene two blocks away. The shrill, piercing sound ripped into his brain like a spike being driven in. Tears flowed from his eyes because of the searing pain. He tried to connect with Pat, but suddenly realized the device he had so carefully planted was now gone.

"That sonuvabitch! How did he do it?" he moaned, standing up and kicking Bobby in the side as the boy lay sleeping on the floor.

He grabbed a bottle of Tylenol from his knapsack and swallowed a handful--at least eight or ten-- in one gulp, and then washed it down with a huge swig of Johnnie Walker Black. He took another swig and swished it around his cheeks and tongue like mouthwash before swallowing it. He kicked Bobby one more time causing the boy to moan and writhe on the floor.

"Listen, I'm going out to get some food. If you try to escape,

I'll go and kill your mom, your dad, and your grandpa, got it?"

Bobby sobbed out, "Uh huh." He sniffled under the wrapping on his mouth, still bound and blindfolded.

The man stepped to the front door and placed a Do Not Disturb sign on the handle, then drove off in the latest stolen SUV he had at his disposal. While he cruised along looking for a fast food restaurant, thinking about Pat and the removal of the listening device, two things occurred to him. First, he had a sense--weak and unclear--that Pat had not completely removed the hidden mental microphone. There was some remnant remaining, something that gave him a loose connection to him. He could not quite put his arms around it, but if his intuition was right, he might still be able to keep tabs on Pat in some way. He knew he could no longer see through Pat's eyes, or hear the words he spoke, or read the things he thought, but he knew he still had a hook of some kind there that waited for him to exploit. As he came to this realization he broke out into a smile, rubbing his head with one hand while his headache started to subside.

But the other thing he came to realize threatened to bring the pain back. He had a mental image of Pat standing on a pitcher's mound with the killer himself at bat. He watched as Pat wound up for a fast ball, leg rising just before his right arm rocketed the small black glass baseball straight at him. But instead of a perfect pitch down the middle, the ball whistled toward him high and to the left. Before he could react, the ball beaned him in the head, crushing right through the plastic helmet, then through his skull, and burrowing itself deep inside the southpaw killer's brain. The pain was nearly unbearable. The psycho clutched the steering wheel tightly, realizing now that his headache resulted from this mental assault, and realizing now that Pat had more than removed the device from his brain...Pat had implanted it in the killer's mind. His sudden worry that Pat could invade his thoughts and know where he was at the moment sent a panic up his spine.

The killer slammed on his brakes, screeching to a halt on a busy intersection in Anacostia. Cars behind and next to him came to a sudden horn-blaring stop, trying to avoid an accident. He hit the gas and made a sharp U-turn, spinning his wheels wildly, turning so harshly his vehicle almost seemed to want to tip over. He floored the gas and sped down the highway back to the motel. He parked abruptly in front of his motel door and popped the back hatch door open for a quick insertion ...of Bobby. He nearly kicked the room door open in his hysterical haste to retrieve the boy and make a getaway. He tossed Bobby into the SUV with no regard for his welfare. The boy thumped to a stop after sliding in a few feet.

The lad let out a loud, but muttered, "Ouch!"

"Shut up!" he groused at the boy as they sped off again.

Like Pat at this moment, driving aimlessly around the Washington, DC metropolitan area, the killer had no particular place to go. He was worried now, checking his mirrors constantly for tails, unsure if he had been made or not. He needed a plan, but with his concentration on survival right now, nothing coherent was emerging. He drove. And pounded the dashboard. And drove. And screamed.

Pat cruised around trying to make sense of all that happened to him. He tried his hardest to pick up images of the killer, but all he received was a snow pattern like a television set with no signal. Occasionally, a jagged ghost image would appear but quickly fade into the mass of black and white dots chasing each other on the mental screen. For reasons unknown to him at the moment, he headed away from Dr. Jacobsen's Arlington neighborhood toward Interstate 395. He took the highway north toward the District, crossing over the South West Freeway until it dumped him out on the other side on Interstate 295 in Anacostia. He exited near the Washington Navy Yard and drove aimlessly in this area. His surroundings were a blur as he paid no attention at all to the vehicles near him. Subconsciously he made the sign of the cross and began to pray out loud.

"Blessed Virgin Mary, I cannot help but feel I am close to this guy right now. Guide me to him. Stay with me. Protect my family and keep them safe. Amen."

A comforting feeling came over him with his prayer. A sense of warmth and love he typically felt when the Mother of God touched his soul. He knew instantly she was with him at this moment.

Without conscious thought, he found himself traversing the main streets and roads of Anacostia...Martin Luther King, Jr. Avenue, to Alabama Avenue, to the Suitland Parkway. He definitely stood out as not belonging there. In his white Subaru Outback with Virginia license plates, the clean-cut federal agent in a raid jacket and tactical sunglasses drew lots of stares and snickers from local residents of the cruel and dangerous streets of the DC ghetto. Young men, congregating on street corners wearing their gang colors, signaled each other as he approached...not sure if he was lost, or crazy, or a police lure of some kind. The normal level of activity began to drop off as he drove, but he still managed to see some of it. There were sleight-of-hand drug deals made with the same precision as old Cold War-era brush passes American spies used to transfer secrets to Soviet agents around the world. There were daytime hookers in skin tight dresses that accentuated their large curves, who slipped into doorways adorned in multi-color graffiti paint. The only clear thought about the place to enter Pat's mind was how cities like the District created such abject poverty and desperation for its citizens…the worst misery bought with the best taxpayer money.

He rounded a corner, nearly hitting a trash can that had been knocked down into the street, with its filthy contents spilled out. When he swerved to avoid the mess, he spotted a large Chevy Suburban speeding toward him. The driver seemed distracted, making occasionally jerky motions with the wheel as if angry or disturbed. As he got closer, now no more than twenty yards ahead of him, Pat's synapses came alive with electricity. The subtle something that lay hidden beneath the fabric of the sodium pentothal cocktail the night before suddenly emerged. When he imagined himself launching the fantastic fastball at the brick wall, he had actually imbedded the listening device inside the killer's mind. While not functioning perfectly, it provided him with a beacon of sorts, a homing signal to lock onto and use to follow his nemesis. For the first time in this strange, twisted, and relentless game of tracking and trapping, Pat now had a clear image of the killer's face. He had the upper hand at the moment, and knew he had to exploit it.

It was also clear that the killer instantly recognized Pat. He gunned his engine and raced past him on the busy Anacostia road, perilously swerving to avoid cars in front and on the sides. He weaved in and around them, screeching his tires and kicking up loose dirt and gravel.

Pat slammed his brakes and put his car in reverse, accelerating rapidly to spin his sedan into a sharp curve, then straightened the wheel and shot out down the same road in pursuit. His Subaru was ill-equipped for a high-speed chase, but it was all he had. It also did not present a convincing cop profile, barren of lights and sirens, so it did not command the kind of respect he needed at the moment. Most other drivers on the street became aggressive in trying to block him; others just passive-aggressively pretended not to notice him honking his horn and jerking his car behind them to urge them on.

"Come on! Move!" he shouted, smacking the dashboard. He watched the SUV gradually shrink in size as it pulled ahead of him faster than he could catch up.

He saw a break up ahead when the driver in front of him switched lanes to make a turn, leaving an open space. He floored the gas, swerved into the right lane, then the left, gaining momentum now with a lane-changing rhythm that propelled him along briskly. The SUV made a sharp turn onto Minnesota Avenue as Pat made measurable progress in catching up. He was gaining enough ground now that the license plate became visible. Pat grabbed his cell phone and dialed the emergency operator.

"Hello, I'm Special Agent Pat O'Donnell, U. S. Air Force. I'm in pursuit of a late model Chevy Suburban traveling southbound on Minnesota Avenue in Anacostia. The driver is a murder suspect and he is believed to have an abducted child with him."

"Sir, what is the vehicle's description?" the operator asked.

Pat provided the information, nearly clipping the right rear end of a Nissan Sentra that had slowed unexpectedly, forcing him to swerve into the right lane to avoid a collision. Although the operator wanted Pat to stay on the line with him, he hung up to keep both hands on the wheel. He was within a few yards of the SUV now when it suddenly took a sharp right turn onto the Suitland Parkway headed toward downtown and the Capitol Mall area. It was mid-afternoon, and traffic was relatively light as the Chevy Suburban emerged from an underpass beneath Interstate 295, making a high speed bounce up a steep hill within line of sight of the United States Capitol building. Pat was in hot pursuit, busting through two red lights, once almost getting T-boned by a semi-truck coming at a clip from his left. He fishtailed for several feet until he regained control of his sedan and gunned the engine to make up for lost time. He was only seconds behind the SUV when it went under the freeway, and when Pat flew up the same hill, he saw the SUV take a sharp right turn onto D Street, nearly tipping over. Sensing he had an opportunity, Pat raced ahead to the intersection, slammed his brakes on the approach to force his rear end into a slide for a much sharper turn. He was in the inside lane and about even with the SUV that was on his left side.

With his Beretta in hand, Pat rolled the window down and

aimed up at the driver. He fired off one round, but found the combination of the killer's elevation and his own inability to drive at a high rate of speed, while aiming a gun at the same time, proved to be a nearly impossible task. It was nothing like the Hogan's Alley simulator. The bullet struck the SUV's passenger window and exited through the front windshield, but not before it fractured the side window into thousands of glass gravel chunks that were held together precariously. The killer swerved to the right hard, striking the Subaru, crushing the left fender and shearing off his side view mirror. Pat fired two more rounds in rapid succession, the first one missing completely, while the second one struck the passenger window again, causing it to collapse into a snowstorm of glass all over the busy road.

The killer shot out ahead of Pat, crossing his lane directly in front of him. He slammed on his brakes forcing Pat to do the same, along with a sharp left turn of his wheel to avoid a rear-end collision. Pat spun around two times, ending up on the wrong side of the road, facing the opposite direction. By the time he regained control and aimed his sedan back onto D Street heading east, the SUV was no longer in sight. He knew he needed to get out of there fast. With all the commotion and the shootout he was in on a busy workday in Washington, DC, the area would soon drown in a sea of police cars. He headed up through some smaller streets until he sat in front of a row of old brownstones on A Street in the city's southeast quadrant.

"Dammit!" he screamed making two fists and pounding the steering wheel.

Knowing he had some kind of fuzzy psychic link to the killer, he concentrated hard on trying to identify the virtual GPS signal emanating from the psycho's brain. Like the snowy television screen impression he had just hours before, he glimpsed an occasional outline of the SUV. He tried to pickle the image, to lock it down and head toward it, but he didn't know how to do it. Like an old television with rabbit ears antennae, he did his mental best to twist and turn his brain to find the optimum signal. But he simply could not paint the target. It was moving and not fixed, making the task nearly impossible.

In the background he heard the wail of sirens as police cars crisscrossed the roads all around him in the search for the SUV and for him. Pat knew it would not be long before the killer ditched his latest stolen vehicle, heisted another one, and forced him to start all over again in the search.

But how do I go about finding the right frequency to latch onto? How do I locate this guy? Mary, please help me! he thought, burying his face in his hands in anguish.

~ 30 ~

"Jake, I need your help," Pat said, clutching his cell phone tightly to his ear. He sat in his car, still outside a row of old brownstone apartments in one of Washington, DC's highest crime neighborhoods.

"Huh, I'm kinda hung over here, Pat. What do you need?"

"Look, it's complicated. I'm hot on this guy's tail right now, but I need help tuning in to his signal!"

"His what? You're not making any sense," he grumbled with a yawn.

"I'll explain when I get there. I'm on my way to your place, get ready because you're comin' with me," Pat shouted, flipping his phone off without waiting for him to respond.

He pulled away from the curb, hands trembling with worry over the prospect of being unable to locate and take down the killer. It was early evening and rush hour traffic was beginning to build as he backtracked through the District to Interstate 395. He knew the fastest way there was to take the HOV lanes south, but the restrictions were already in effect. He ran the risk he'd be spotted by an overzealous highway patrolman. The last thing he needed at this moment was a delay…he had to get over to Arlington fast, and precious time was running out.

It was anything but easy. The buildup was heavy and thick, and the interstate looked like a giant parking lot as he approached it. He eased onto the HOV lanes after what seemed like at least forty-five minutes of rubbernecking. Although they were also busy with commuters headed out to the suburbs, the high occupancy vehicle lanes were a welcome relief from the stop-and-go traffic he had been in. He breezed along--or so it felt--at no more than thirty miles per hour, but that's all he really needed to make up for lost time.

Arlington was close by, and within ten minutes he was off the freeway and deep inside the side roads leading to Dr. Jacobsen's apartment. He parked his sedan, got out, and stood in shock at the condition of his car. The last time he used the Subaru like this was when he raced home to rescue Erin from the clutches of FBI Agent Desantis. He nearly broke the rear axle jumping across the Woodrow Wilson Bridge's open expanse when it began to rise to let a ship pass by in the Potomac River below. His insurance company was furious at him, and almost declined to cover the damage.

It may be time for a new car, he thought, shaking his head as he stepped up to the apartment door and rang the buzzer.

Jake opened it slowly, shielding his eyes when the setting sun's light struck his face. In his post-drunken sickly condition, he had spent the day in total darkness, clutching the sides of the sofa to keep it from spinning him into a vomiting state of dizziness.

"You look like shit, Jake. Sorry to do this man, but I need your help," Pat said stepping into the dark, dank, and booze-reeked apartment. There were still a couple of sleeping bodies on the floor, although he really couldn't tell if they were men or women at this point.

"Jeeze, Pat. Come on in, let's talk in my bedroom again. Don't worry, Susie is gone," he chuckled, recalling how the barely-legal-age teenager had hit upon him the night before.

He sat on the edge of the bed while Jake fell down face first, head on a pillow, and groaned. Pat related everything to him...the high speed chase, the shootout, the smashed up car, and the certainty he had now that by symbolically lobbing his fastball at the killer while in his drug-induced state the night before, that Pat now had some ability to track him.

"Jake? You awake?" he asked nudging his shoulder.

"I'm still with you. Listen, I don't want to use the truth serum again because it knocked you out last night, but how about we try hypnosis?"

"I dunno, I didn't like it the last time we tried it. You think it will work?"

"Not sure, Pat. But it's the only option I see right now where we can at least get you back on your feet fast to go find this guy," he said nearly heaving as he leaned over the side of the bed.

"You're all I got. Let's do this, Jake."

Dr. Jacobsen grumbled, holding his aching head as he pulled a shiny medallion on a chain from his nightstand. Just as he did weeks earlier in Pat's office, he asked him to concentrate on the object in an effort to fatigue his eyes. Within moments, Pat was in a deep hypnotic state, surprising Jake, who was pretty sure he couldn't pull it off considering his hangover.

"Pat, I want you to concentrate on all the images you received today when you started to experience the fuzzy television snow thing. Mentally adjust the antennae until the signal seems strongest."

Pat tried. At first it was difficult to reconnect, because, just as he surmised following the high speed chase, the killer was now behind the wheel of a new car. The change in vehicles from an SUV to a compact sedan, with Bobby cramped in the trunk and getting weaker by the moment , was an effort by the psycho to confuse Pat. It worked for a moment, but not well. Once he had the scent, he locked down onto the maniac's special signature, and would not let go.

"Identify and memorize the signal, Pat. Don't let go of it. When I count to three, you will wake up, and the killer's frequency will be burned into your mind until this ordeal is over."

He woke with a renewed sense of strength. Just like the high-tech satellites he used in the course of his work as a super secret agent, in the CRYSTAL ROUNDUP program, Pat had the signal pickled. He knew instantly where he needed to head to home in on the killer. He looked at Jake.

"You are coming with me. I need you in case I lose this signal. It's our only chance."

"Noooo, Pat. Look, you're not even supposed to be doing this operational stuff, let alone me. No way!"

"Yes you are!" Pat snapped, grabbing Jake by the collar and dragging him off the bed. He pushed him along, under protest, to his car and shoved him in the passenger side. Just after firing up his engine, he reached down to his ankle and pulled his Kel-Tec handgun from his concealed holster. "Here, I know you hate guns, but you need to be armed if you're riding with me."

Jake was visibly repulsed. It was not just the fact he was

hung over like a frat boy, it was, of course, his loathing of handguns. "No way, Pat. I don't even want to see it!" He turned to look away.

"Alright, but you listen to me, and follow my lead. Okay?" He snapped it back into his ankle holster.

"You got it. Just keep that thing away from me."

They sped off in a dust spray as Pat gunned his engine…off to downtown Washington, DC.

Pat concentrated on the killer, aware now that he had punched a hole in his defenses when he pitched the mental wiretap back to him. He received weak signals, at best, but enough to give him important insight into his current mental state. The killer had tried to outsmart Pat, assuming he would never think to look for him close to where they had their shootout. But he was wrong. With the advantage now of his mental GPS system closing in on the psycho's signal, it didn't matter where he was or what he drove.

Traffic was almost non-existent heading into town, and as they approached the off ramp to the 14th Street Bridge, which would lead them into the bowels of the District, the sun was setting and dusk had arrived.

Pat's mind was on autopilot again, like it was earlier that day, but this time it was a more conscious and aware sense. He drove toward the killer with silent determination, the snowy television image gradually becoming clearer and more detailed as he got closer. When he approached Constitution Avenue, he veered left, heading west, then north toward George Washington University. Within moments, the image on his mental screen became much clearer. With every inch he drove, the image became sharper until the black and white screen faded, only to be replaced by a full, color-rich screen that seemed three dimensional to him. He knew exactly where he needed to go.

The alley was nestled among a cluster of old tall buildings near the university's hospital. The killer's signal pulled Pat right to him like a laser-guided bomb to its target. He slowed as he approached the alley. It was now dark night, making it difficult to see down into the narrow lane that was wedged between office buildings and restaurants.

"Let's get out here. He's not in his car, so when we get to it, I want you to free Bobby from the trunk and call the police. Tell them a federal agent needs assistance."

Jake had not really even begun to snap out of his throbbing hangover. He just mumbled in response to Pat, but stayed close and tight behind him as the two crept down the alley slowly. It occurred to him as he slid along the tall buildings, back pressed against the cool walls, that the scene was eerily-reminiscent of his experiences in the OSI's Hogan's Alley firearms simulator. He was nervous for sure, worried that if he fired too quickly, he would take out an innocent civilian like Lucy Liu. If he hesitated, he would get killed. Somewhere in that perfect middle was a sweet spot in time he had to find again. It had been lost over the past year and a half since he killed Vicky Desantis.

The car came into view. They sneaked up on it silently and found it empty inside as Pat predicted, but the muffled sobs from the trunk were unmistakable. Pat pointed in silence to Jake, instructing him to pop the trunk open using a driver side lever. They both smiled when they saw Bobby wrapped in a blanket. Pat put a finger to his lips to tell him to remain quiet as he unwrapped him, handing Jake a pocketknife to cut his ties. Jake stayed with Bobby while Pat continued his frightening journey into the alley.

His heart pounded as he crept along, trying to stay as low as he could. It was pitch black now, and he had advanced no more than fifteen feet. Up ahead he could barely make out the outline of a utility van parked close to the right. Glancing behind him, he could hardly see the sedan where Jake and Bobby waited despite a dim amount of moonlight that flickered in and out of the alley. When he turned around again, he caught the momentary glint of a metal object from behind the van. He aimed his weapon and was about to fire two rounds, but he stopped himself. He had no clear idea if the shimmer he saw was the killer with a weapon, or if it was an innocent person like he feared. He wiped his brow, then opened his eyes as wide as he could. He needed to be certain this time.

His hesitation was a terrible mistake. Making virtually no sound at all, a bullet ripped quietly through the killer's silencer. By the time Pat saw the suppressed muzzle flash, it was too late. The bullet struck his right shoulder knocking the Beretta out of his hand. His gun flew backwards toward the sedan behind him. He fell to the ground in searing pain. It was the first time he had ever been shot for real, and tales of the pain he had heard about over the years did not do justice to the reality he faced now. It was far worse than the mental pain he felt when he was inside Woody's memory the day he searched for clues about the killer. The psycho rushed up and stood over him laughing. For the first time, the two men stared at each other, face to face. His smile was sickening, and his laugh was mocking as he aimed his handgun at Pat's head. Pat managed to sit up with his back to the wall.

"Well, Pat. Nice to finally meet you. Cool trick with the fastball you hit me with last night. But it looks like the bad guy wins this round. Any message you want me to pass on to Sean and Sara before I go have some fun with them?" he taunted.

"You leave them alone!" he screamed. He knew he had to distract him, if even for a second, so that he could withdraw his backup gun. He pulled his right leg up so his ankle holster would be within reach. "My partner's right behind you, asshole."

The killer never looked away. "You mean Jasper? He's still with Bobby at the car."

He knew all he could do at this point was to make a virtual suicide move since the freak didn't buy the lie. Despite his wound and the horrific pain in his shoulder, he quickly reached forward to his ankle and pulled the miniature semiautomatic from its holster. He raised it up and was about to fire, when the gun suddenly, and mysteriously, flew from his hand as if ripped away by an invisible force. It landed three feet away.

The killer laughed. "Oh my! You didn't know I was psychokinetic, Pat? This is so tasty. Unless you have a second back up, which I doubt, I suppose this is the end."

He slowly unscrewed the silencer and placed it in his pocket, then once again aimed at his head. "I want you to have the full effect, you know, the big boom of death! Good-bye, Pat. It's been fun!" The freak's face morphed in front of him for a split second. Just like his Hogan's Alley vision of the red-faced, green-eyed demon, Pat saw the malevolent face of evil implanted on this man for a moment.

Pat rolled to his right and tried to creep toward his Kel-Tec pistol, but his arm was so weak, he advanced mere inches. The very last sound he heard was a thunderous explosion. Then, as if a black hole had formed in the alley where he lay, all sight and sound and thought came to a crushing single point in front of him. And then, everything stopped.

~ 31 ~

Standing five feet behind Pat's body was Jake. He held the Beretta in both hands, awkwardly gripping it, his hands shaking violently. He had just fired off one round that struck the killer in the lower abdomen. It was the first time in his life he had fired a weapon, let alone held one. Although he aimed for his chest, his inexperienced, jerky trigger finger sent the round downward. It was just as well. The psycho wore body armor and would have been unaffected if Jake's aim had been true. The maniac looked down at the blood flowing from his gut, dripping onto Pat's face. He growled angrily at him, lifted his gun, and was about to fire when Jake's amateur hands pulled the trigger sooner than he intended. The explosion ripped through the alley, and this second round pierced right through the killer's throat and out the back left side of his neck, just missing his spinal cord. Jake dropped the weapon when the killer went down in a thud. He rushed over to Pat and began to shake him.

"Pat? Pat? Are you alive?"

"What happened?" he sighed, coming back through the fog of having passed out briefly from the searing pain and loss of blood.

"I shot him Pat, I killed that guy! I can't believe I did this," Jake cried, shaking like a leaf.

"Oh God, thank you Buddy," he said, sitting up, still burning from the sharp pain of a bullet lodged in his shoulder.

Pat looked at the psycho lying on his back in pools of blood around his neck and waist. He saw the bloodstained bottom edge of the bullet-proof vest sandwiched between the killer's shirt and abdomen.

Jake continued his lament. "I, I, I had no idea what I was doing, Pat. God, I feel awful about this!"

"Looks to me to be two perfect shots, considering his body armor," Pat said with a painful wince and a small, grateful smile.

He wiped the droplets of the killer's blood from his face, thinking all along it was his own. He looked to his right and slid over to pick up his backup pistol. He tried to stand, but the pain was gripping him. Jake helped him up.

When he stood up, something strange and invisible seemingly brushed his left cheek gently. It felt like a small bird or butterfly had gracefully fluttered past and touched him. He had no idea that the Archangel Michael was standing there. It was Saint Michael's first stop of the evening, and he had an important mission to secure before moving on to one more venue for the night en route to Heaven. When Michael stretched his wings, a few white feathers touched Pat's face. On purpose.

Pat reached up with his left hand to scratch his face when he felt the mild tickle, and when he did, his eyes caught movement off to his left. The psycho, face and hands bloodied, air wheezing in and out of his lungs spasmodically through the clean hole in his throat, had grabbed his gun once again. The killer began to pull back on the trigger with both hands and all his might, aiming right at him. Pat's strong hand was out of commission from the bullet wound. He gripped the Kel-Tec in his weak, left hand, instinctively pointed it at the man, and fired two rounds rapidly. Instead of aiming at center mass as he was trained to do, he aimed at his head, knowing this was the only way he would be able to take out his body-armor-wearing target. Both rounds hit the psycho in the forehead, no more than a half inch apart. His skull exploded like a bomb.

As soon as the killer's soul departed the earth, Pat knew instantly he had been cured. Those fears he held since shooting and killing FBI Agent Vicky Desantis over one year before—fears of getting into a shootout, and probably hesitating, or firing too soon and killing the wrong person--vanished when he took the man out. He knew immediately there would never be another Lucy Liu-like Hogan's Alley firing range incident…simulated or real. The Expert Marksman…the legendary OSI Special Agent, regarded by his peers and superiors as one of the finest investigators, counterintelligence agents, and counterterrorism operators the organization ever produced…was back again. He was restored, reset, resurrected.

In addition to the realization that he was now mentally healed when it came to his firearms prowess, he also felt like another giant weight had been lifted from his shoulders. He was hardly aware of it over the past few weeks, but the killer's mental hold on him grew in strength steadily, sapping his physical and mental might. He dropped to the ground again, his back to the wall, and set the handgun down. He let out a soft cry...of thanks. He placed a hand on his chest and caressed his Saint Michael medallion through his bloodstained shirt.

Pat reached with his left hand for his TOP SECRET PDA phone. He wanted to call Colonel Helmsley, but the PDA's case was empty. He knew that somewhere over the last twenty-four hours he had lost it…sometime between the high-speed chase with the killer the day before and the alley gunfight this evening.

"Jake, grab my wallet and call that number on the florist card the Boss gave me," he groaned.

Dr. Jacobsen complied, remembering to use the fax number for the password.

"There, that should do it. That thing should be toast right now."

He and Jake applied pressure to the gunshot wound, trying to stop the steady, gushing blood loss, as the wail of police sirens grew louder and louder.

~ 32 ~

It was several days following his surgery to remove the bullet before Pat was finally able to have any visitors other than Sara. Sean and Erin giggled while playing a card game right on his bed, at his feet, while he slept. Sara and Pat's mom sat in two easy chairs drifting in and out of naps. His white-haired mother held a set of Rosary beads in tired, wrinkled hands, having fallen asleep following her third recitation of the long series of prayers. He started to come to, blinking the bright fluorescent light from his eyes.

"Is somebody going to give me a hug?" he mumbled in tired words.

"DADDY!" both children shouted together.

Erin nuzzled up on his left side and planted kisses on his cheeks. Sean approached him more gingerly from the right, not wanting to upset the giant bandage affixed to his shoulder and arm.

"Hey, Dad, I'm glad you're okay!" he said giving his father a gentle kiss on the cheek, holding his right hand tightly.

"It's so good to see you guys. And you, Sorcha. And you Mom!" he said with a big grin once he realized who was in his room at that moment.

"We've been prayin' for ya, Sonny!" his mom said with a hint of an Irish brogue and a warm, wide smile.

"We're so happy you're fine, Baby," Sara said moving to his bed and wedging herself in next to Erin for her own share of kisses.

"Look at me!" he said, eyeing up the myriad of cables and tubes attaching him to machines and IV bags. "I look like a science experiment! Ouch, that really hurts!" he cried when he lifted his arms up too high.

"Quit your complaining, Patrick!" came a familiar voice.

He looked across the room to his right, and squinted through dopey-hazed eyes to see for himself if his instincts were true. The image slowly came into focus. On a bed near the window, he saw Dr. Woodrow Wilson Davis. His head was bandaged, along with his arms, but his smile and kind eyes were both familiar and comforting. His bed was raised up forty-five degrees so he could rest semi-prone. Grace Davis stood by his bed, caressing her husband's face and smiling broadly at Pat. When he and Pat made eye contact, Woody raised a few fingers on his right hand in a wave. Tears streamed from Pat's eyes once his brain processed the scene, once he realized with certainty it was all real.

"God bless you, Woody. When did you come out of the coma? I've been praying so hard for you."

He smiled. "Three days ago, same night you killed that maniac. It was the strangest thing, but I had a dream Grace was sitting here caressing my face. Her fingers were light like feathers. But when I opened my eyes, the room was empty!"

"I feel so guilty about that, Honey!" Grace Davis said, giving his hand a squeeze. "But I ran out for a quick bite to eat in the cafeteria, and when I got back the place was swarming with doctors and nurses, all around Pookie, talking with him!"

"Pookie? I won't even go there, Woody!" Pat laughed.

"Well, when I heard you were here, I insisted they make us bunkmates."

Thank you, God. Thank you, Mary, Pat thought. "It's so good to see you, Woody."

A deep voice came from the doorway. "Did we come at a bad time?" Colonel Helmsley asked with a grin.

They all looked over and saw the colonel, Dr. Jacobsen, and General Swank standing there. Jake had a bouquet of flowers in his hands. "It's from the Attorney General and the CCVC staff," he said placing them on Pat's nightstand that was already crowded with several flower bunches and get-well cards.

"Thanks, guys; it's great to see you all."

"I have something else for you Major O'Donnell," the stern-looking general said gruffly.

For a spilt-second Pat had a mental flashback to all those times General Swank verbally abused him with his crotchety and grumpy demeanor. His eyes widened instinctively, suddenly fearing it was business-as-usual with the old man. But a smile broke out on Swank's face. He reached over to Pat and placed two silver oak leaf clusters in his left hand.

"Congratulations, Lieutenant Colonel O'Donnell. Compliments of the Secretary of the Air Force."

"What? How? I'm not up for promotion for another year!"

"Well, you were considered for early promotion, but the board didn't select you. When the Secretary got the list, he looked for your name. Not seeing it there, he penciled it in."

"Congrats, Pat!" Colonel Helmsley added, pretending for a moment he was about to punch him in his bandaged shoulder.

"I'm so proud of you, Honey!" Sara exclaimed, just as shocked as Pat was at the news.

"Unbelievable. Thanks, Sir." He gripped the metal rank insignia in his hand tightly.

The general placed a hand over his clenched fist. "No, thank you, Pat. For everything. For bringing my grandson home safely, and my daughter-in-law."

"Are Janet and your son getting back together?"

"They're going to give it a try, and my wife and I are committed to helping them work through their problems. As a family."

Pat nodded and smiled. "That's great news."

"Well, I need to leave, folks. Pat, thanks again and God bless," the general said before he turned and walked away.

The colonel looked at Sara and then Grace. "I hate to do this, but may Jake and I have a few minutes alone with Pat and Dr. Davis?"

"Okay, sure, John. I'll take the gang down to the cafeteria and spend some of that pay raise. It's dinner time anyway," Sara laughed. She gave Colonel Helmsley a hug before herding the children from the bed.

"I'll join you," Grace Davis announced, taking the cue.

Once the door to the hospital room was shut, and the four men were in it alone, it was silent for a few seconds, with just the occasional beep from a piece of medical equipment.

The colonel's demeanor quickly changed. "Pat, I have half a mind to take that rank back! What were you thinking? You never should have gone it alone!"

"Sorry, Sir. I know it broke the rules, but I didn't see any other end to this. This guy had to be taken out."

The colonel glared at him for a few seconds, but then suddenly rolled his eyes and let out a sigh. "Oh hell, I know that. Look, I'm not really mad at you. Damnit, you dun good! Just promise me that in the future you will trust me. I may not always agree with you, but you will need my top cover!"

"I promise, Boss." He looked at Jake. "You dun good, too, Buddy. Thanks for watching my six."

Dr. Jacobsen's face was drawn, suggesting to Pat he had agonized over the incident these past several days. He braced himself for another lame lecture about the evil of handguns.

"I hated having to do it, Pat. But I'm glad you're safe."

He could tell there was something more Jake wanted to say, but was holding back for some reason. "What is it?" Pat asked.

"Well, this is probably going to sound weird and all, but I don't think we were alone in that alley. I mean--"

"I know we weren't alone out there," Pat said with a smile, his left hand subconsciously caressing his Saint Michael medallion over his gown.

Jake nodded. "Yeah, well I was also sorta wondering if you would mind if I attended church with you sometime?"

Pat's eyes welled with tears as he suddenly recalled the words the Blessed Virgin whispered to him at Easter Mass, *We are all God's children, even those with whom we squabble.*

He took Jake's hand and held it tightly. "I'd be honored, Jake. And if you want, I can take you to the range sometime and give you some shooting practice."

"Don't push your luck! Church will do just fine, for now!"

"Now this is what I call a team!" Dr. Davis said from across the room.

The colonel grinned a look of both happiness and relief. Then he cleared his throat.

"Gentlemen, let me bring you up to speed on a few things. Before he died, our killer mailed Dr. Davis's report to Fox News. When their reporters approached the Justice Department for comment, the AG's spokesperson laughed and asked them, 'What sounds more silly to you? A constellation of high-tech satellites snapping pictures of everything, or some super-psychic soothsayer on the government payroll?'"

"I take it the reporters agreed the latter scenario was less probable?" Pat asked.

The colonel chuckled. "It worked perfectly. They took the comment to be an indirect confirmation of the satellite report. If anything, they are now more convinced than ever such technology exists."

"I'd say we're in the clear on this one," Woody offered.

"So what about the bad guy? What do we know about him?" Pat asked.

The colonel gave him a thorough rundown on the killer's criminal history, to include the fact that he kept a meticulous journal about his killing spree. "We originally linked him to eighteen murders. It really was twenty-two. Bobby was close to being his next victim, but thanks to you and Jake, he's safe at home with his parents."

"Jake, what do you make of the fact this guy had some kind of psychokinetic ability? My gun literally was ripped from my hands and tossed a few feet away!"

"We've never seen it before. Honestly, this has always been the stuff of science fiction or fantasy. It's the first confirmed case of it I've ever heard about. In a way, it's kinda sad this guy's dead. I would love to have studied him…" he said, his voice trailing off as he saw Pat's visible reaction.

"He's better off where he is right now!" Pat smirked.

"Oh, we found your PDA. Well, what was left of it, I should say. It was a molten blob of goo next to the sedan in the alley," the colonel said.

"That's good, I was a little worried about that thing, but I sure miss it."

"Ha, wait to you see what we have in store for the future! You think that was cool!"

Pat closed his eyes for a moment, and appeared to be deep in thought. Actually, he was praying. Giving thanks not just to God, but to the Virgin Mary and Saint Michael for once again seeing him through another tough task. As he prayed, he felt that special warmth and closeness to the Mother of God he oftentimes experienced when he was deep in prayer. Once again she spoke to his heart in soft, gentle whispers. He nodded his head as she spoke, drawing some confused looks from the other three. Finally, he opened his moist eyes.

"Gentlemen, we have a lot of work to do. There are many children who need our help. But there's more…something weird is going on somewhere far, far away. I don't know yet what it is, or when it will happen, but we're going to embark on our strangest journey yet. This one is especially important to God."

The Author

Colonel Michael "Mike" Angley retired from the United States Air Force in September 2007 following a rewarding 25 year career as a Special Agent with the Air Force Office of Special Investigations (OSI). He held thirteen different assignments throughout the world, among which were five tours as a Commander of various units, to include two Air Force OSI Squadrons and a Region, the equivalent of a Wing.

Mike is a seasoned criminal investigator and a counterintelligence and counterterrorism specialist. Following the 1996 Khobar Towers terrorist attack in Saudi Arabia, he was dispatched to command all OSI units throughout the Middle East, with responsibility for 23 countries. During his tenure, he and his teams effectively neutralized numerous terrorist threats to U.S. forces in the region, to include an imminent threat to senior Department of Defense officials. Earlier in his career, while commanding an OSI unit in northern Japan, Mike conducted an operation that effectively blocked a KGB agent's efforts to steal critical U.S. technology, and thereby stymied Soviet military advances for years. In 1999 he was Chief of Counterintelligence within the Directorate of Intelligence, U.S. Strategic Command. His office competed for the prestigious Killian Award, a White House level honor that annually recognizes the very best intelligence unit in the entire U.S. government. His unit came in as first runner-up for this significant honor.

Mike has an M.A. in National Security Affairs from the U.S. Naval Postgraduate School, Monterey, CA, and a B.A. (summa cum laude) in Criminal Justice and Psychology from King's College, Wilkes-Barre, PA. He is a former National Defense Fellow and Adjunct Professor of International Relations at Florida International University, Miami, FL, and is an Honor Graduate of the Defense Language Institute's Korean language program.

Mike and Evelyn, his wife of 23 years, make their home in Colorado Springs, CO. They have three children, and they recently adopted a beagle puppy named Brynn.

Acknowledgments

There are so many people to whom I am grateful for making this dream a reality. My family, for sure...which is why this book is dedicated to them.

I also want to acknowledge my critique partner and editor, Barbara Weingartner as well as the young lady who designed the cover art, Jaquellyn Tramble. Thanks once again for pulling my fanny out of the fire!

Kudos to my friend and fellow writer, John Wills, for graciously writing this book's Foreword. Thanks, John...and may God grace you with your own writing as you continue to inspire readers.

- **Title:** ***Child Finder***™
- **Author: Mike Angley**
- **Price: $27.95**
- **Publisher: TotalRecall Publications, Inc.**
- **Format: HARDCOVER, 6.14" x 9.21"**
- **Number of pages: 320**
- **13-digit ISBN: 978-1-59095-827-8**
- **Publication: June 9, 2009**

Inspired by Real Life Experiences

Follow the Paranormal Adventures of an Air Force Special Agent as the Government Exploits His Psychic Abilities to Rescue Abducted Children

Major Patrick O'Donnell, an Air Force Special Agent assigned to the Pentagon, begins experiencing haunting nightmares about children who have been abducted and murdered—*before* their bodies are found. It quickly becomes apparent that he has a special psychic gift that the government is all too eager to exploit.

Agent O'Donnell is drawn into a TOP SECRET ***black world*** community overseen by the FBI that leverages his skills to solve child abductions. Soon he discovers that this ***black world*** has an even darker underbelly when those close to him begin to die mysteriously.

Advance Praise

This compelling debut novel, the first in a trilogy, features a memorable protagonist who is a combination of devoted father and mystic. For fans of supernatural thrillers and those who enjoy the TV show Medium, this is a real find.

The author is a retired U.S. Air Force agent whose real-life experiences inspired this novel.

--Library Journal 6/1/2009

Author, Colonel Michael "Mike" Angley, USAF (ret) enjoyed a rewarding 25-year career as a Special Agent with the Air Force Office of Special Investigations (OSI). He is a seasoned criminal investigator and a counterintelligence and counterterrorism specialist. He received extensive training in Undercover Operations and Informant Management, and early in his career performed undercover work for the Air Force.

Mike uses his extensive forensic background to provide authentic, fascinating details into how government law enforcement agencies do their work.

LaVergne, TN USA
15 December 2009

167046LV00004B/10/P

9 781590 958292